GAME
OVER

◆

TAYLOR KEATING

TOR®

paranormal romance

A TOM DOHERTY ASSOCIATES BOOK
NEW YORK

GAME OVER

A Tor Book
Published by Tom Doherty Associates, LLC
175 Fifth Avenue
New York, NY 10010

www.tor-forge.com

Tor® is a registered trademark of Tom Doherty Associates, LLC.

ISBN 978-0-7653-6547-7

First Edition: November 2010

Printed in the United States of America

0 9 8 7 6 5 4 3 2 1

For Heather Osborn for believing in Taylor Keating and the worlds she creates.

For Terry Wadden, my high school English teacher, who once said he'd read anything I ever wrote. Teachers really do make a difference. And for my husband, who'll probably read none of it, but loves me anyway.

For the talented Anne MacFarlane for her support, honesty, and enthusiasm.

For Tim Wacey and his incredible love of books. I can't express how much I appreciate the adventure that you've given my daughter. Barely a day goes by where she does not say, "oh, and Tim did this, and Tim said that." You truly are a wonderful man, one of a kind. I really enjoyed your brief visit last summer. I wish we lived closer so we could sit and chat about books all day.

GAME
OVER

PROLOGUE

Annia clutched a hand to the swell of her stomach, gritting her teeth against a fresh wave of pain.

It was too soon for the baby to be coming. Not now, not when she and Calen were running for their lives.

Calen gripped her free hand, urging her along in the darkness, unaware that the baby wasn't going to wait any longer, and Annia was afraid to tell him so.

"You have to keep moving," he coaxed her anxiously, love and concern thickening his voice. Annia would never get over the wonder of loving him, or of him loving her. He was a Guardian, a protector of the Fae, and it was forbidden for their two races to mix. They had a similar purpose in the universe—they spread life—but whereas the Fae brought their earth magic to other worlds, the Guardians brought a talent for technology.

She and Calen had both been meant to save a dying world. Annia feared that not only could they not save this world, they couldn't save themselves either.

Another explosion rocked the ground beneath their feet and Annia stumbled. Calen caught her before she could fall. "Oof," he grunted, teasing her, trying to make her laugh despite the precariousness of their situation. "You've put on weight since we first met. Are you so sure of me that you're letting yourself go?"

Annia did laugh at that, although unshed tears tugged at her lashes. This time when the contraction came it caught her by surprise and she couldn't stifle a small gasp of pain.

"Oh no," Calen breathed against her temple, wrapping her tight in his arms as understanding dawned. "Nia, my love, you have to jump. Save yourself. I promise, I will follow."

"No!" Annia slid her hands up his back, absorbing as much of his warmth and the fresh, clean, achingly familiar scent of him as she could. She pressed her face to his chest. "I've told you, the baby is half Guardian. I don't know if it can jump with me. I won't take that chance. I won't risk its life."

They'd had this argument for several days now. She wouldn't leave him, and he had not had time to fix the damaged transporter he wore beneath his skin at the small of his back. Even if he'd been able to fix it, there was no guarantee that he could transport both her and their child without making major adjustments. Annia had no doubt that he could make those adjustments—he was a Guardian, and technology came as easily to him as breathing—but they had run out of time. They'd been discovered, and now they were being hunted.

They'd been so stupid. They hadn't stopped to consider that the biotechnology lab they'd tried to break into might possibly be protected. Worse, the biorobotics left as watchmen had been programmed to seek and destroy. Clearly, the owners of the lab hadn't wanted their secrets exposed to the outside world. Annia shivered. Considering what she and Calen had found inside, she wasn't surprised.

Calen's head swung to the left and right as he searched for a safe place to hide, although Annia knew in her heart that it was hopeless. Despite the darkness, and the thick forest overgrowth, the mountainside offered no true haven against bioengineered life forms.

Calen knew it, too.

"Annia," he said, and his tone no longer held the undercurrent of love she'd come to expect from him, but the stern command of a Guardian. "You will save your Fae soul. You will jump. If the baby holds the magic of a Fae, then between us we will have saved two precious souls."

She knew he was right. A Fae soul, and all its

earth magic, could not be replaced if lost, and Fae numbers were already dangerously diminished. If there was a chance that this baby possessed a Fae soul, then she and Calen owed it to the worlds to ensure that it survived. They owed it to the worlds to ensure that Annia's soul survived as well.

Yet Annia didn't know how she could do so if she no longer had Calen at her side.

The cracking of underbrush grew louder and closer.

"Now!" Calen ordered. "Jump!"

Annia took one last precious second to kiss him good-bye. As she started to turn, she caught a flare of red light from the corner of her eye. The rest happened in a blur. She heard Calen shout as he leapt to shield her, and then a blast of heat struck like a fist to the small of her back. She tried to jump but she knew in her heart she'd hesitated too long.

The jump was incomplete. She pitched forward to her hands and knees, uncertain and uncaring of where she'd landed. The heat in her back became a blinding wave of pain. Another knife of pain sliced through her stomach. She panted through the contraction, trying desperately to remain conscious, concentrating on the fact that her baby was still with her and ignoring the fact that Calen was not.

Warm yellow light beckoned her through the trees. Annia tried to stand but couldn't. As this new life with its magic Fae soul emerged into a foreign, troubled world where no Fae should ever be born, Annia felt her own soul slowly slipping away. Desperation gave her the strength to let out a final agonizing scream for help that rocked the darkness of the night.

◆ ◆

"Did you hear that?"

David Weston cocked his head to one side, listening intently to see if the sound would repeat itself, but heard nothing more.

His wife paused by the open window, the night air stirring white organdy curtains. She frowned as she wiped her dishwater-damp hands on the legs of her jeans. "I don't know what that was," she said, "but it gave me the shivers."

David rose from his chair at the kitchen table and went to the door, reaching for his boots on the rubber floor mat beside it.

"Where do you think you're going?" his wife demanded.

Glancing up, he tugged his shoelaces tight. "I'm going to see what that was. Lock the door behind me."

She started to protest, then pressed her lips together in silent disapproval when she saw that he was going to go no matter what she said.

He took his flashlight off a nearby shelf, stepped out onto the verandah, and waited for her to shoot the dead bolt home behind him before he descended the stairs and crossed the yard.

He swung the flashlight in wide circles as he walked. These were not good times to be wandering the mountain in daylight, let alone late at night, not with so many desperate people displaced by the war.

Still, their small farm was well off the beaten track. They didn't get many visitors, desperate or otherwise, and there was little enough human kindness left in the world as it was. David couldn't bring himself to contribute to its total demise. If someone needed help he'd willingly provide it.

It didn't take long for him to find her, or for him to realize that he'd found her too late.

It was not too late, however, for the newborn infant lying bloody at her side, its tiny chest heaving as it sucked in its first breaths of life. David's experience was limited mostly to animal births, but common sense lent him a helping hand. He tied off the umbilical cord with one of the laces from his boots, wrapped the infant in his shirt, and then, promising to come back and bury the poor woman as soon as he could so that animals couldn't get at her, he took the baby and headed for the house.

He stepped onto the verandah, the bundled infant in his large, work-roughened hands. He examined it closely in the light gleaming from the kitchen window, wondering what on earth was likely to happen to the poor little soul.

The mother was a vagrant—one of many—and if David and his wife were to call Children's Services, this child would end up in a group home where no one would care what became of it.

The baby opened its eyes, seeming almost to stare back into his. David wiped its grime-crusted cheek with the tail of his shirt and fell instantly in love.

He banged on the door, calling for his wife to unlock it for him. He winced a little at the shock on her face when she opened the door, not knowing quite how to explain a situation he didn't understand himself.

He held out the tiny bundle to her. "You'll never guess what I found down by the river."

CHAPTER ONE

♦

If not for the sword held high above her head or her ability to wield it like a Samurai warrior when the situation required, River Weston knew she could kiss her ass good-bye.

But it wasn't just her ass she was worrying about. Without the necessary skills to fight off the packs of wild dogs hiding in the shadows—beasts fondly known by the team as the Hellhounds—they'd peel her skin from her body and indulge in a late-night snack.

Of course she couldn't forget about the demons hot on her trail either, or how delighted they'd be to separate her head from her body and wear it as a trophy.

Either way she'd lose her soul, and dammit, she wasn't about to let that happen. Again.

River's heart monitor gave a little blip of warning, and she took a few deep breaths to center herself. Then, with stealth and precision, she pressed her back against an abandoned concrete structure and eased forward through the shadows. Although the streets appeared deserted, she knew they were anything but. Between every vacant building and alleyway, creatures modeled after the make-believe monsters of children's bedtime stories watched her—waiting for an opportune moment to attack. These creatures were smart, organized, and lethal, and if River wasn't careful, she'd never make it to the Soul Man's lair in one piece.

Sprays of light from overhead streetlamps fanned the blood-drenched sidewalk. A coppery, pungent stench clogged her nostrils, causing her stomach to churn. River lowered her sword and shifted it to one hand. So much blood, so much carnage, yet no bodies to be seen, although she knew all too well what these depraved monsters did to their victims.

Stifling a shiver she pressed herself deeper into the shadows and crab-walked forward, her eyes continually scanning and cataloguing her surroundings, searching for motion while seeking signs that her comrade, Sever, was nearby.

Beads of sweat trickled between her breasts, but she'd learned long ago to distance herself from the discomfort and concentrate only on the hunt.

Off in the distance a hound barked a warning, followed by a low growl swallowed by the night. The faint smell of smoke drifted in on a howling wind, dusting debris into her eyes. She gave a quick blink, not daring to take her trained gaze off the shifting shadows.

Her damp skin barely registered the increasing chill of the night. She drew another slow, steadying breath and noted the heavy clouds knitting together overhead, accompanied by a faint rumble of thunder. The rain would soon be here.

A bright firefly whipped past her head. With lightning speed River reached out, grabbed it with her free hand, and dropped it into the rucksack dangling from her shoulder. Even though a firefly brought only minimal amounts of energy, every bit of strength would be needed in her final battle against the Soul Man.

Making herself one with her surroundings, she moved with a practiced agility. But despite her best efforts, she feared that each tread of her military-issue combat boots on the dangerously tranquil street might give away her coordinates.

River was partial to solitude. At any other time, on any other night, she would have longed for such peace and quiet. But this solitude was different. It was menacing, dark, dangerous. Her gaze skated over the rooftops. Hellhounds were out there watching, waiting. She felt them, sensed them, and tasted them with every fiber of her being.

God, what a rush.

She glanced at the silent com-link on her wrist

and orchestrated her next move. If she could make it to the movie theater—the safe house—on the other side of the street, she could rest and gather strength while she signaled Sever. She couldn't move on to the Soul Man's lair without him.

Suddenly, her skin prickled in warning the way it always did when demons pinpointed her location. If she didn't get to the safe house as soon as possible, the hunter was about to become the hunted.

Gunfire rang out behind her and she picked up her pace, putting more distance between herself and the approaching demons until she could better position herself for an all-out attack.

A low growl cut through the silence and a movement in the shadows caught her eyes.

Shit.

She bolted, darting across the cracked and pitted street at an inhuman speed.

Before she could make it to the safe house a pack of Hellhounds rushed at her, a frothy mixture of saliva and fresh blood dripping from their fangs.

Both hands tightened around the hilt of her sword, and using slow movements intended to distract and intimidate, River twisted, counting the Hellhounds circling her. Even she was impressed by their numbers, and felt a small twinge of pride that she warranted so many.

There was little time for self-congratulations. Violence erupted around her as one hound raced forward, hitting her with such force it would have driven a lesser woman to her knees. Dark lips peeled back to reveal razor-sharp fangs and River's thigh ached in response. She wasn't oblivious to the damage those fangs could inflict.

Survival instincts kicking in, River cut her sword through the air, driving the blade deep into the belly of the beast. A pained expression ripped across its muzzle as it collapsed onto the ground. Its sharp yelp, combined with the spray of fresh blood, fueled the other hounds into action.

One beast latched onto River's thigh, zeroing in on her weakness, its fangs slicing through her flesh like a hot knife through butter. Wincing, her sword slipped from her hand and she dropped like a snared gazelle. Her heart monitor blared and the com-link on her wrist flashed a red light of warning.

Trying to see through the blinding pain, River groped for her sword. The second her hand connected with it a round of shots scattered through the air. The rapid-fire rain of bullets took down a few Hellhounds while the others scurried back to the shadows. River knew the bullets would only temporarily stun the hounds and wouldn't keep them down for long. The only way to kill one of those fuckers was with the cold blade of a sword.

River glanced up to see Sever approaching. Intense gray eyes locked on hers.

She ripped the torn sleeve from her camo jacket and tied it around her bloodied thigh. Her heart monitor fell silent and the red light on her com-link blinked out.

"About time you showed," she said.

He leaned against the ridiculously oversized Uzi Nick had insisted on designing for him. "Been busy."

River grinned, happy to see him. "That's a smart mouth you've got there." She made a mental note to adjust his attitude when this was all over.

Her gaze panned over him, taking pleasure in a well-muscled man in face paint and battle fatigues. Sever was the picture of perfection. The ideal man, straight out of her fantasies—or rather, her imagination.

"You hurt?" she asked.

His answering grin was a mixture of sweet honey and determined grit. He shouldered his gun. Weapon or no weapon, this man was a trained warrior. A hunter. A predator. And was never to be underestimated.

"I've been better."

Sever held his hand out to her. As she reached for it, a spray of bullets ricocheted off the towering buildings above their heads. Grenade fire followed.

A horrendous explosion erupted inside an old warehouse. What she could only assume was C-4 tore one building from its roots.

It seemed the demons had found them.

Sever grabbed her hand, maneuvering his body to protect hers, and hauled her to her feet. "Let's go."

Protecting her back was Sever's job, although River was of two minds about that. Strategy, however, was all hers.

The Wizard or the Soul Man's lair?

Thunder crackled in the air overhead, accompanying the first flashes of lightning. A few fat drops of rain splattered her cheeks and bare arm.

She had to get to the safe house first. Then she needed a few more moments to think.

The safe house was only two doors down in the abandoned movie theater sporting boarded windows and a crazy, tilted neon sign that flashed an ad for *Spaceballs*. Under cover of Sever's return fire they made it inside without further injury to themselves, although River thought she heard three demons fall behind them.

Three wouldn't be enough.

River jammed the blade of her sword into a panel on the side of the building and the door to the safe house swung open. They darted inside, the door hissed shut behind them, and silence fell.

She spun in a circle, examining the room carefully in the unnatural, filtered light. She knew the room by heart, although its contents were never quite the same. What she'd find inside depended on what she'd collected in the outside world.

A few scraggly weeds crept through the cracks in the stone foundation of the safe house and twisted up the walls. Disappointment dampened her initial thrill at making it to the house alive. There weren't enough plants to give her the power she'd need to successfully complete the mission. She tapped the weeds with the dull edge of her sword, drawing as much power from them as she could, as she tried to make up her mind what to do next. Her sword's blade strengthened, but only slightly.

"Hurry it up." Nick's impatient, tinny voice blared through her com-link. "You're over by about five minutes and I want you out of there."

Sever stood by impassively, his weapon slung over his shoulder and his arms folded across his broad chest, waiting for her to make up her mind.

Door number one summoned the Wizard. Door number two led straight to the Soul Man's lair.

River glanced at her com-link, considered the amount of time Nick would likely allow her, and decided what the hell, she might as well live life on the edge. She hitched her rucksack higher on her shoulder.

Door number two it was. "Come on."

Sever followed close on her heels as she stepped through the door.

The Soul Man's lair never failed to astonish her. It resembled a long medieval hall, its low ceiling supported by a tunnel of carefully pillared archways crafted from chiseled stone and crumbling mortar. Deep, smoke-blackened fireplaces, large enough for several big men to stand within, lined the walls to the left and the right.

Their footsteps echoed eerily against the polished granite floor as they moved forward into an unnatural stillness. The damp coolness inside the lair wrapped around her and chilled her bones. River fought to steady her breathing and keep her heart rate down to an acceptable level.

Sever, of course, looked as if he was out for nothing more than a casual stroll. Most of the time she enjoyed his calm steadiness. At other times, like now, it annoyed the hell out of her. She tossed her rucksack into one of the empty fireplaces out of harm's way, but close enough for her to retrieve if necessary. Its contents were sparse, but every little thing she'd collected had a purpose, however minor.

A low whine rent the air and she ducked as the first fireball shot past her left ear. It caught Sever on the shoulder, but he shrugged it off.

River lifted her sword, its slightly curved steel

blade glinting blue in the flashes of light from the unleashed fireballs, and deflected the next three.

The Soul Man stepped from behind a pillar, robes billowing around his long legs as he hefted more fireballs in thin, bony white hands, letting River know he was toying with her. A cowl covered his head and hid his face.

River's heart monitor let out a sharp *beep*.

"Careful, River," Nick warned on the other end of her com-link.

That wasn't good. When Nick started fussing about vitals, it meant he was serious. He was going to pull her out.

"Relax," River said, reluctantly making a decision that might buy her more time. Disappointment curdled the pit of her stomach. "I'm going to let Sever handle this one. I'm just going to observe."

As the Soul Man lifted his hands to release his next round, Sever stepped in front of River. He grunted as a fireball glanced off his chest, a direct hit.

Each time one of those fireballs hit him, it was going to do him more and more harm, and River knew Sever wasn't going to make it. She had to put the little time he bought her to good use.

She pulled her gaze away from Sever and the Soul Man, needing to find out more about his lair and the dark, deadly secrets it held.

A slight smell of sulfur and hot plastic stung her

nostrils, and the faint ring of thunder through the thick stone walls told her the storm outside must be almost directly overhead.

Without warning, a lightning bolt shot from one of the fireplace chimneys and scorched the floor at her feet, knocking her flat on her ass. She skidded a few feet across the stones, the aftershocks of electricity lifting her hair. She fell backward, hitting her head on the floor, stunning her for a few seconds.

"What the hell?" she heard Nick yell.

Sever, too, was caught off guard. He half turned to see what was happening, and as he did, a well-aimed fireball nailed him square in the back of the head. He dropped to his knees and pitched forward, collapsing like a marionette.

The Soul Man never faltered.

River, trying desperately to gather her wits, reached for the sword that lay on the floor a few inches beyond her scrabbling fingers.

"You're mine, River Weston," the Soul Man said, his voice crackling like brittle bones. Full-blown panic clawed at River's frozen chest. Her heart monitor screeched and she heard Nick swearing a blue streak in response.

This wasn't how it was supposed to be.

Her fingers wrapped around the hilt of her sword and she swung it upward, aiming at the Soul Man's knees. The blade swept through him and he laughed, a terrible, soul-chilling sound that sent a rush of adrenaline to her brain.

Run!

River dropped the sword and grabbed for her helmet.

CHAPTER **TWO**

♦

Heart still racing, River dropped her gaming helmet beside the length of wood she used as a makeshift sword.

"Son of a bitch," she bit out in disappointment as Nick stepped onto the circular gaming platform and went to work on removing her monitors.

"Christ, River. Are you trying to get yourself killed?"

"Killed?" River ripped the last monitor from her chest and glanced over at the program still running on Nick's monitor. *Error//K:61253.10 end_function* flashed in bright neon lights. "How can I get myself killed when you're hovering over me like a little old lady?"

Nick's blue eyes narrowed. "Bungee jumping with an extralong cord is safer than what you just did. If I don't take care of you, who will?"

She'd actually scared him, she saw. She grinned, trying to lighten his mood. "Sever?"

He didn't smile back. "Sever? Sometimes I wonder if you really designed him for his abilities. Maybe if you spent less time watching his ass and more time covering your own you'd be able to defeat the Soul Man."

She stepped from the rubber gaming platform, plunked herself into Nick's chair, and took a slug of his Red Bull.

"Something just isn't right. I need more time inside the game to figure it out," she said.

"You're an adrenaline junkie, River. That's what isn't right."

She couldn't deny it. Regardless, that didn't change the fact that she needed more time to figure out why she couldn't take down the Soul Man and win the game. She'd written the code, for Christ's sake. All she had to do was weaken the Soul Man with lightning and then take him down with her sword, yet every time she reached his lair her program seemed to take on a life of its own.

"All I need is five more minutes."

She took in Nick's watchful expression and noted the exhausted lines on his face.

"You can't have them. Your vitals were off the chart. Any more time inside that game, and you and I both know what could happen." He drove his hands deep into his pockets. "I have no desire to stand in front of a judge and explain why you went into cardiac arrest when I was supposed to be monitoring you. At the very least we're talking criminal negligence causing bodily harm."

She rolled her eyes and took another slug of his Red Bull, even though she was already far too wired. She punched a few keys and rebooted her program. "Get real. The legal system isn't that efficient. It would take a team of investigators years to figure out what happened, and that's only assuming they'd care. You're safe. Let's go over the subroutine code again."

Nick reached past her shoulder, plucked the near-empty can of Red Bull from her hand, and spun her around to face him. He slanted his head, his dark, disheveled hair falling forward. "Better yet, let's call it a night. The rest of the team is waiting for us at Andy's Pub and you look like you could use a good stiff drink to bring you down. I know I could."

With rumors running rampant that competitors were close to creating and marketing a similar inter-active kick-ass adventure game geared toward the rich and bored, and upper management making noises about taking away funding for what was becoming an alarmingly overbudget project, River was far from ready to quit for the night. Not when she was so close to figuring out that final code.

This was her brainchild. Her baby. She'd poured her heart and soul into it and she'd do anything to see it succeed. The rich and bored might be the only ones able to afford it at first, but she had high hopes that it would someday offer a semblance of normality to people who'd lost all use of their physical bodies.

Her mom would have loved it. Watching her waste away had been almost more than River could bear.

She made a grab for the Red Bull, but Nick easily pulled it out of her reach.

"Come on, Nick. Just give me five more minutes, okay?"

"You and your five minutes." Nick studied her, an annoying little habit he had, especially when he thought she wasn't looking, and dangled the can of Red Bull in front of her eyes. "You've already worked too hard. Your reflexes are way off. You should've had that." He tossed the can into the trash.

River sighed, knowing he was right and unhappy about it.

"You don't get it," she said, frustration sharpening her tone. "I'd seriously sell my soul for this game to work."

Unease washed over Nick's handsome face. "You shouldn't say things like that."

River was a little tired of Nick and his crazy

superstitions. Ever since some lame-ass politician had leaked a secret government study on children's fairy tales to the press, speculation as to whether or not the "monsters under the bed" were fact or fiction had gotten completely out of hand. All the so-called study really proved to River was that the government had learned nothing from the Great War, and would waste money on anything.

Public paranoia and government waste weren't all bad, of course. She'd based Soul Quest on one of those old bedtime stories—although how a parent could expect a child to sleep after hearing stories like that was beyond her. Soul Quest was adults only.

And her generation was going to grab it up. That was where the money was.

She pulled her best innocent face and gave Nick the pleading look that always got her what she wanted from him. "If we don't get this game done on time someone else will."

Nick threw back his head and stared at the ceiling for a few seconds before finally conceding defeat. He pinched the bridge of his nose between a thumb and forefinger. "Five minutes with the subroutine, River. No more."

River grabbed another Red Bull from their small fridge, popped it open, and went to work, determined to make every minute count. Fingers flying across the keyboard, she ran through her program, checking and double-checking the code.

As she went for another swig of her drink, her elbow collided with Nick's cell phone. She reached out and grabbed it before it could sail off the desk and smash to the floor.

She flashed Nick a triumphant smile. "See? Nothing wrong with these reflexes."

Momentarily distracted, she barely caught the string of code out of the corner of her eye as it suddenly flashed on her screen. Her head whipped around with a start, but before she could get a better look, it vanished. One second it was there, the next instant it was gone.

Was that what she thought it was?

Maybe prolonged neural stimulation really was playing tricks with her brain. Insanity was another potential side effect of the game. She rubbed her temples in an attempt to ward off an impending headache. Although she hated to admit it, she was beginning to think Nick was right and that it was well past time for her to call it a night. She was tired, and that was unusual for her.

River blew a heavy sigh and reached for her monitor to power it down when all of a sudden, the code flashed again.

Pulse leaping, she licked her lips and glanced at Nick, who was leaning in the doorway, chatting with the security guard making his evening rounds. Fingers poised over the power button, she turned her attention back to her monitor and waited a moment longer. When it flashed a third time she shifted in her chair, grabbed a pen, and jotted it down. She took a moment to study the string of code, comparing it to the failed subroutine she'd keyed in earlier, noting how similar it appeared to the one she'd written for the final fight scene.

Had one of her team members figured it out and left it for her to find? Or was she losing her mind?

Nothing ventured, nothing gained. River moved her cursor over the string of numbers and symbols, inserting the new data. It wouldn't hurt to try it.

The minute she inserted the code she felt an odd tingling in her bloodstream—a heady mixture of anticipation and dread. Her pulse hammering, she stole another longing glance at the gaming platform.

There was no way in hell Nick would let her go back in.

The security guard continued on his way and Nick turned back to her, tapping his watch. "Time's up. Ready to call it a night?"

"I'm fine, Nick. Playing the game didn't hurt me a bit." At least she didn't think it had. No need to mention the sudden appearance of new code until she'd tested it. "What you really should be worried about is figuring out what's going on in the final scene with the Soul Man. We've got to make the ending believable. How do we kill something that's supposed to already be dead?"

"You'll figure it out. I have faith in you. You're the best software engineer I know."

"Which is why this is driving me so crazy." Her heart settling back into a steady rhythm, River saved the program and powered down her computer.

"Let's go."

♦ ♦

Twenty minutes later, River pushed through the heavy wooden doors of Andy's Pub with Nick at her side. The warmth of the pub washed over them, pushing back the cold, crisp autumn air. River unzipped her windbreaker and stole a glance at Nick's tall, athletic form as he moved a little closer to her, his body conveying without words that he'd rather be somewhere else—somewhere private. When her gaze collided with his, sexual energy hit her hard and fast.

Not tonight honey, I've got a headache.

Okay, so maybe she didn't have a headache. What she did have was her mind set on getting back to the compound and testing the new code. Which meant Nick would have to take care of his own needs. A pity really, because she would have enjoyed the fringe benefits of their friendship tonight if she didn't have more pressing matters on her plate.

River took note of her friend Andy tending bar, then turned to wave to her three teammates who were already relaxing over drinks and finger food.

She gestured with her head for Nick to go on ahead without her. "I'll grab our drinks and meet you at the table. I want to say hello to Andy first."

She did want to say hello to her friend, but she also wanted to ensure that her drink was alcohol free. If Nick heard her order anything less than a whiskey and Red Bull it would raise his suspicions.

"Hey, Andy, how's it going?" River asked, sidling up to the bar, taking in her friend's waist-length dark curly hair and tight uniform. Even at fifty the woman still had a killer body. She also had the stamina and drive of a twenty-year-old. River should know, since they took the same karate classes together.

Andy's emerald eyes lit with joy. Always ready with a quick, genuine smile, she held her arms out.

"River, how are you? You haven't been by in ages. Get on over here," she said, her smile as wide as her arms.

Andy smelled like home, peppery sage and earthy. She practically climbed over the counter for a hug.

"I've been crazy busy." It occurred to River that

she and the rest of her research team had been living in this mountain town for a little over two years, yet outside the compound Andy was their only friend. Their top-secret project automatically made them outcasts in an isolated town that didn't welcome strangers. River, born at the tail end of the war, didn't really remember it, but for many people it was as if it had happened yesterday. It didn't help matters that the virus that had triggered the war mutated and occasionally resurfaced.

Andy was the only person River knew of who'd contracted the virus and survived. That made it all the more surprising that she was willing to touch people, and that people were willing to touch her. But Andy was a people magnet.

When Andy's arms loosened, River eased away. "How've you been?"

Andy's smile widened. "Good. Better, now that you're here."

River chuckled. "You're good for my ego."

"And you're good for my soul." Andy shook her head in mock amazement as she poured a beer from the tap, and added, "I swear, you're a magician, River. Every time you touch me it gives me strength and lifts my spirits."

Like one of the cowboys from the next province over, River tipped an imaginary Stetson. "I do what I can, ma'am."

Andy laughed and wiped her hands on her apron. "What can I get for you tonight, honey? The usual?"

"The usual for Nick, make mine a virgin." She paused and then added in a lower tone, "But I want it to look like it has alcohol in it."

Andy narrowed her beautiful eyes. "Are you up to no good, River?"

"Of course."

"River . . ."

River held her hands up. "Don't go all motherly on me, Andy."

River's thoughts drifted to her own mother for the second time that day—an amazing, caring woman who hadn't been as lucky as Andy. A former nurse, she'd taught River all about nurturing. Her hands-on training had started in the garden, showing River that through a loving touch she could have the biggest, lushest garden in town.

Her mother had also taught her to be strong, independent, and self-reliant. At fourteen, when River had blossomed into a woman, her mother had signed them both up for self-defense classes, insisting that with River's tiny build and small frame, she needed to learn to defend herself. In other words, her mother had prepared her for the real world. River often wondered if her mother had been preparing her for anything else. If so, she'd never know.

That was the mother whose loss she felt most deeply, the one who could never be replaced.

She hadn't had the time or inclination to go searching for her biological mother, nor had she ever wanted to hurt her adoptive mother by doing so.

Although at times, she did wonder.

"Here you go, hon," Andy said, hauling her thoughts back to the bar. River glanced at the two drinks, unable to tell which was hers. Andy pushed one of the glasses forward and winked. "No one will ever be the wiser."

"Thank you, ma'am."

River settled her imaginary hat back on her head and with that, made her way across the room toward her team.

Her gaze panned the near-empty bar, taking in the patrons. On one side, a few men in business suits sat in a booth, papers spread before them. On the other, a pack of cowboys mingled with the local girls. An old country song blared from an antique jukebox Andy had scrounged up from the prewar era. Andy kept the oddest assortment of antiques in her pub. Nick had teased her incessantly about the butter churn in one corner and called her "milkmaid" after she proved she knew how to use it.

River shot the locals a smile, and although they all responded, their answering smiles never quite reached their eyes. No surprise there.

The truth was, not only did River feel like an outsider in the town, she often felt like an outsider with her own team. They all got along well, and had a great camaraderie, but there was something she couldn't quite put her finger on that left her feeling a bit like an outcast. It had been no different for her when she was growing up in the small town of Hammonds either. The war had taught people to fear the unknown, and the few other kids living there had always kept a distance from her because she was adopted. When she left Hammonds for good, she left that behind her. Not even Nick or Andy knew. River liked being herself. She didn't like being defined by standards other people set.

Enough of that. River approached her team and plastered on another smile. She handed Nick his drink and took in the three sets of glassy eyes staring back at her.

"Been here long?" she asked, amusement lacing her voice.

Marsha Day, tall, blond, and stacked, grinned back. Why Nick wasn't sleeping with her, River would never know.

Then again, maybe he was.

"Hey, River, have you killed the bogeyman yet?" Marsha asked.

River didn't bother to keep the annoyance out of her voice. "It's the Soul Man, and no, not yet."

And she wondered why she had no friends. Okay,

so maybe she was a little defensive of her game, and maybe she didn't like anyone not taking it seriously. But Marsha could be such a competitive bitch sometimes.

"Bogeyman, Soul Man. Either way, the things you've got in that game scare the shit out of me," Tanner Gracie piped in.

River rolled her eyes. "*Either way,* they're not real, Tanner. They're make-believe creatures from fairy tales."

"Says who?" Johnny Jacobs asked, leaning in close and deepening his voice to promote the stupid conspiracy theory that monsters were on the loose and the government was covering up for them.

River noted how quiet Nick remained on the subject. "Says me," she replied. "I've got a good imagination. I don't need the government giving me lame ideas."

Tanner tossed his car keys at her. Barely missing a beat, she took a sip of her virgin and snapped them out of the air. A familiar drinking game. Toss objects at the freaky fast girl and see if she could catch them. River didn't mind, normally. Tonight, she was on edge.

Tanner folded his arms, a cocky grin pulling at the corners of his plump lips. "Hey, River. With your lightning speed, maybe you're one of those fairy-tale creatures, too."

River picked up an empty beer can and lobbed it at Tanner. It hit him between the eyebrows and a round of laughter erupted.

"And maybe with your extra *sloooow*"—she paused to stretch that word out—"sensory receptors, you're one of those fairy-tale monsters."

"You think?" Tanner asked, his bright green eyes hopeful as he rubbed his forehead.

Never one to be politically correct, Johnny bit into his mozzarella stick and around a mouthful of cheese said, "Yeah, we could call you Fucktard Man."

Tanner grinned. "Hey, I like that." He glanced around the table and crooked an arm, showing off a pudgy bicep. "You all heard Johnny, from now on it's Fucktard Man."

After another round of laughter they all fell into easy conversation, quietly discussing the game, the code, and the problem River was having defeating the Soul Man.

Although they'd yet to come up with any concrete solutions, River finished off her fake drink and stretched. After a good show of exhaustion, she glanced at her watch.

"I guess I should get going. It's been a long week."

Nick leaned in, his gaze brushing over her face. "You want me to walk you?"

That was his subtle way of asking if she was interested in a little "Nick" cap.

"No, I'm good." She grinned and gestured toward Tanner. "Unlike Tanner, I'm not afraid the Soul Man's going to get me."

"I hear he's not nearly as scary as Fucktard Man," Johnny said.

River chuckled and shot Tanner a glance. He wasn't much taller than she was, but he was a whole lot heavier. All that extra weight would be more of a handicap than an asset in a fight. "I'm pretty sure I can take him down."

Tanner steepled his hands in a thankful prayer. "Finally, my dreams have come true. I've been wishing for months for River Weston to go down on me."

"Your dreams are my nightmares, Tanner. You're Fucktard Man, remember? A fairy-tale monster."

With that she zipped up her jacket and stepped out into the night, her team's laughter slowly fading away behind her.

Once she was sure Nick wasn't following, she hustled back to the compound.

CHAPTER THREE

♦

"I'd sell my soul for this game to work."

Those nine simple words, and more important the conviction behind them, were music to the Dark Lord's ears.

From a scorch-marked throne deep inside his private sanctuary, the Dark Lord tipped his bald head sideways, glancing every so often into the seeing stones in the crucible beside him that linked the living world to his own prison. His nails tapped one blackened armrest as a subtle smile turned up the corners of his mouth.

She might have had no idea what she'd tapped into when she began stealing from his program or uttered those fateful words, but she would. Once a mortal being accepted the help he offered, they enabled him to mark their soul—to watch over it and collect it upon death.

The marvelous thing about mortals was what fragile, predictable creatures they tended to be. Centuries had passed since the last time one of them had offered up his soul in trade. River Weston had accepted the code. And he knew that she would soon be back to try it out.

A shifting of shadows in the room brought his head up.

"Step aside, love," he whispered to the woman sitting on his armrest. With a slight flick of his fingers he pushed her away. She squirreled backward to join the others crouched patiently in a corner.

He didn't spare them a glance. Once they gave up the fight for their souls they were hardly worth his attention. They served mostly as a power source for his prison, and lately they weren't even good for that.

The program was failing.

The Dark Lord rose. His reflection gleamed in the polished granite floor as he stood over the seeing stones and peered into River's world.

She was back, just as he'd known she'd be, hunched over her computer, working late into the night even though sleep tugged hard at her eyelids.

He watched her lift a drink to her lips and take a small sip. As she went to set the can back on her desk she missed. In one fluid movement, she reached out to grab it seconds before it fell to the floor. Her eyes never once left the monitor.

He examined her more closely as she gathered her long hair away from her weary face, tying it behind her. With her black hair, light blue eyes, slight frame, and flawless skin, she was the most exquisite woman he'd seen in a long time. Her physical form didn't interest him nearly as much as her soul, however. There was something different about this particular woman's soul.

Without warning, the image in the stones flickered as his program froze. His sanctuary and servants vanished, and all that remained was a vast wasteland of blowing dust and searing desert.

A burst of helpless fury curled through him. He'd ruled this world since the Guardians and the Fae had trapped him in it, then forgotten him. He was the last, and the mightiest, of the immortals. He'd found a way to alter his virtual prison enough so that he could claim the souls of those who reached out to him.

Unfortunately, his tampering had not been without cost. Now he stood on the brink of a fatal error with no way to escape. When the program finally failed he'd become nothing more than an empty consciousness adrift on a world unfit for biological life, contained by Fae magic and unable to function as more than a thought. A fate far worse than any death.

The error in the program corrected itself, his prison reformed, and he quickly ran through his safety checks to determine how much damage was done.

Minimal. This time.

He turned his attention back to the woman

captured in the stones and watched her as a grow-ing sense of hope overrode the hated tingle of fear.

The Guardians had put him here, but the magic of a Fae could get him out. If this woman was what he thought she was, she might be the answer to the greatest of his problems—and he intended to have her.

But he couldn't claim her until her soul departed its body, and she looked so young. He doubted if he had much time left before the program shorted out completely—but thankfully, accidents happened every day.

Movement in the seeing stones to the left earned his full attention. Nostrils flaring, he watched the shifting images. A man paced in a cell like a caged animal, and the Dark Lord's excitement at the thought of a Fae turned to a slow-burning frustration at his inability to fully claim the soul of his Guardian prize.

Chase Hawkins' soul had been drifting through space. Curiosity had brought it too close to the Dark Lord's prison, and the adjustments to the program gave him the means to capture it.

By rights, when a soul separated from its bio-logical body, consciousness ceased to exist and the mind shut the body down. This Guardian's mind, however, remained tied to his soul and it was prov-ing to be a little . . . out of the ordinary. Somewhere out there in the Guardian's mortal world, someone was keeping Hawkins' biological body alive—and Hawkins trusted him enough to believe in that.

The Dark Lord needed to convince Hawkins' mind that his body was dead, and he needed to do that before whoever kept Hawkins' body alive found some way to retrieve his soul. If the Dark Lord lost the Guardian soul he'd captured, there was a good chance that Hawkins would hook up with whoever was keeping him alive and come back looking for him, and the Dark Lord was in no position to fight that kind of war. The Guardians had forgotten him, and the Dark Lord didn't want them reminded, now that freedom was within his grasp.

As though knowing he was being observed, Hawkins turned. A slow, lazy smirk curled his lips.

The Dark Lord tapped his chin with steepled fingers. No matter how much he tortured him, the man refused to die. And now the Dark Lord might have a Fae to contend with.

But was River Weston really Fae, or was she another Guardian trap? Had someone finally come to rescue Hawkins?

Did it matter? Once River plugged in the code he'd given her and put on her gaming headgear, her body might remain in her world but her mind would be his to do with as he pleased. She'd accepted his code, and that code opened all sorts of possibilities.

She'd unwittingly tapped into his prison through the final level in her game. He'd initially thought she'd managed to tap into it because she was a Guardian. Now he suspected she'd tapped into it through Fae magic. By accepting the code he'd offered, she'd granted him access to her game. And the closer she got to his sanctuary, the more control he would have over it—as well as any magic she might possess.

He curled his fingers into fists. The problem was that the more he played with her game, the more frequent the errors in his program became.

He regarded the two images before him in the seeing stones. Until the arrival of Chase Hawkins, he'd almost forgotten how much he hated the Guardians and the Fae for trapping him here, then abandoning him as if he were of no consequence whatsoever.

If he inserted Hawkins into the game with the River, he just might be able to find a way to solve his problems once and for all.

In order for River's game to truly work, someone had to be defeated in the final level. The Dark Lord had no worries of that someone being him. But if he could manage to defeat the Guardian as well, he could then have two souls for the price of one. Chase Hawkins' soul could rot in this Guardian prison for all of eternity. The Dark Lord would make certain the experience was a pleasant one.

But River Weston's?

Her soul opened up worlds of possibilities for him, and he intended to explore them all.

♦ ♦

Hawk would be damned before he let that bastard know how much he hated being watched.

He recounted the number of stones on the outer wall of his cell. Sometimes there were twenty-eight, sometimes thirty-two. It would seem that someone was having programming issues. Interesting.

He'd lost track of how long he'd been stuck in this miserable little hellhole, although he doubted if he'd know for certain how much real time had passed anyway. All he knew was that wherever he was, reality played a very small part in it.

He dropped onto the gray-blanketed cot with its one wobbly leg and threw an arm over his eyes.

When he'd volunteered for an experimental research program in soul migration, he hadn't really known what he was getting himself into. His wife and daughter were gone, killed in a transporter accident, and he had nothing more to lose. But his mind was as healthy as the rest of him, and he had more than enough training to help him keep it that way. He was a military man—a weapons expert— and the researchers had been inclined to agree that he was the perfect candidate for the program.

They'd explained the process. It was based on

research of out-of-body, life-after-death experiences, and the conclusion that the body, the soul, and the mind were all linked, but separate from each other. The plan was that researchers would stress his body to the point that his soul believed it was dead. Then, when his brain ceased to show signs of life, his body would be cryogenically frozen. It was his logical mind that would keep his soul and his body linked.

In most reported out-of-body experiences, it was sheer strength of will that brought the people back. He was supposed to let his soul drift, to see if he could sense the presence of the Fae, then return to his body when his consciousness warned him it was time. Monitors hooked to formerly unmapped parts of his brain would alert the researchers when mental activity resumed. Then they'd begin mapping his brain as his body was brought slowly back to normal temperature.

They had assured Hawk that his body could be kept for him for at least a year, and he believed it. These were people he worked closely with, and whom he'd known for a long time. He'd literally trusted them with his life on any number of occasions.

But they'd also warned him that they had no accurate data on how long a body could be kept frozen beyond a year before deterioration began to set in.

He also knew that no matter how advanced technology became, something as simple as a power failure could hasten his demise. If someone flipped the wrong switch and his body died, the Dark Lord who'd shanghaied his soul would have it forever.

Or at least until the next glitch in his program.

Yes, Hawk had felt it. That, combined with the fluctuating number of stones in his cell wall, gave him hope. If he waited until the next time the Dark Lord's virtual program shorted itself out, he might just be able to escape. For him, it was the equivalent of an unlocked cell door.

That's where his strength of mind and willpower came back into play. While on one level he knew that this world was not real, a great deal of effort had gone into making it as realistic as possible, and there were plenty of things that Hawk's mortal mind just couldn't get past.

The trouble was that normally a mind needed to shut itself down periodically and get some rest. Despite the cot conveniently supplied for him, sleep wasn't an option. Not if he wanted to keep his somewhat slippery grip on reality. He had no idea what he'd wake up to.

Two servants approached the door of his cell. Demon servants were one of the changes the Dark Lord had made to the program. Massive, ugly monsters with blood-red skin as hard as steel and arms and legs like tree trunks. Hawk had already learned not to waste his time fighting them. They might not be able to kill him, but they could make him wish he were dead.

As one unlocked the cell the other jerked him out by the back of his shirt, lifting him so that his feet dangled a few inches off the ground.

Every time he left his cell, the route through the Dark Lord's lair was a little different. Sometimes it followed a long hall lined with other cells, all filled with the sounds of tortured and broken prisoners, although there was nothing for Hawk to actually see. At other times the route was short and direct, or even nonexistent.

Reality in this world was whatever the Dark Lord chose to make it. Hawk hadn't yet found a way to create his own route through the lair.

Today, the route was short and direct. With a demon on each side of him, Hawk stepped into the chamber and took in the sight of his captor peering intently into the crucible filled with magic stones.

Those magic stones had been Hawk's first clue as to who the monster he dealt with truly was— the last of the Dark Lords, imprisoned by the Guardians so long ago that no one believed him to be more than a children's evil bedtime story. The fact that this was a prison, in spite of the enhancements the Dark Lord had managed to make, confirmed it.

Hawk might not be able to escape, but neither could the Dark Lord.

The Dark Lord turned slowly. Pure hatred danced in his cold black eyes as they locked on Hawk.

With his hands shackled behind his back, Hawk stood before him, now clad in a single loincloth. The Dark Lord's gaze left his face and scanned his bared body, lingering over the purple scars on his flesh. Scars that he'd personally given him. Hawk actually liked those raised, puckered welts. They reminded him that so far, he hadn't been broken.

He didn't, however, much care for the loincloth. He wondered what the sick little bastard had in mind for him this time. Whatever it was, he wasn't going to cooperate.

"You can dress me up, but you can't take me out," Hawk taunted, a less-than-subtle dig that the Dark Lord was also a prisoner. Hawk looked over the Dark Lord's shoulder at the stones he'd been watching so closely. "Is she another one of your sick fuck tests for me?"

He'd carefully wiped those words of all emotion before delivering them. Sooner or later he would find a way to make the Dark Lord pay. He'd get back to his own body and warn his people that the monster was out there, waiting and watching, and they would find a way to put an end to him. Revenge had given Hawk something to plan, something to fight for. One more reason to go on.

The Dark Lord stepped closer until the two stood eye to eye. Without tearing his gaze from Hawk, he called on Vienna, one of the poor, tormented souls haunting the corners of the lair.

Hawk faltered backward. A low groan crawled out of his throat. His body shifted.

Not again.

"I want you to understand that I'm not always a cruel bastard."

It was a lie. They both knew it.

Hawk steeled his spine as Vienna crept from her corner. The Dark Lord nodded to her and she dropped to her knees in front of Hawk. Her movements were slow, deliberate. She nestled herself in between his legs and unceremoniously tore away the loincloth.

"Crisos," Hawkins cursed. "What more can you possibly do to me?"

The Dark Lord grinned. "That depends. I have a little game I want you to play."

Sweat collected on Hawk's brow. "Do you really think I'm going to offer you my soul because you've found me a plaything?"

He felt so sorry for her. She was one of the souls the Dark Lord had managed to break. She didn't deserve this any more than he did. The difference was, she no longer cared. He could see that in her utterly empty, lifeless eyes.

"If you did, you could have this all the time."

"I don't want this," Hawk bit out, furious that the Dark Lord could find ways to control him no matter how hard he fought against it. "I've never wanted this."

The Dark Lord glanced down. "It would appear otherwise."

Hawk groaned. His jaw clenched.

The Dark Lord waved his hand and nodded toward the crucible. "You see that woman in the stones?"

With effort, Hawk shot the stones a glance and then moaned deep in his throat as Vienna drew in his thickness.

"What about her?" His voice came out rough, gravelly.

"She is mine." A slow grin curled the Dark Lord's lips. "She has just traded her soul for a favor, and I don't want to wait until she has met with death to claim her. I want her now."

Hawk's whole body tightened, and his voice dropped an octave. Swallowing hard, he struggled to find his words. They came out broken, fractured. "Then. Go. Claim. Her." Soft mewling sounds came from the poor creature between his legs. Hawk bit down on his bottom lip, fighting a losing battle for control. He sucked in a ragged breath.

The Dark Lord let out a frustrated, long-suffering sigh. "If only it were so easy. River Weston is playing a virtual reality game against the ultimate evil warrior, the Soul Man." He paused, his lips twitching, and then he added, "Quite flattering, really." He linked his long fingers and continued. "The object of the game is for the player to defeat the Soul Man in the final level. Should she lose the battle, she loses her soul. So far, her game has failed in the final level every time she's played."

Hawk gritted his teeth, his eyebrows arching as he labored for breath. "What the hell . . ." He sucked in air. "Does this have . . ." His hips jerked forward. "To do with me?"

"Everything, actually, since you are going to take the place of the game's computer-generated warrior."

Hawkins pulled back, trying to break free, tortured that his body responded so readily to the woman on her knees before him. He fisted his hands and rattled his shackles, hating the control the Dark Lord had over them both.

"River Weston is about to find out that the difficulty level of the game has gone way, way up. I plan on inserting you into the game with her, and I want to ensure that she reaches that final level." He paused as though for effect. "Then I will release your soul, and you can rejoin your body back in your own world."

The Dark Lord snapped his fingers, gesturing for Vienna to finish.

The breath rushed from Hawk's lungs, his whole body trembling with his release. He sagged against the stone wall and threw his head back against its cool surface. Vienna licked her lips and stood, moving quietly to the Dark Lord's side.

"You really are a sick bastard," Hawk said. He shook his head, disgusted with all three of them. "Why would I believe you?"

The Dark Lord grinned. "Because you're a man who will do anything to get his life back. What is your alternative?"

Hawk snarled, righting himself. "Go to hell."

The Dark Lord's gaze dropped below Hawk's waistline. "Hell is what you make of it. Sometimes, you can even enjoy it."

He looked back into Hawk's eyes, and the coldness of them almost made Hawk shiver. Almost. He was still his own man.

"I want your answer," his tormentor said. His eyes narrowed. "And I want it now. Or I'm going to peel the flesh from Vienna's bones while you watch."

The little start of fear in the woman, the soft noise low in her throat, made Hawk sick to his stomach. Maybe there was still a bit of life left in her, after all.

He thought about the woman whose image he'd caught briefly in those magic stones. Was she real, as the Dark Lord claimed, or was she another test for him?

Or was she simply another poor, tormented soul who had yet to be broken?

He wouldn't be responsible for the suffering of another. Neither did he have to trust anyone or do anything he didn't want to. All he really had to do was wait out the failure in the Dark Lord's program and hope like hell that his body was waiting for him. What difference did it make if he waited out that failure in this program, or in some virtual game?

His eyes flashed to Vienna, her expression vacant once more, and he made up his mind.

"Bring it on," Hawk said.

CHAPTER **FOUR**

Nick Sutton normally enjoyed playing with fire. But playing with River was more like playing with molten steel.

He rolled up the collar of his jacket against the damp chill of the evening as he left the warmth of the pub and stepped outside onto the dimly lit street. It was still early fall, but already the sunny days were giving way to the gray rainy weather of a mountain winter.

He began the steep climb to his apartment past tall, narrow townhouses fronting the sidewalk with their carefully cultivated, microscopic yards. In the months since he'd moved here, he'd developed good quads. One of the perks.

River was another. She was totally hot and he liked sleeping with her. They'd fallen into a fun little relationship that she wasn't taking too seriously, which was a relief, but he never knew when she'd dig in her heels and insist on getting her own way about something.

Like that game. River was so focused on it that she constantly disregarded her own safety, and he suspected the safety of the others, too. Her obsession had nothing to do with money. All any of them would ever get from it was their normal salary and maybe a nice bonus.

Something else drove River, and Nick hoped like hell it wasn't because of what they said she was. He liked her. He liked her a lot. And the thought of having to turn her in made it hard to look at himself in the mirror sometimes.

As he walked, Nick paid attention to his surroundings. The street seemed deserted, and the crime rate in this area was one of the lowest in the country, although that still wasn't much to brag about, and it never paid to be careless. Who knew what lurked in the darkness?

But even when one paid attention, some of the things that dwelt in the night couldn't easily be detected by the average human senses. Nick wasn't prepared for the shadow that shifted from the face of one stippled building, or the arm that caught him around the neck and yanked him off his feet into the short driveway between two dark houses.

He caught a faint whiff of wet fur and immediately stopped struggling, knowing it would only trigger a predatory reaction. Unfortunately there wasn't much he could do to hide his fear. Jesus, he hated werewolves, especially right before a full moon. This quiet little mountain town was about to become the crime capital of the country for the next few days.

"Nick," the wolf whispered, his breath hot and damp against Nick's ear. "I haven't seen you in a dog's age. How the hell have you been?"

"Can't complain," Nick rasped. "Do you think you could let up a little on the old larynx there, Bane?"

The wolf let him go and Nick rubbed his throat. They sometimes didn't realize their own strength. And sometimes, they did.

Bane slouched against the townhouse beside a green recycling bin and took a deep, appreciative breath of whatever the homeowner had thrown out.

As Nick's eyes adjusted to the darkness, he tried to read Bane's mood.

Even he had to admit that Bane was one beautiful man. Dark hair, thick and shiny and the source of the faint, wet-fur smell, fell to a pair of broad, powerful shoulders. Eyes, black pools tonight, were normally a deep, chocolate brown. Lean hipped and long limbed, Bane gave off such a rush of animal magnetism steeped in pheromones that Nick often thought he could be tempted to do him—if his own inclinations drifted in that direction, which they didn't.

Playful, Nick decided. That was the kind of mood Bane was in, and it scared the shit out of him.

"So," Bane said, examining his fingers. "How is little Red Riding Hood? Been visiting her grandma lately?"

Jesus. Nick swallowed hard and thanked God River'd blown him off for the evening.

"She's a gamer, and a total workaholic. The only place she visits is the compound."

Bane laughed softly. "She doesn't spend all her time there. I can smell her on you."

Nick was going to bluff this out, even though he knew it was pointless. "Of course you can. We work together."

"You work with lots of people. You just came from a crowded bar. But I don't smell anyone else on you the way I smell her." Bane curled up his nose. "Although I do smell something on you. I just can't quite figure out what it is."

"Are you here bothering me because you're jealous I'm getting some and you're not?" Nick asked, keeping his voice low and even. "Or do you have a better reason?"

"You don't seem to be 'getting some' tonight," Bane observed, lifting one mocking brow. He gestured with his chin. "Her apartment's in that direction."

It chilled Nick to the bone that Bane knew where River lived, and even though of course he'd know that, Nick didn't like it.

"But," Bane continued, "it so happens I do have a better reason for being here. The department thinks you're wasting their time and money. That you might be getting a little too . . . involved."

Why, Nick mused dully, did it come as a surprise to him that they'd arrived at this conclusion? Because they were government, and government was the worst chronic waster of time and money? Had he really thought they'd let him drift along this way forever?

In all honesty, he'd thought they'd at least give him until the game was in full production.

"You're barking up the wrong tree," Nick said. "They wasted their own time and money by starting this whole investigation. River's got a great mind and some good reflexes, but other than that, she's nothing special."

Bane watched him for a long moment with eyes that could see quite well in the dark, sniffing the air to see if Nick lied. Nick's smell would give him away even if his expression didn't.

As it happened, Nick truly believed the department was wrong. River was human.

"Maybe she's nothing special as far as the department is concerned," Bane finally said, "but she seems to be something special to you."

"She's good in bed," Nick said impatiently. "Look. If I pull out now, River is going to ask questions. So is management, and they are totally suspicious when it comes to investors and competitors. Is that what the department wants? For management to find out who some of their game's investors really are?"

He knew he'd scored a direct hit with that last observation. The BiMiP—Bioengineered Military Program—had bought into the game as a way of keeping tabs on both Nick and River. They might be chronic wasters of time and money, but they always covered their assets. Management for the company producing the game wouldn't take kindly to handing over control of a potential jackpot to a government department more interested in experimentation than in profit.

Bane mulled that over. "Since you're right about that, and you can't pull out just yet, you may as well keep on watching her."

He flipped his hair out of his eyes, the wet-fur smell strong enough now to weaken Nick's knees. Werewolves, unlike the fairy tales, didn't turn into actual animals. It was the way they behaved that made them inhuman, and when their smell was strong, that was when their behavior was at its worst.

Nick didn't doubt for a second that the department's investment in the game was the only thing currently saving his life.

Bane slipped off into the night, leaving Nick badly shaken. He waited a long time to make certain the werewolf was really gone.

Then, just in case, he continued walking uphill toward his own apartment, his mind racing.

He'd made such a mistake getting involved in that government study. They could call it "Homeland Security" if they liked, but what kind of crazy bastards wanted to bring monsters to life? Smart people pulled the covers over their heads at night and went back to sleep. They didn't make sleep impossible.

And if the public ever caught wind of what had happened to the politician who'd leaked the story . . . Cancer didn't rip off a man's arms and stuff them up his ass. Bioengineered trolls did things like that. They might live under bridges most of the time, but they could be lured out if the price was right.

Nick walked a few more blocks before deciding Bane wasn't following him. Then he cut down a side street and began to run, his soft-soled shoes slapping too loud on the concrete. He didn't think Bane would touch her, not when that little threat about investors pretty much covered her, too, but he needed to know for sure that she was okay.

When he got to her building he let himself into the foyer with the key she'd given him. He didn't bother to wait for the elevator. Her apartment was on the second floor, so he took the stairs.

Unlocking the door to her apartment he closed his eyes, his heart pounding almost as hard as hers had earlier back in the game. If he hooked a monitor up to himself right now, it would be blasting all kinds of alarms.

He pushed the door open, terrified of what he might find inside, but her apartment was si'ent and undisturbed. The telltale scent of wet fur was absent.

So, however, was River.

Nick searched the apartment, ducking through a slew of overgrown plants and ornamental trees. Her place looked like a tropical forest. With an uncomfortable sense of urgency he paced from the tiny living room and cramped kitchen to the bedroom with its too-large four-poster bed, then rested the back of his head against an off-white wall and closed his eyes again.

Anger, based partly on relief, replaced his worry. It didn't take psychic abilities to realize that the real reason she hadn't wanted him to come over this evening wasn't because she was too tired, which would have been the truth, because she never got enough sleep.

She hadn't wanted him to come over because she'd intended to go back to work on the game.

♦ ♦

This was someone's idea of a game?

Hawk's palm skirted over the knife sheath anchored to his outer thigh as he took in his camouflage combat gear, familiarizing himself with his array of weapons. He glanced around, scanning the hot, humid, primitive surroundings. The Dark Lord had altered his perceptions once again, leading him to believe he was in a different world, one resembling a tropical rain forest.

Now he knew where he was, but he still had no idea who he was supposed to be.

"Sever, where are you?"

The female voice crackled through the communications link strapped to his wrist, answering his question.

So, he was Sever. And the voice, he assumed, eyeing the com-link, must belong to the gamer the Dark Lord said he wanted brought to him. Anger shook through him. He wasn't playing anyone's game. No more than he had to in order to keep his mind in one piece. After that, all he intended to do was wait out that weakness in the Dark Lord's program. Either that, or he was going to have to find some way to exploit it.

Hawk stepped from the shadows, his large body cutting a path through the overgrown shrubs and towering deciduous trees. High overheard a canopy of leaves blocked the sky and kept his body shrouded in darkness. The leafy blades also provided coverage, keeping the rain from totally drenching his combat attire.

With unease curling around him he stalked forward, determined to figure out what the Dark Lord had orchestrated this time to convince him he was dead.

As he ruffled the foliage, animals cried in warning, alerting others that a predator had invaded their territory. Their shrill calls blocked out the sucking sounds his heavy boots made with every step.

The voice crackled again. "What's taking you so long?"

River, the Dark Lord had called her.

"Where are you?" Hawk asked.

A short pause and then, "Check your com-link for the coordinates. You'd better haul ass. There are a couple of Ferals closing in around us."

Using the GPS on the com-link, Hawk easily tracked her down. It occurred to him that this was the first time the Dark Lord had pitted him against a woman. His face tensed. At least in battle. Did the Dark Lord think he'd falter if he came up against a pretty face?

Not fucking likely. Anger flared through him, hot and fast. If a kill needed to be made, he'd make it. He knew the drill. As a trained soldier deployed to hostile worlds, he'd come up against both sexes. This was nothing new.

First, however, he needed to establish if she was friend or foe. Either she was another sick fuck test set in place to kill him, or she was a tortured soul that the Dark Lord hadn't yet broken. His money was on the fuck test.

He pushed forward, continually scanning for predators. His long legs ate up the jungle floor. A moment later he found River standing in a clearing, also dressed in fatigues, a slightly curved saber held ready for battle.

Hawk drew his own sword from its scabbard. Thick brush crushed beneath his military boots as he closed the short distance between them.

River spun around. When she spotted him she lowered her sword, relaxing. "Oh, it's you."

He didn't lower his own. Instead, he moved quickly, and positioned the tip of his blade over her heart. She gave him a questioning glance as he checked her over. With his feet planted, and his shoulders squared, he took his time sizing up his opponent.

The top of her head barely reached his chest. Her blue eyes were big, soft, almost transparent. The long dark strands of hair that slipped from her helmet framed her face and clung to her cheeks. She was tiny, almost doll-like, and honesty gleamed in those too-big eyes of hers.

But he knew better than to trust her. He'd been tricked and tested enough to know all about betrayal.

Dark hair fell over his eyes when he lowered his head to meet her gaze. One well-shaped eyebrow shot up, confusion and a dawning wariness evident in her expression.

"You were expecting someone else?" Hawk asked, and stepped closer, his large body dominating hers as he considered his next move. Lightning split open the skies and the rain came harder, washing the dirt and insects from his fatigues and streaking down her mud-spattered cheeks.

River didn't flinch from the point of his blade and she didn't retreat.

"I wasn't expecting this turn of events," she said evenly.

Hawk watched her pulse jump at the base of her throat as she stood her ground and tightened her hands around her sword. Narrowing her eyes, she studied him in return. Confusion mixed with annoyance as she considered his actions, but she showed no signs of fear. Clearly she didn't think she had anything to be afraid of.

"What exactly were you expecting?" he asked.

She shook her head, ignoring his question. "What is going on with my program? And why are we back in the primitive world? We should have entered at the start of the postapocalyptic world where we left off. I know I saved the data." She glanced at her com-link and continued to speak to herself. "That's what I get for taking shortcuts. The new code must have messed up other data sequences."

He didn't have the patience for this. To regain her attention, he flicked his sword, slicing a cut in one sleeve of her combats. "Code?"

That caught her off guard. With lightning speed, she stepped back, tossed her rucksack to the side, and raised her sword. "What the hell are you doing?"

"Who are you?" he asked, advancing a few steps. If she belonged to the Dark Lord, he wanted to know. Turning his body sideways he widened his

feet, the movement intended to threaten and pro-
voke her into action.

River reacted instinctively to his combative stance.
The free strands of her long hair flared around her
face as she spun around. With amazing speed she
delivered a roundhouse kick, her foot driving toward
his head.

She hadn't put everything she had into it, testing
him, and even still, Hawk barely had time to block
it. In response, he used every ounce of strength he
possessed and matched her kick with a spinning
back kick of his own. His heel connected with her
jaw. She cried out, flung backward by the blow,
landing in a lump a few feet away.

Gaze intense and mouth set in a grim line, she
touched her face with the back of her hand and
said, "Jesus, Sever, what the hell is wrong with
you?"

That blow would have killed her if this were real
life. It probably should have killed her anyway.

Unless she knew that it wouldn't.

He quickly advanced, dropped to his knees on
top of her, grabbed her arms, and pinned them to
her sides. "Who are you? And don't make me ask it
again."

"I'm *River.*" Her breathing grew heavy, labored,
and after a few unsavory expletives, she whispered
under her breath, "And you're not supposed to be

acting like this. Get *off* me. I need to go back and fix this glitch."

That caught his attention. "What glitch?"

"This is not how the game is supposed to go."

Good enough for him. Hawk mentally searched for the weakness in the program, but if there was one, it wasn't big enough for him to use. Maybe if he continued to fight her, the weakness would grow.

He caught the wet-fur scent of an animal. Senses finely tuned, he sniffed the air and catalogued their surroundings. He shifted his attention from her to whatever lurked somewhere in the shadows.

River gestured with a bob of her chin. "The Ferals are closing in. Get off me so we can fight."

Hawk hesitated. Was she something the Dark Lord had created to test him, or was she another unbroken soul? If he fought her, was he helping the Dark Lord break her?

He wanted to escape, yes. But did he want his freedom at the expense of another's?

Keeping her in his peripheral vision, Hawk stood and turned in the direction of the scent. In one swift movement, a Feral, as River had called it, rushed from the shadows and pounced. Hawk stepped forward, meeting it head on. The animal went up on its hindquarters and he sank a punch dagger into its belly, twisting until all signs of life slipped from its body.

He stepped back without taking his gaze from the animal. He recognized the hound as one of the beasts that inhabited the Dark Lord's program, but it wasn't quite right. It was smaller, and not quite as fierce.

Twigs crunched beneath River's feet as she stood, and he turned to look at her. She dusted off her hands and said, "Now you're finally playing the game like you're supposed to."

He turned to her and steadied his sword. "This is no game."

"Sorry to break it to you, but it's a virtual video game, Sever. I designed it, and I designed you, and you're not doing what you're supposed to be doing."

She looked like a pissed-off munchkin. Somebody needed to set her straight. "If this is your virtual video game, why does it contain creatures from the Dark Lord's world?"

She gave him a quizzical look. "Dark Lord?"

A snarl on the other side of the trees reached his ears. They didn't have time for this right now. Hounds traveled in packs and more would be closing in shortly.

He wasn't going to trust her, but he wasn't going to abandon her either. He needed to keep her close until he found out if she was working with the Dark Lord, or if she, too, was in danger of losing her soul.

They needed to move. Now. He held his hand out to her and she eyed it tentatively. He pitched his voice low. "If you want to live, come with me."

"Shit. Something is really messed up with my game," she bit out. "Strategy is *mine.*"

She might be in danger of losing her soul, but Hawk had just lost the last little bit of his patience. "You might think this is a game, River, but believe me, if you die in here, you die for real."

She backed away from him, her eyes filling with dismay. "I should have listened to Nick. I'm in no condition to play tonight. I need to end this now."

She reached up and pulled off her helmet. Her eyes widened as she glanced around them. Whatever she'd expected to happen obviously hadn't.

Hats off to the little bastard, Hawk thought. If he'd created her, she was pretty damned realistic. He didn't dare get his hopes up that this was really her game and just might be his ticket to freedom. Life hadn't been that good to him lately.

She looked at Hawk. Full-blown panic edged her voice, bordering on hysteria.

"Why the hell am I still here?"

CHAPTER FIVE

♦

Bane flipped his thick hair out of his eyes. Nick was playing it too cautious with River Weston and the bosses were tired of it. That's why they'd called in the big gun.

Separate her from the others, they'd said to him. All he'd been told was to find a way to shut down the compound for a few days so they could find out if she was using magic to enhance the game without any witnesses around. No one had set any restrictions on how he should do it.

But while Bane might be a lone wolf, he understood pack behavior. Start bringing them down one by one, and the rest would turn on you.

The solution was not to bring them down one by one, but to take them all out at the same time, or as close to it as possible. The bosses wanted River alive for sure, and Nick was, well, sort of on Bane's side—although he wouldn't bet his paycheck on that—so that left the rest of the gamers as the expendable crewmembers. The redshirts.

Still, if someone was using magic to enhance the game, Bane didn't think it was River. Neither did he think she was Fae. Magic smelled funny and made his nose and throat burn. River Weston didn't smell funny and she didn't make his nose burn.

Tonight though, Nick had. He'd been in contact with someone who'd been in contact with magic. That was a lot of contacting, but Bane felt confident that whoever it was, the contact had been recent.

The lights from the town twinkled and glittered on the soft blanket of darkness spread out below him as he loped down the steep, empty street, following Nick's scent in the direction from which he'd come. He knew Nick was on his way to check out River's apartment. Just as he knew River was back at the compound, working diligently on that game his bosses were so interested in.

Bane also knew that when he reached the last place Nick had been, he'd find the redshirts. All three of them. He ran the tip of his tongue over the sharp edges of his canines in anticipation. Drunk gamers weren't much of a challenge for a were. This would be as easy as hunting sheep in a pen.

But Nick, now. Nick would be a challenge. He was smart and he had a healthy dose of self-preservation. Someday Bane was going to get the order to take him out, and good old Nick was going to do some serious running. For Bane, it was all about the thrill of the hunt. Killing the prey was the bonus.

Nick's trail led him to a part of the town he'd avoided until now. Bane didn't care for the smell of it. It wasn't so much the smell of magic, although that was bad enough, but more a sense of something groping for his soul. Bane didn't like anything touching his soul. He didn't have much of it to spare and what he had, he liked to ignore.

He slouched against a grimy brick wall in an even grimier alleyway across from the bar's main entrance, prepared to wait as long as it took for the gamers to appear. There weren't a lot of other people in the bar so there weren't likely to be witnesses, although witnesses didn't bother Bane. Humans were easily taken care of. Man-made disasters explained away a lot. A natural gas line, perhaps. Those things hadn't been properly maintained since early in the last war. The police wouldn't waste their budget investigating if another one "accidentally" blew.

He didn't have to wait long. The gamers were total lightweights when it came to drinking. He could smell the girlie drinks on them from here. The three of them emerged into the night, zipping their coats and complaining about the cold. He could see them clearly, backlit by the bright light from the bar's open door.

He decided to go after the fat one first. Not only did he look like a fairly easy warm-up, but anyone who referred to himself as "Fucktard Man" was begging to get his ass bitten off.

Bane had hoped the three of them would stick together for a few blocks and he could take care of them all at once. After all, it was late at night and there was a werewolf in town. They should be cautious. Instead, they said their good-byes and headed off in two different directions.

He sniffed the breeze again. The trashy-looking blonde wearing way too much perfume and hairspray was doing doggy-style with Fucktard Man. That made him question both their taste.

Change of plans. He couldn't go after them all at once. Plan B was to follow the single guy and rip out his throat, but make it so the others would hear his screams. The screaming should bring them running back to see what was happening to a member of their pack.

Bane made note of the direction the other two took before following his first target.

The tall skinny guy with the bad skin walked along as if he hadn't a care in the world, hands crammed into his jacket pockets, whistling a song so badly out of tune that Bane's sensitive ears ached and made him want to howl. Tone-deaf people shouldn't be allowed to listen to music, much less try to replicate it.

Broken glass crunched under the skinny guy's feet. He stopped suddenly, bent down, and looked to be tying his shoe. Bane wondered if this was a

trick, and if the skinny guy knew he was being followed or had some small sense of impending danger, then decided to go for it anyway. He didn't want
the other gamers getting too far away. He wanted to
turn this into a credible disaster scene, and he didn't
want to have to carry Fatso any great distance to
make the scenario work.

Bane moved in swiftly, grabbed the skinny guy
around the neck with just enough slack to allow him
to let out a bloodcurdling, deeply satisfying scream,
then bit into the jugular.

The thing about going for the jugular was that it
tended to be messy. Very messy. The skinny guy's
heels pounded against the sidewalk as Bane held
him down, letting the blood run off the sidewalk
and into the gutter, listening hard for the sound of
running footsteps.

He heard them all right. But they were running
away from, and not toward, him. *Shit.* So much for
pack behavior. What was *wrong* with people? Did
they not give a rat's ass at all about what happened
to one of their own?

He dropped the cooling body, the back of its head
striking the concrete with a loud thud. Then he
broke into a steady run, determined to salvage what
he could of the whole snafu. It looked like he was
going to be dragging Fucktard Man's fat ass around
after all.

This time, however, he was going to have to keep the blood to a minimum. Sweat beaded on his upper lip. A trail of blood leading to the scene of an explosion was going to make even an indifferent and unenthusiastic police force take notice.

And if the police noticed, his bosses would as well.

He caught up with the other pair between a boarded-up dry cleaner's and a coffee shop with an off-kilter but still functional flashing red Closed sign in the front window. The woman was slower than the man, which made sense since her women's shoes weren't meant for running. But at the same time it was clear that Fucktard Man had no concept at all of what it meant to protect a mate.

This was another one of the many reasons Bane had little but contempt for the human race. The world was truly a fucked-up place these days.

Bane broke the woman's neck with a quick flick of his wrists, then followed the terrified squeals of the final gamer. The squealing, along with the smell of wet blood on his own clothes, kicked Bane's predatory instincts into overdrive. The hell with being tidy. Bane wasn't going for the jugular this time. He decided to go for the entrails. This guy was going to suffer.

Tearing out entrails was just as satisfying as one

might expect. But the cleanup was going to be a bitch.

Bane stared with horror at the mess he'd made, and horror wasn't something he was used to experiencing. But he was here in this armpit of a mountain town with no one to think through the cleanup for him. Natural gas lines were as clever as he got, mostly because they'd worked for him in the past.

He didn't trust Nick enough to go to him for help, and besides, if Nick refused to help him he'd have to turn around and kill him, too. That would piss the bosses off even more than they were going to be already.

The blast of a Browning 125 double-barreled shotgun, circa 1984, blew a hole in the glass windowpane of the coffee shop just above Bane's head and wiped out its already sketchy Closed sign.

Bane threw himself sideways and rolled around the corner of the building. The clatter of spent shells bouncing off asphalt told him the shooter was on the other side of the street. The air reeked of gunpowder and magic.

"Show yourself, you hairy-toed, smelly little bastard," a woman's angry voice shouted from the shadows.

If she hadn't been able to hit him using a shotgun and magic, then whoever she was, she was seriously out of practice with both and Bane wasn't about to stick around and let her practice on him. Cleanup was now the least of his worries. He had a magic-wielding, shotgun-toting, pissed-off crazy woman gunning for him. Come tomorrow he was going to have equally pissed-off bosses who'd make tearing out his entrails appear like an attractive proposition.

If they caught him. This might be a good time for him to practice his more basic wolf skill sets and get back to nature for a while.

Bane took off in a crouching, weaving run, another blast of the shotgun drifting across his fleeing ass.

♦ ♦

How very interesting.

The Dark Lord leaned forward, his attention completely focused on the drama unfolding within the seeing stones as Hawkins and the gamer squared off against each other.

This might quite possibly be the first time in the history of the universe that a Guardian had ever struck a Fae. Either the Guardian's control was slipping so he couldn't recognize a Fae . . . or River wasn't Fae.

The Dark Lord now had another reason to hope that she was, because if so, her game was about to become even more interesting. He needed to get her to use her magic in order to be certain. He also needed to make certain the Guardian didn't start to trust her, although there wasn't much danger of that. Chase Hawkins was suspicious to the point of paranoia.

Even so he had no intention of making things easy for either one of them. There was no reason to take a chance when he was holding all the cards.

What more could he throw at them?

◆ ◆

River stared at the gaming helmet on the ground at her feet and tried hard not to throw up. She'd never had a panic attack before in her life, but there was a first time for everything.

Intense eyes zeroed in on her in a foreign, terror-inducing way. Nausea and light-headedness reared up in response.

"Where else should you be?" Sever asked in response to her question.

If she were smart she'd be tucked in her bed, snuggled up with Nick and enjoying a little late-night destressing session. Instead she was stuck in a virtual nightmare, the bleeping com-link strapped to her wrist useless until morning when the other members of the team showed up for work.

If she lived that long. Her heart was pounding so hard she wondered her ribs didn't crack.

She needed to pull herself together or the team was going to find her cold, stiff body plastered to the gaming platform in the morning. Almost as bad, two years of hard work would be thrown out the window. The legal system might not be what it used to be, but investors would never dare risk the kind of lawsuits that would follow if the game's safety was called into question. Today's generation made a career out of suing companies.

But she wasn't cold or stiff yet.

Purposely positioning her back against a damp, fungus-crusted tree trunk—partly to support herself because it seemed highly unlikely her knees could be forced to do so, and partly to better situate herself for battle—she studied the alien warrior looming over her beneath the dripping jungle foliage.

The differences were subtle, but nonetheless they were there. Her unconscious eye began to take note of the variances, some so small as to be insignificant, while others so glaringly off that she couldn't explain the discrepancies away. His thick hair was longer and slightly darker than the mock-ups, his strong, angular face free of the silly warrior paint Tanner had insisted on. His eyes weren't gray. Instead they were blacker and harder than Sever's— tortured, distrustful eyes filled with a mixture of suspicion, apprehension, and . . . hope?

What was he hoping? For her to get him out of the game, too?

Dream on, buddy. Virtuality was a one-way street. Players got into the game. Computer-generated warriors didn't get out.

River shifted against the tree and ignored the dampness seeping through the back of her shirt as she concentrated more fully on this stranger's body language, and his almost militant stance. He lacked Sever's calm steadiness—a steadiness that used to annoy the hell out of her, but that she now suddenly found herself longing for.

She concentrated, and yet the sword she clutched in her hand still felt like real metal, not the lightweight piece of wood she used to simulate a weapon when she played the game. She touched her finger to the tip of the blade and let out a small gasp when it pierced her flesh, drops of crimson blood seeping from the deep nick. Even though she knew it was nothing more than a psychological response, that had felt far too real.

Sever's warning words echoed in her mind. *If you die in here, you die for real.*

Maybe it was her mind that had died. Or maybe her body was already gone but her mind hadn't caught up with it yet. Sort of a "chicken with its head cut off" situation. Her hand went to her throat, not caring for that image.

"Where else should you be?" Sever repeated, his deep voice and impatient tone demanding a response.

A gust of wind came out of nowhere, blowing debris over her face. The wind was artificial, something they'd added to the game room for extra effect, but the tingle of dirt was a newer feature that River hadn't quite gotten used to. Tanner was totally into making the experience as realistic as possible. At the moment it was just a touch too real for her liking.

She wiped her bloody finger on her fatigues, blinked the dirt from her eyes, and took a moment to calm herself, but her addled brain could barely keep up with her racing thoughts.

"Who are you?" she demanded in return, dodging his question with one of her own.

He scanned the ground, the thick jungle around them, and the treetops before his gaze refocused on her. "The name's Hawk."

"Hawk?"

"Yeah. Who the hell is Sever?"

"You're Sever. You have to be," she said, more to convince herself than him. "The brawns to my brain."

His lips quirked up at that. "Afraid not."

Oh, God, what was happening? Her vision went a little fuzzy around the edges. Nick's dark predictions were about to come true and her brain was going to explode.

Sever—or rather, Hawk—caught her by surprise, grabbing her by the arm and yanking her so hard that she barreled into his chest. The top of her head connected with his chin. That felt pretty real, too. She would have met with more cushioning if she'd hit a brick wall.

She tried to shove herself away from him as a piercing noise rose from the depths of the jungle, and in that instant it occurred to her that Hawk was protecting her from something closing in on her from behind. She'd been so wrapped up in her thoughts she'd forgotten the danger.

The squawking sounds in the jungle threw her off again. She'd written this as a beginner's level, with simple Ferals and limited danger. She didn't remember anything that squawked.

Fucktard Man was going to get his ass kicked when she got her hands on him.

Returning to fight mode she peeled herself off Hawk's chest and spun around, prepared to kill the approaching creature with a blow from her sword.

Except when she turned, she found herself face to face with some sort of prehistoric monster that didn't belong in her virtual video game. Or anyone's. And while Nick was right about her—she really was a total adrenaline junkie—this was more excitement than even she could handle. She had to be in total control of any situation. Sweat broke out on her skin, preceding the terrible likelihood that she was about to be violently ill, but with a giant mental effort River pulled herself together. She had to try to understand this. To get herself out of the game and back to her own reality.

She needed to think of this as a challenge. She loved challenges—they were something she could handle.

Hawk grabbed her by the back of her shirt, lifted her feet clear off the soggy ground, and swung her behind his larger body, his voice lacking any warmth or kindness as he ordered, "Snap out of it."

He was right. There was no room for hesitation in this virtual game. Especially when she was no longer confident of the rules.

Although one rule seemed comfortingly intact. Sever, or Hawk, or whoever he was, protected her back. Strategy was still River's specialty.

She dropped to the ground as the leathery, vulturelike monstrosity eyeballing her took flight, then swooped down at them. Its sharp beak, easily as long as her body, glanced off the blade of the sword Hawk swung in an upward arc. River bit back a scream, determined to do her part and come up with a plan. No way was she going to show any weakness.

This was a *game*.

"What is that thing?" she asked, her voice sounding so close to normal she actually felt proud.

The bloodthirsty bird dove past them again, its claws coming far too close before climbing higher and higher above them in the darkening sky. River grabbed her sword and jumped to her feet. Sever might be programmed to protect her, but this wasn't the Sever she knew and she had a vested interest in protecting her back herself. She poised the sword high over her head and braced herself for the next attack.

Hawk pressed his back against hers, a warrior move she'd written into the code. She had no idea who this man really was, or what he was doing in her game, but it gave her a measure of comfort to know that he'd at least taken on Sever's fighting techniques and abilities.

"You really don't know what it is?" he asked, disbelief thick in his tone.

"I never designed it, so how would I know?"

"It's an Uultur."

River pressed one hand over her eyes to block the sun and peered into the sky to size up their winged opponent. Obsidian eyes were set deep inside a silvery bald head, its long neck leading to a leathery, lizardlike body. A thin membrane of pale orange skin stretched from its legs to the tips of four finger-like appendages, and its mouth possessed a full set of pointy teeth that looked as if they could easily tear through human flesh.

If you die in here, you die for real.

River had never seen anything like it. If she had, she would have remembered. Had that new code created this creature? Where had that code come from in the first place?

Maybe she should have asked herself that question before she inserted the code into her program. She eyed Hawk suspiciously. Had someone tapped into her program? And was that someone playing with her? Or worse, against her?

She wanted answers, but first she had to deal with the current crisis. She cast Hawk a suspicious glance. "What is it, some sort of cross between a vulture and a pterodactyl?"

"Something like that."

He was looking at her as if she should have known what that crazy thing was. She widened her stance and rooted her feet in the thick jungle floor, the setting sun reflecting off her blade as she held it steady in front of her. He thought she was lying.

"So okay, you didn't design it. How can you be sure you know how to kill it?" Hawk asked.

She angled her head to regard him, wondering what he was up to and not certain she'd like it, whatever it was. "Are you trying to tell me that my sword won't work?"

He pointed upward. "You're about to find out."

The creature dove, coming at them at breakneck speed. Hawk stepped back, leaving her undefended in the center of the clearing.

So, unlike her computer-designed warrior Sever, she couldn't count on Hawk to watch her back. How chivalrous.

Out of the corner of her eye she caught Hawk watching her, as if sizing up her performance. He seemed to be waiting for something to happen, but what, she didn't know.

The Uultur, easily three times her size, flapped its long wings and aimed for River's sword as if attracted to the light reflecting off the blade. She didn't like that thing coming at her from the sky. A sword really wasn't the best weapon in this instance. She gripped the hilt tighter, standing steady. Her pulse kicked up a notch as she calculated the best angle to use the sword to take out the beast in one strike, wondering where its heart might be.

Maybe she didn't have to use a sword. She'd planted weapons far more appropriate to this level than that in the game.

"Like some help?" Hawk inquired, an edge in his voice. He didn't sound quite so sure of himself now. Whatever he'd been expecting, it didn't seem to be happening for him.

"Under a boulder," she shouted at him. "There are bows and arrows under boulders in this level. Crack a boulder with your sword!"

Hawk sifted through the foliage with the tip of his sword. "Found one."

The bird made an ungodly, high-pitched sound and thrust its razorlike claws forward. River considered the awful possibility that it might scoop her up, carry her off to its nest, and pick her bones clean before she was entirely dead. Her stomach plummeted. What had she gotten herself into?

The whine of an arrow breezed past her face. A split second later its fletching protruded from the creature's scrawny neck. The Uultur squealed, flapping its wings to remain airborne before losing that battle and flopping to the ground in a steaming pile of death. River gagged from the stench of decay it released.

Even Tanner wouldn't have added a smell that bad. Something had seriously changed in her program.

She rounded on Hawk, angry that he hadn't stepped in to help her sooner. "Could you have been any slower with that bow and arrow?"

"The shot wasn't mine," he said grimly as he slung the bow and quiver of arrows over his shoulder.

Of course the shot was his. River was about to call him on that lie when his head went up with a start and he sniffed at the air, lifting a hand for her to be silent.

She rubbed her aching temples with shaky fingers. "Look—"

Hawk clapped a hand over her mouth and nodded upward. She followed the movement. A flock of Uultur were closing in from the west. As they circled from above their large, winged bodies eclipsed the last light of the setting sun, prematurely turning twilight into night.

Hawk moved close and pressed his mouth to her ear, his body shielding hers. As though she was about to fall for a false display of manly protectiveness from him again. The second she blinked he'd be gone.

"We need to move," he said.

She might have designed Sever from her own taste preferences, but this guy took alpha warrior to a whole new level. *Asshole.*

This was still her game. She picked up her rucksack from where she'd tossed it and hitched it over her shoulder. "Then follow me," she said to him.

He shot her a dark look.

River quickly concluded that she'd have to somehow convince him to follow her. She intended to find out what was happening to her program. She needed him with her, and kept alive long enough for her to get those answers. They'd be the next meal for the Uultur if she didn't find the nearest safe house in time. As tempting as it was to let him find his own way, she really did want him alive and still in the game. At least for a little while.

"I'm not asking you to trust me. But if *you* want to live, follow *me*. Otherwise, you're on your own." She steadied herself, fully expecting him to go his own way. He hardly seemed the type to relinquish control easily. Sever certainly wouldn't.

Neither would she.

A flicker of movement caught her attention. The sharp blade of his sword had begun to deteriorate, a sure sign that they needed to get to the safe house, and fast. Hers couldn't be too far behind.

"You'd better hurry up and make your decision," she said. With a nod she indicated his sword. She wasn't going to stand there and debate the issue and risk her own life in the process. If he didn't start moving, she'd have to get the answers she needed some other way.

Hawk glanced upward at the sky, running his finger along the melting edge of his sword. His jaw tightened, nostrils flaring. Then, to her surprise and relief, he held his hand out and gestured for her to lead the way. Dark, unreadable eyes drilled into hers.

"Smart move," she murmured, averting her own

gaze. She really didn't like it when he looked at her like that. It made her skin burn.

With her sword still whole and held at the ready, River led them deeper into the damp jungle. Her boots sank into the soft ground as she inhaled, pulling the rich, familiar smells into her lungs, and letting her senses guide the way. This was supposed to be an easy level. She'd been through the primitive jungle level a dozen times before, but she darted a glance around, completely unsure of herself now and wary of what could go wrong next. She cut a path with her sword and sent up a silent prayer of hope that the safe house would still be intact, and where she'd put it. If not, she wasn't sure what her next move would be, because right now she needed a quiet, safe spot to catch her breath and figure out what was going on.

The game was unpredictable at the best of times. Before this was over, it was probably going to get a hell of a lot worse. At least her vitals were back near the normal range.

Either that, or she was already dead.

CHAPTER SIX

♦

Hawk wondered what it meant, if anything, that the mysterious River hadn't known what to do with an Uultur. He also wondered what it meant that he hadn't been the one to fire off that arrow.

He let her guide the way, keeping pace behind her, fully aware that she could be leading him into a trap but deciding, what the hell? What was the worst thing that could happen to him now? Another impromptu blow job at the little bastard's command?

He gritted his teeth, gambling on her being as misplaced in this reality as he was, although her insistence that this was her game remained unsettling. She didn't seem to want him dead though, at least for now, so he was willing to return the favor.

For the moment. Anything to keep the Dark Lord from getting something he wanted—and as long as it suited Hawk.

She moved through the jungle with an eerie skill, dodging dangling vines and camouflaged boa constrictors with equal dexterity. While that creeped him out and made him even edgier, he nevertheless found himself impressed by her speed and endurance. In a virtual world the pace she was setting required strength of mind, not body, and River's strength pretty much matched his own.

Of course, he hadn't been himself lately.

When they came to a cluster of eucalyptus trees at the edge of the jungle, River looked around to ensure it was safe before ducking under the drooping branch of a tree. She jammed her sword into the thick trunk and pulled, and its bark peeled away, mimicking a door. River stepped inside.

She glanced back at him. "Quick, get in the safe house."

The entrance wasn't designed for someone Hawk's size. He had to wedge himself in sideways. Once he stepped through the threshold, though, he entered a bright, spacious room.

He touched the tip of one careful finger to blue walls created to resemble the sky. Very realistic looking, but the feel of wood underneath was unmistakable. Other than that, he could have sworn he'd entered the world of the Fae, the fabled Garden of Eden, where all life began. Tropical ferns and flowers littered the floor. Scattered coconut, banana, and various deciduous trees had trunks carved into chairs with comfortably shaped backrests.

No way had the Dark Lord programmed this. He didn't have the imagination. Maybe she really did have a part in designing this game.

Keeping a careful eye on him, River set her rucksack against a tree, removed her sword from its scabbard, and worked her way around the room, touching her blade to the fruit, looking more confident in here than she had back in the clearing. Little jolts of lightning danced along the length of the metal. As her blade grew sharper the fruit it touched decomposed, presumably disintegrating into the dirt floor to provide nutrients for new life to grow.

Nice trick. While the Dark Lord restored his virtual energy from stolen souls, River gathered hers from fake fruit.

Hawk settled himself into one of the carved chairs and proceeded to remove his weaponry, or what was left of it. He would have tried River's trick to restore it except she'd stripped the trees of fruit, leaving none for him. He'd bet that was deliberate.

She stashed her restored sword into its sheath, leaned it against a tree, then came to stand beside him. She planted one hand on a slim hip. "Who are you?" she asked. "And how did you end up in my game?"

She was pretty cocky for someone half his size. He contemplated his flickering sword. Of course, at the moment she had a lot more energy than he did. But she'd also stood her ground against both him and an Uultur, and that took guts.

Still, he wasn't in an especially good mood. He

raised his eyebrows. "You keep saying that. What makes you think it's really your game?"

"I designed it, and I want to know why you're messing with it."

Hawk would have laughed if he remembered how. She truly thought she was playing her game. If she was telling the truth—and Hawk wasn't yet convinced that she was—it would mean that somewhere in this whole bizarre mess there really was a game.

That possibility was the only thing keeping him here with her. If there was a game, there was a way to beat it. But if this was part of the sick little bastard's virtual prison, one created by the Guardians that even Hawk couldn't escape, then how could it also be a game?

Hawk planted his elbows on his knees and leaned forward. This had to be too good to be true. He wondered if the Dark Lord could see them right now.

"So this is all a game to you?" he asked, watching her closely.

"Yes!" She sounded impatient now, her eyes sparking with frustration. "But it's messed up."

"What if that's because you aren't in your game anymore?"

"Of course I am. How else would I know about this safe house?"

"How come you didn't know about the Uultur?"

She crinkled her nose and shot back, "How come you did?"

Fair enough.

"Uultur are prehistoric birds from the Dark Lord's world," he explained. "The Guardians probably thought they'd add a nice, homey touch for a warm and friendly guy."

She gave a baffled, disbelieving shake of her head. "Dark Lord? You mean the Soul Man? And who are the Guardians? I created this game, the Soul Man, and even you. There are no Dark Lords, Guardians, or Uultur." She shuddered. "Those things are another glitch in the program. I bet Tanner was messing around again. If he doesn't cut it out we'll never get this game on the market." She tapped the com-link on her wrist. "At least my vitals are back to normal."

Hawk tried to follow her bouncing logic. "What are you talking about?"

"My V-I-T-A-L-S." She spelled it out slowly for him, as if he were mentally challenged. She waved the com-link under his nose. "This tells me how my body is reacting to the stress of the game. It links me to my gaming platform and computer."

By Guardian standards, that com-link was fairly archaic technology. For other worlds it was cutting edge. As he mentally ran through all the worlds the Guardians had visited, he could think of several that might have progressed to the point that they could produce such technology themselves. There was only one where he hoped it hadn't.

He examined the com-link on his own wrist more closely. He pressed a button and the tiny microchip inside popped out.

Immediately, the safe room disappeared and he found himself back in the Dark Lord's lair, staring into the Dark Lord's astonished face with what he knew had to be an equally stupid, astonished expression on his own.

Then River was standing over him with his wrist and the com-link in her hand, the microchip safely back in place.

"Don't take it apart again," she said. "You disappear when you do that."

Did he ever. Hawk didn't like where he'd disappeared to either. This safe house might not be real, but it was a hell of a lot better than the reality he'd lived with for the better part of a year.

"Let me see yours," he demanded, holding out his hand for her to give it to him.

She jerked her arm away. "Why? So you can make me disappear instead?"

Smart. If he took her com-link apart and she remained in the game, then she really was a player. That meant her soul was still her own. If her soul was her own, then maybe, just maybe, Hawk could find a way to use that to his advantage.

"You don't strike me as stupid," he said. "According to you I'm in this game as a part of the scenery. If you're in this game as a player, as you keep saying, then my taking your com-link apart won't have any effect on you. The real com-link is with your body. These ones are built with 3-D imagery, correct?" She nodded, and he beckoned with his fingers. "Hand it over." He sighed when she didn't move. "I promise I won't damage it. I just want to see how you built it." With 3-D imagery, each illustration could be drawn piece by piece and assembled exactly as if it were real. He could take it apart and put it back together again just as if it were the real com-link, depending on the level of detail the illustrator had used.

Curiosity, not trust, won her over. She wanted to know what would happen next. She was a definite thrill seeker.

A true gamer.

And, as Hawk examined the com-link she handed him, simple as it was he could also see that she possessed real Guardian technology. This was something he might have been able to build himself, given the time and the resources. That meant she was telling him at least the partial truth.

So who was she, and where had she come from?

Hawk had been a mind and a soul drifting in space, trapped when he'd stopped to investigate what had looked like an abandoned world. His body was still on his own world, cared for by his people. If River's mind and soul were here in the game, where was her body?

"What was the last thing you were doing before you entered the game?" Hawk asked her.

"I was at my computer, testing a new code."

"This code. What's it for?"

"I had a problem with my program," she explained. "In the final sequence where the player battles the Soul Man, the game keeps freezing for no apparent reason. I can't seem to kill him. All I get is an error message."

Hawk mulled that over. "Perhaps that's because only an immortal can kill an immortal," he mused. "That fact might not change, even in a virtual world."

If Hawk couldn't kill the Dark Lord, not even in a virtual world, then his only hope of escape became the error in the Dark Lord's prison program. And it didn't take a programming genius to figure out that River's error and the Dark Lord's failing program were most likely related. Her error happened in the final level. That meant Hawk had to get to it.

She was looking at him as if he were insane, which put him on the defensive because he wondered about that himself. Then she turned her attention back to the com-link she'd refastened to her wrist. She pressed a button and cursed low when nothing happened.

Hawk glanced at his own com-link before shooting her a suspicious look. "Who's on the other end of these things?"

Her head came up. "Nick. My . . . assistant."

That little hesitation was interesting. "Where, exactly, is this Nick?"

She sniffed. "Probably asleep."

"That's not what I meant. Where is your body right now?"

"On a gaming platform in the compound."

Hawk pinched the bridge of his nose and tried not to choke her. "Can you be a little more specific? Where's this compound?"

"In a small community on the west coast of British Columbia."

British Columbia. Hawk searched his memories. *Earth. She was from* Earth. The Dark Lord's world. A place even the gentle Fae had finally agreed was beyond salvation. Unease tap-danced in the pit of his stomach. This wasn't good.

"Can Nick stop the game?" Hawk asked.

"Not at the moment."

"Why not?"

River avoided his eyes. "He's not there. I wasn't supposed to go into the game alone."

She absently tucked a strand of long black hair behind one ear, bent forward, and touched her palm to the root of a tree. Succulent red fruit blossomed before his eyes. Hawk jerked back with a start at the faint brush of magic. *What the hell?*

"How did you do that?"

She seemed startled by the question, her blue eyes widening. She gestured toward the fruit that had suddenly materialized on the low-hanging branches as if it were something that happened every day. "That?"

"Yes, that."

"It's written into the program. We use the energy from these plants to restore our weapons." His body tightened when she stepped close, drew his sword from its scabbard, and tapped it against the smooth-skinned hollow fruit.

He clenched his jaw hard enough to grind bone. He didn't care how good someone's technology was, magic couldn't be programmed, and he knew of only one race that could create life with magic the way she just had—virtual reality or not. Not even the Dark Lords could do it.

Only the Fae.

He'd had no experience of his own with the Fae. His chest squeezed, the pain real even if the body he used was not. Traveling to endangered worlds with the Fae had been his dead wife's role, not his. All

Guardians, however, could recognize Fae magic. When magic was released it had a distinctive scent as well as touch.

He couldn't sense any magic in River. He couldn't smell it on her either. But he'd felt it, or at least he thought he had. His chest started to rise and fall in a panicky rhythm he couldn't control. Had his mind finally short-circuited?

He didn't want to go too far down that road. "Tell me more about this code you were working on."

He didn't miss the way she kept his sword between them, and decided he would take it from her if she got too jumpy. She might not be able to kill him outright, but he wasn't ready to face the Dark Lord again if she caught him off guard. Not when he just might be able to use River to his own advantage.

"I was working on the final level when this new string of code suddenly appeared on my computer." She rolled one shoulder. "I did a little copy and paste, got back onto my platform, and voilà, I end up here with you, unable to find my way out." She frowned. "But I'm in the wrong level. I don't understand how that could have happened."

She was a gamer. Of course she'd try the code. The Dark Lord's words came back to Hawk. River had wanted her game to work badly enough to trade her soul for it. While Hawk couldn't imagine why she would do such a thing, obviously she'd meant the words or the Dark Lord wouldn't have a claim on her soul.

He thought about that. It was possible she'd meant the words, but had she *believed* them?

Whether she'd believed them or not wasn't really important to Hawk at the moment. *He* didn't believe that if he managed to kill her and convince her she was dead as the Dark Lord wanted, the Dark Lord would release Hawk's soul and let him go.

What Hawk did believe was that River could somehow tap into magic, she knew how to use Guardian technology, and she still possessed her own body and soul. Therefore she could be useful to him, particularly in that final level. How could he explain this in a way that would earn her trust without making him sound crazy?

He bounced a fist off his thigh, thinking hard. He was a lost soul trapped in a virtual prison, masquerading as a warrior in a gamer's screwed-up program. Sounding crazy wasn't his biggest concern.

He tried to think of common ground, something she could identify with that would be shared by both their worlds. Something she could believe, or at least understand. He'd never heard of a world yet that didn't have children's stories. If his world told stories about the Dark Lord, then so might hers. Earth, after all, was where the Dark Lords had ruled.

River took a cautious step back, clearly uncomfortable with his silence. "What?"

"Do you believe in fairy tales, River?" he asked.

She went quiet, all big eyes and nervous tension. "No."

"Well I do, and the Guardians have stories about your 'Soul Man.' To us, he's the last of the immortal Dark Lords. He feeds on souls for restoring his energy, and his energy is dark magic. A very long time ago he made the mistake of stealing a soul the Guardians were sworn to protect. The Guardians managed to trap him with the help of the Fae—the weavers of earth magic, the bringers of life. Somehow you've tapped into his prison with your game."

Hawk told her then of the immortal Dark Lords, and of how they'd ruled the earth world with their magic during that period of time known as the Dark Ages. He told her about the Guardians, whose world existed solely through technology, and of the Fae, who brought magic and life to all the worlds. He explained how the Guardians protected the magical souls of the Fae, because a Fae's soul was finite. When one ceased to exist, another would never replace it. Rebirth was what kept a Fae soul and its magic alive. A Fae soul was the most valuable thing in all the universe. A Guardian would sacrifice his or her own soul a thousand times over to protect a single Fae, because without the Fae, there would be no life. That was why Hawk was here. He'd accepted a task to find out why Fae soul numbers were dwindling. He'd allowed his mind and soul to be separated from his body in order to follow them.

What Hawk didn't tell her was that he, too, would offer himself to the Dark Lord this instant and suffer the consequences for all of eternity in exchange for the life of a Fae. The depth of his feelings on that was something he didn't think he could adequately convey, and therefore he didn't bother to try.

River was listening, but Hawk couldn't tell if she believed him or not. "Did you say anything before you accepted that new code?" he finished. "Anything that might make him think you'd give up your soul?"

She swallowed. "I can't remember. Maybe. Why?"

"Because if you said it, and meant it, I'm really afraid that's exactly what you may have done." He leaned forward, and she took another small step back in response. "How badly did you want this game to work? How much were you willing to sacrifice for it?"

A lot. Hawk could see it in her eyes. He could also see her growing fear, which was good, because fear might keep her alive.

"How do I know you're not messing with my program?" she countered. "How do I know you're not messing with my *mind*?"

He understood her concern. Hawk worried about his own mind, too, far more than his body or soul, because the mind was the fragile link that tied a body to its soul. Break the mind, break the link.

He stood, lifted his shirt, and exposed his scars. "Because the Dark Lord is after my soul, too. Or at least he's trying to claim it."

Her cheeks went white at the sight of the scars, and she couldn't take her eyes from them. They were thick and ugly and red. Hawk had been proud of them because they were a symbol that the Dark Lord hadn't broken him. Now, seeing them through her eyes, he was disgusted with himself that they were even still on him. Just how weak had he grown?

Hawk could read the uncertainty on her face. The dangers to the body, she could accept. It was the danger to her mind she was having difficulty with.

"Why can't he claim your soul?" she asked.

"My real body is still alive in my world, just like yours is still alive back in your compound," Hawk explained. "Your mind is what is protecting you. If you die in this world you can die for real, River. All it takes is for your mind to believe that you're dead."

He fingered the scars. Gritting his teeth, slowly, one by one, he made them disappear. Her eyes were even wider when he'd finished. "I believe I'm alive," he said. "I can protect myself. But the longer the Dark Lord holds me here, the harder it is for me to believe. That makes it harder and harder for me to heal." He lowered his shirt. "And when danger comes at you faster than your mind can rationalize, that split second when your mind accepts the danger as reality is the split second that can make the difference between life and death."

Understanding lit her eyes.

"Of course," she said. "None of this is real. It's all a simulation." She glanced at the tiny cut on the tip of her finger.

Hawk held his breath in relief as the cut disappeared. She might not trust him yet, but at least she believed.

◆ ◆

River watched the cut on her finger vanish as if it had never existed and decided that whatever happened, she was going to survive.

Whether Hawk spoke the truth about where he'd come from and this Dark Lord who'd captured him, or someone had programmed the words into him, it was reality as he knew it and he truly believed. She had no reason to trust him other than the suffering she read in his eyes. No one could fake so much pain. No one could program it either.

At least not in her world.

She sank to the ground, into the soft, lush, familiar vegetation she'd created. The earth was warm and comfortable, and she was exhausted both physically and mentally. She could see no reason why she shouldn't fall asleep right now and wait inside the safe house for morning to come and Nick to rescue her. All the Red Bull she'd consumed was long gone from her system. Her eyelids dropped.

"Open your eyes!" Hawk barked at her, and she straightened with a startled snap of her head. "You can't go to sleep. If you sleep, you won't know for certain what reality you'll wake up to. Will it be your reality? Or a dream? Or something that was programmed?"

River massaged the skin under her eyes with the tips of her fingers. He was right. She could understand the logic in that. She hoped her body could understand it as well, because right now, she didn't think it was all that willing to cooperate.

"Okay," she agreed with grudging grace. "But let's stay where we are for a few more hours." All she had to do was survive until morning, when the rest of the team came to work. They would find her and extract her. Then she could go home and sleep for the rest of the week.

She fixed her attention on the bright, skylike walls of the safe house. She blinked, thinking at first her eyes were playing tricks on her, but no, the voxels—the units defining the 3-D imagery—had shifted apart. The walls rippled, began to cascade, and she leapt to her feet.

The next thing she knew, she and Hawk stood at the center of a vast wasteland. Red dust swirled around them on a hot, stinging desert wind.

No longer in the safe house, and suddenly weaponless, Hawk grabbed her shirt and hauled her to his side. River clutched his sleeve with the howling wind whipping hair and sand into her face, terrified and trying not to be.

She had to shout to make herself heard. Heat seared her lungs as she drew in a breath. "This is no error in my game."

Hawk shook his head, shielding his face as best he could. "No," he confirmed, his voice grim. "It's a glitch in the prison's program. So why am I still Sever?" He glanced at his wrist where the com-link remained. "Ah," he said. His fingers flew to the button that released the microchip.

If he released that chip he would disappear, River thought wildly. Was he planning to abandon her here?

Before she could ask, the error in the program corrected itself and they were back in the safe house.

Hawk took his fingers off the com-link. River's hand went to her raw throat. The awful burning sensation slowly eased as she reminded herself she hadn't really been harmed.

The same couldn't be said for her safe house. She looked around in dismay. The beautiful room she'd spent so many hours building was no longer lush and green. Instead, the plants were wilting and the sky had gone gray. The earth wasn't warm and soft, but crackled like brittle glass beneath their feet.

"Look out!"

River ducked instinctively, throwing her arms over her head as an ugly, red little troll-like creature swung from the branches of a nearby eucalyptus and missed her face with its booted feet by mere inches. Hawk's sword hissed through the air as it caught its belly on the return swing, gutting it from stem to stern, spraying blood and gore around the room and drenching their hair, skin, and clothing.

"One of yours?" Hawk asked, nudging the body with his toe, and River nodded, breathless.

"It's called a wichtlein. It appears in the next two levels. In the first of the levels it causes rock slides. In the second level it trashes buildings, and it's also poisonous. I don't know how it got in here."

Hawk wiped streams of blood off his face with the crook of his elbow. "We need to avoid unpleasant surprises. I don't think we can stay safe in here any longer."

She didn't think so either. But neither did she think she should go out in the game with him, not when the levels were going to grow increasingly more complex. Not if she couldn't trust him. Sever was supposed to watch her back. Hawk's only interest was himself.

"Were you going to leave me out there?" she asked him.

He paused in the process of wiping down his blade with the frond of a dying fern. "Pardon?"

"You reached for your com-link out there in that dust bowl," she said. "Were you going to remove the microchip again?"

"Yes." Her heart gave an unpleasant lurch. He met her gaze. "I wanted to see if I could escape through that malfunction, and if your game's com-link was all that kept me in place." He shrugged. "If I'd disappeared, you would have brought me back again."

She might have if she were able. Had he even considered the possibility that maybe she couldn't this time?

Another question suddenly leapt into River's brain, one she should have considered more seriously sooner.

He'd just saved her from a wichtlein, true. But if

Hawk hadn't saved her from the Uultur earlier—
and why should he lie about being a jerk?—then
who had shot that arrow?

◆ ◆

The Dark Lord flipped the crucible of seeing stones
off its pedestal with the tips of his fingers, sending
it to the floor with a crash and the stones scattering
across the room like multicolored marbles.

"Pick them up," he snarled at the terrified souls
trembling nearby.

Fresh scorch marks blackened the stone walls
from floor to ceiling. The acrid tang of smoke thickened the air. What had they done to make his program collapse like that?

He hadn't expected to win the game quickly or
easily. He knew from experience that the Guardian
was too tough for that, and if the woman was Fae,
she'd have some tricks of her own. She'd had the
ability to tap into his prison in the first place.

But that arrow had been unexpected. So had their
disappearance into a sanctuary through a door in a
tree. She'd managed to find a way to hide from him
and he didn't like that. He didn't like that at all, and
he'd tried to smash his way in.

He sat back and tapped clasped fingers against
his chin. The Guardian was far too suspicious to
form an alliance with the woman. The Dark Lord

had tried that tactic before and failed. He doubted very much if she could accomplish what he had not.

Yet he had come to think of himself as lord and master of this world and he didn't care for the reminder that he was nothing more than a prisoner, long forgotten by captors who no longer feared him as they should. He'd learned to run the Guardians' program, altering it in small ways to amuse himself, but he couldn't escape it no matter what he tried, not even using the limited magic he'd managed to recoup through the capture of a few unwary souls.

The program's impending failure, just when he'd found a possible passage to freedom, was too great a threat. The most recent error made it impossible for him to pull the Guardian out now, even if he wanted to. Every time he inserted something into her game, his program malfunctioned. He'd have to be careful what obstacles he threw into the game from now on. He'd have to make them count.

The seeing stones, back in their crucible on its pedestal, beckoned him again. He stirred them, then leveled the glittering mound so that he could see more clearly the images the stones projected.

He scanned the next level. He knew the game quite intimately because River Weston had stolen parts of it from his prison. Those were the areas where he had the greatest control.

There. He'd insert an obstacle at the door of the next safe house. Let them try to enter it now.

But there was something odd about the construction of the level, and it made him frown. The latest error in the program seemed to have altered the game as well.

He had no idea what that might mean.

CHAPTER SEVEN

♦

Nick slammed the door to his apartment behind him with unnecessary force. The neighbor next door pounded on the flimsy dividing wall in protest.

The kitchen phone rang and he snatched it off the hook, fully expecting it to be River and intending to give her an uncensored opinion of her evening activities. She needed someone to keep an eye on her. She always played too long.

The voice on the other end of the line was as unwelcome as it was unexpected.

"I wonder what you've been up to all evening?" Amusement tinged General Amos Kaye's words.

Nick rested his back against the wall and held the phone between his shoulder and his chin to free his shaking hands as he tried to figure out what Kaye might want.

Amos Kaye was the sort of man who gave the military a bad reputation, assuming the general population ever figured out what it was that he did. A geneticist in a former life, in the days before and during the war that had almost decimated the world's entire human population, he'd spearheaded experiments that brought monsters like Bane out of nightmares and into reality. The plan, as Nick understood it, had been to create an army of supersoldiers to protect the nation's borders. They'd ended up with soldiers scarier than hell.

Once the war was over and everyone lost—that had been an unexpected outcome for the world's great leaders, Nick thought with little humor—Kaye had been appointed to cleanup duty on the Homeland Security team.

Kaye, however, was a scientist through and through. Making monsters was what he did best. He was a little sketchier on maintaining control over them.

But for a scientist he had some interesting, rather offbeat beliefs. Magic was one of them. He'd hired Nick to investigate River's special talents, and Nick took the job because he'd assumed it would be easy money, and it was, but it had a few pitfalls. He should have requested danger pay.

"Amos, my man." It always bugged Kaye that Nick didn't do the whole respect thing and call him

"General," or even "sir." That was one of the few perks of being a civilian. "I've been hanging out with Bane."

"And yet you're still alive. I had no idea you and Bane were such good friends."

That comment about him still being alive sounded a little too pointed, especially since chances were good that Bane was going to be busy this evening. Nick thought he might try a bit of respect after all. "What can I do for you?"

"You can haul your ass back to the compound and find out what your girlfriend is up to."

"I don't need to haul my ass anywhere to find that out," Nick replied. "She's trying to figure out what's wrong with the final level."

"What *is* wrong with the final level?" Kaye asked.

Nick really didn't like to tell him because Kaye was crazy enough to read more into it than he should. "It's a game built with underdeveloped technology from before the war, and the technology has some quirks to it. River's com-link microchip is more of a micromachine, programmed to carry out any number of functions, and it hasn't been perfected yet." The crazy geneticist who'd once bioengineered human mutants from machine parts should understand that, but the progression of time hadn't made Kaye less crazy. "Her main character turns on her in the final level. She can't figure out a way to beat him."

"What do you mean, 'turns on her'?"

"Poor choice of words," Nick said hastily. He hadn't forgotten he was angry with River, but he wasn't ready to sell her out either. He slid down the wall to sit on the cold kitchen tiles. "She's made him impossible to beat and she won't change him."

"Won't, or can't?" Kaye mused.

"Won't." Nick was definite about that. River was stubborn and hated to admit to mistakes. Probably because she so seldom made any. Now there was an irritating quality in a woman.

"You're sleeping with her. Haven't you noticed anything . . . unusual about her?"

Jesus. Did he have no privacy at all? If Nick had known Kaye was going to watch him this close he would never have crawled into bed with River in the first place. Fun and games. That was all he'd expected from this assignment. But this wasn't fun anymore, and it was certainly no game.

"Yes. She snores." She also had a fixation with Sever, but Nick didn't bring that up. It was a guy thing. His ego wouldn't let him acknowledge the competition.

He could tell Kaye wasn't amused.

"I expect you to keep a closer watch on her from now on," Kaye said. "Find out why she can't fix her program. Perhaps it's not the program at all. Perhaps she's managed to re-create something that everyone thought was gone forever."

Or perhaps, Nick thought as he listened to the click on the other end of the line as Amos Kaye hung up on him, River had caught the attention of a crazy old fuck who made the Soul Man look like Santa Claus.

The status of her vitals while she played a game was the least of his worries.

Right now, Nick was far more worried about the status of his own.

♦ ♦

As Hawk finished wiping down his sword and started to peel off his blood-soaked jacket, River's discreet glances panned the length of him, taking in every small detail.

Whoever he was in reality, as Sever he was totally hot. Nick had even more reason to be jealous than he thought, because Hawk added a certain male . . . *something* to the character that she could never have programmed.

And even though Hawk really did look like he hadn't slept in months, he also looked like he hadn't yet been beaten into submission either—if everything he was telling her was true and he really was being beaten. But what other explanation could there be? If she couldn't deny that she was trapped inside her own game, unable to get her mind back to her body, why should she be surprised that someone else was in the same position?

As long as they both weren't really dead.

She swallowed a yawn. Thank God Andy had made her that fake drink or she just might be willing to sell her soul for another Red Bull.

Even though it was going to cost them in energy—and they needed all the energy they could get—she took two measured steps across the decaying safe house floor to her control panel, flipped it open, and stuck in her sword. As she cashed in credits, a door slid back and she reached inside to grab two new sets of clothes. No way could they go back out there with the scent of blood on them, attracting more Ferals—pack animals that were going to become far more organized and far more unpredictable in each subsequent level. This wasn't just a game of physical strength, it was also a game of wit.

She tossed Hawk a clean set of fatigues. "Here."

"Thanks."

As grudging gratitude flitted across his face, sympathy welled up inside her. River had always been a soft touch for the socially skill-less. What kind of torture had he been through to make it so difficult for him to say thank you for a simple kindness?

She stepped behind a coconut tree to give them both some privacy, but as she peeled off the soiled gear, her mind was running a marathon. Did she believe everything Hawk had told her?

She had to laugh. She was standing behind a coconut tree, getting ready to bury wet, stinking clothes drenched in troll demon's blood so that Ferals couldn't sniff them out. If all this could be created, why shouldn't she believe Hawk? Why couldn't there be something bigger than a virtual game at large in the universe?

River stole a quick glance over her shoulder at the door to the next level. She didn't want to sit around all night waiting for someone to rescue her, worrying that her brain could explode, when she might be able to get back to her body by beating the game.

But she'd never beaten the Soul Man before. Of course, she'd never had the same amount of motivation to beat him.

She rolled that around in her head for a moment and decided the next course of action should be to gather enough energy to summon the Wizard. That meant it was time to take down a few more Ferals—every kill increased their energy, which could be cashed in for weapons, clothing, and entry into the nearest safe house—and make her way to the next level of the game.

She hoped there weren't any more Uultur out there, or that if there were, Hawk would be a bit faster with a weapon this time. She should have planted rocket launchers in the game.

She patted her thigh. Perhaps the Wizard would have some suggestions for killing the Soul Man. But what was it Hawk had told her?

Only an immortal can kill an immortal. As far as she knew they didn't have any immortals kicking around in the game, ready to do their bidding. There had to be another way. There just had to be. Because River had no intention of being beaten at her own game.

After changing into fresh clothes, she stepped out from behind the tree in time to catch Hawk with his pants down—literally. She retreated behind the tree. If she hadn't already admitted that Hawk couldn't be her Sever, she'd be convinced now. Sever hadn't been programmed to change. He was the one true constant in the game. This man was far better proportioned than the anatomically correct warrior she'd crafted.

After making that purely professional observation, she cleared her throat to warn him of her approach.

That had been a wasted effort. Modesty didn't seem to have been programmed into him. Hawk met her glance straight on, sans pants, and something about the way he was looking at her had the fine hairs on her nape rising. He angled his head, his jaw tightening.

"If it takes an immortal to kill an immortal, how are we supposed to terminate the Soul Man?" she asked him.

"I guess that's what we're going to have to find out, isn't it?" He tugged on his pants, drove his sword into the sheath strapped to his waist, and adjusted the quiver on his back. "Are there any rules or strategies I should know before we go on to the next level?"

"I could give you a basic rundown, but with the way things are changing I can't guarantee they'll apply."

"Give me a rundown anyway."

River held up her fingers. "There are three levels. Primitive, which is where we are now. After we gain enough energy we can cash in the credits and enter the modern world, then on into the postapocalyptic world. The Soul Man's lair is in that world. We need to gain enough energy to move from one world to the next, and in each world the game increases in complexity. We save the data from each world as we move on—that way we don't always have to start back in the primitive world if we make a mistake, and we get to pick up where we left off. Well," she amended, "to a certain degree. We start off at the beginning of the world we left off.

"It's also timed. We have an allotted amount of time to complete a level, otherwise we have to start at the beginning of the world we've yet to conquer. At any time, as long as we have enough energy, we can enter a safe house and summon the Wizard."

"Wizard?"

"Yes. The Wizard sees all, knows all, and can help with strategy. I think that's where we should head first. But we need to gather energy to get there."

He glanced around the trashed safe house. "We can't get enough energy from your trees?"

"No. The energy from plants only repairs our weapons. To gain entrance to the safe house, which will open the door to the Wizard's world or to the Soul Man's lair, we need to gain energy from a different life source."

"Life source?"

"Ferals, and other animals that inhabit the jungle." She flashed him a grin, eager to get started. She rummaged through the wreckage in search of her rucksack. "We need to go hunting."

Hawk didn't smile in return, his own face expressionless once more. He was all business as he jerked his chin forward and said, "Then let's get moving."

She found the rucksack. Triumphant, she dusted

it off and shrugged it on. "Hey, strategy is mine, remember?"

He snagged her arm to hold her back when she tried to sweep past him. The air around them charged as he pressed against her, caging her between his chest and the doorframe. He kept his tone low and conversational, but his message was clear.

"Listen up, River. I'm not without my own abilities. If we want to make it through this alive, we have to start working together. I am not just the brawns to your brain. Got it?"

With every ounce of strength she possessed, she pushed at his chest with her elbow until he stepped back. Their gazes collided in challenge.

"We both have our roles to play, and you don't know the game like I do," she countered. There were too many unknowns for her to be able to justify that claim anymore, and Hawk knew it, too, but she made the claim anyway. Call it artistic pride.

Hawk broke eye contact first. He balled his hands into white-knuckled fists.

"And you don't know what a twisted, depraved little bastard your Soul Man truly is," he shot back. "I hope you never have to find out." Shivers skittered down her spine as he flinched at some memory. "He's in a *prison*. It's not some level in your game. I don't know how you've tapped into it, but you have."

He lowered his voice, changing tactics, the hardness in his tone giving way to softness in an obvious attempt to reason with her, because real softness simply wasn't something she'd seen from him yet.

"We can't risk doing anything that might give him a chance to escape. If he gets out of here, we're fucked." Frustration rolled off him. "Your world will be fucked," he continued. "You have no idea what kind of nightmare he'll create for your people. He'll make civil war look like a celebration."

She'd been so worried about getting back to her own reality that she hadn't even considered the need for keeping the Soul Man trapped in his. She wanted to get out of the game. That remained her top priority. But if Hawk was right—and she gave him full marks for credibility—then could she risk releasing the Soul Man on her world? He'd managed to knock her flat on her backside and scare the crap out of her when she'd thought he was nothing more than a virtual character in a game. What damage could he do if he were real?

The beginnings of a headache pulsed behind her eyebrows. How exactly were they now defining reality?

"Why does all of this seem so real to me?" she wondered. "I know it's a game. Or a prison," she added hastily when he opened his mouth. "But I can't tell the difference anymore."

Hawk rubbed the back of his neck. "Have you ever heard of phantom pain?"

River nodded. "That's when someone loses a limb, but they can feel it as if it's still there."

"Exactly. We're detached from our physical bodies, but our minds are telling us how to react to any external stimuli. That's why we have to be careful. It only takes a fraction of a second for an accident to happen. It takes longer for our minds to process what happened, then tell us whether or not it was real."

"That's the premise around the game helmets I developed," River replied. "They tap into our brains' wavelengths, and those wavelengths make our characters react."

"When we go back out that door, you understand that you aren't the only one who's in control now, right? You've created rules for your game, but he's a Dark Lord who has a few tricks of his own. He may be in a prison, but the Guardians aren't monsters. They've given him a little freedom." Hawk's lips thinned. "Maybe a little too much freedom. Someday, that's going to change. Once I get out of here the little bastard's going to have his program seriously restricted, I promise you that."

River wondered again about what had happened

to Hawk to make him so bitter. Perhaps that was simply the way he was. Which meant playing the game with him was going to be such a joy in so many ways.

"Okay, I got it," she said. "The Soul Man has some tricks of his own."

When Hawk opened the door to reenter the primitive world, darkness greeted them. A steamy wind blew the deep rich scent of damp earth past her nostrils and she grasped for any slight sign of friendliness in an eerie, oppressing night. She'd had a totally normal childhood with warm, loving parents. Why had she made this game so grim?

Maybe Hawk's gloomy presence was what made it feel this way. He could use a little blast of sunshine.

Hawk put his mouth close to her ear and she shivered as his warm breath wafted over her neck. "Does it look familiar?"

She pitched her voice low to match his. "Yes, for now. What about you? Do you see anything you recognize?"

"Nothing."

"Good." River inhaled, noting a new energy in the air. She drew the scented wind into her lungs to taste it, and the jolt pulled her awake quicker than a triple shot of espresso.

She was used to sleepless nights. Staying awake to work or play video games wasn't at all uncommon for her. When she played she played hard and when she worked she worked even harder, giving everything she had until she went supernova. But this time she knew she needed to pace herself, since sleep at the end of the night wasn't an option. Not unless the team could get her out in the morning.

But if they got her out, what was going to happen to Hawk?

"How well can you see?" Hawk asked.

She took a tentative step outside and cringed when the gnarled roots of a mangrove tree crushed beneath her boots. Damn. A mangrove could only mean one thing. There was a swamp in the vicinity, and her game had once again taken on a life of its own.

She cursed under her breath, then said, "I was wrong. The water is new."

"What water?"

She shook her foot over the mangrove roots. "This wasn't in this level before. Mangrove trees and shrubs grow in saline, which means things are changing, and somewhere around here we're about to encounter a swamp." She glanced at their combat clothes. One hundred percent cotton. Great. Not only would they suck up water quicker than a sponge, when they dried they were going to shrink in size. If that happened, they currently didn't have enough strength to replace them. Maneuvering in restrictive clothes was another fun game obstacle they didn't need. She furrowed her brow in thought. "I haven't accounted for swamps in this level. It's like the game has wrinkled and things are overlapping," she added, fighting off panic. She drew in a breath and rubbed her temples. "How does a virtual game wrinkle?"

He gave a slow shoulder roll. "Beats me. There are no swamps at all in the prison world."

Her head jerked back with a start, surprised. If there weren't any swamps in the prison world, then how had one ended up in a level that should be jungle?

Her mind reconsidered the Uultur and the arrow that had killed it. Was the Soul Man toying with them?

She peered into the jungle, and just as when she was a child tucked into her bed all safe and sound, her closet door ajar, her mind began creating monsters from the shadowy figures that lingered in the dark.

She didn't want her mind making more monsters for her right now. She didn't think she could tell fast enough that they weren't real.

She angled her head to regard Hawk, knowing she'd given Sever exceptional night vision. "How well can you see?"

Hawk's body tightened behind her. He pushed

his chest into her back and nudged her along. "Well enough. We need to move."

Did he think she was hesitating? She wasn't. At least she didn't think so. She just liked to formulate a plan of action before venturing into the unknown.

Taking her by surprise, he clasped her hand in his, lacing his fingers through hers. Was he planning to drag her through the jungle, or did he also think she needed the moral support? Either way, he didn't need to hold her hand. She was more than capable of keeping pace and taking care of herself. She'd proven that already.

She jerked her hand back, hastily stepped in front of him, and with single-minded determination pushed past the towering mangrove tree.

Except she was so intent on proving herself capable and independent that she missed the slippery embankment leading to the swamp and fell with an undignified thud and small shriek. Her ass hit with a slap, and mud splattered over her clothes and face as she slid downward, her flailing hands unable to grasp anything solid. A moment later she hit a slimy bottom and every orifice in her body filled with muddy, murky water.

She came up sputtering and unsteady, a gurgling sound bubbling from the water around her as the swamp bed sucked at her feet. She flung her sopping rucksack up the embankment. She was tempted to abandon it, but she needed it to carry anything they collected.

"You okay?"

She looked up and caught the silhouette of Hawk staring down at her. "I'm fine."

To his credit he didn't laugh. "Hang tight. I'll find a vine and toss it down to you. You can climb out, then we'll walk around."

"It's too late," River said.

She heard a shuffle, then a curse, and she knew what he'd found. An impenetrable wall of green that he'd never be able to hack his way through, not even with his sword.

"We can't go backward in the game, only forward," she called out to him.

"Of course we can't." He checked his footing, then started toward her—on foot, not ass. "That would be too easy."

"Exactly."

As Hawk made his way down the embankment—upright—she wiped the mud from her com-link and tapped on it. Anytime now her crew would be coming to work, and she prayed they could do something to haul her ass out of here and get her home while her mind was still intact. She stopped short of offering to sell her soul for a hot shower. If Hawk was right, then she needed to start putting a higher price tag on it.

Hawk waded over to her, crowding her space, the radiant heat from his body a somewhat heady reminder that no matter what, he was a man and not just a virtual character. He was a living, breathing human being, like she was, and once her crew got her out of there, together they'd figure out a way to rescue Hawk. No one deserved to have his mind played with this way.

Something brushed up against her leg and she grabbed Hawk's arm, alarm quickly moving through her. When his hard gaze met hers, her pulse jumped at the base of her throat and her com-link beeped as her heart rate trip-hammered.

She pointed downward. "Something's down there!"

"Don't make any sudden movements."

Maybe he'd meant that to sound soothing, but the look on his face was anything but. Whatever had just rippled through the stagnant water and brushed against her thigh couldn't be good. Good things didn't live in swamps. There wasn't one fairy tale that said so.

She nodded, biting her lip, and he made a slight gesture toward a narrow, muddy ledge in the embankment. "Put your arms around my shoulders," he instructed. "And hold your breath."

She did as he told her. The world rolled upside down and for a moment she found herself below the muddy surface. The next instant she found herself shuddering into Hawk's chest as he balanced them on the narrow ledge.

The swamp creature, looking a lot like one of the grain-fed barn rats from her childhood, lifted its head from the murky depths, paused, then slithered back into the water. She could only imagine the diseases a stinking, disgusting swamp rat would carry, and it had touched her.

Ew.

None of this is real, she fiercely reminded herself. *This is not my reality.*

She repeated that mantra over and over until it began to sink in. All she needed to do was keep believing in that until morning.

But initially, it didn't make it any less scary or believable. As Hawk had said, *when danger comes at you faster than your mind can rationalize, it only takes that first split second for your mind to accept the danger as reality.*

And that split second could make the difference between life and death.

She darted a glance downward and looked at Hawk in the dim light, the whites of his eyes stark against his mud-caked face. Punch-drunk exhaustion, combined with the sudden adrenaline rush, made River want to laugh—hysterically. Then she wanted to kick the Soul Man's ass, and anyone else's who might be messing with her program and, quite possibly, her mind.

"You okay?" Hawk asked.

"Was that what I thought it was?"

"Yeah, it was."

A shiver moved down her spine. Okay, Ferals she could handle. Even badass demon trolls she could handle. But if there was one thing she couldn't handle it was rats. Her fear stemmed from her childhood when a big ugly bastard had cornered her in her father's barn, and her father had killed it with a pitchfork. It was irrational to harbor such fears, she knew, but nonetheless the phobia remained. That was why she'd never written one into her program.

Did the Soul Man somehow know her deepest fears? Was he in her head, reading her thoughts?

Was he watching?

She was still lying on top of Hawk, the awareness of their awkward position slowly pushing past her panic as his body transferred warmth to hers. His face might be expressionless, but there was something in his gaze that singed her nerve endings and brought heat to her cheeks when his eyes met hers.

He shifted uncomfortably beneath her. She braced her arms on either side of his head and pushed up and away from him. The gooey mud sealing their bodies together made a sucking sound as she separated her torso from his.

He cleared his throat and for the first time she saw an emotion untainted by anger and distrust enter his eyes. She could tell that her closeness disturbed him.

"Am I crushing you?" she asked. It was kind of a stupid question to ask, but she had to say something to cover the awkward moment. It wasn't every day she found herself glued to a strange man.

"Oh yeah." He sounded amused by the question. His chest rumbled when he spoke, vibrating through her smaller frame. "You're a tank."

River, ignoring the churning in her belly, leaned over slightly and peered into the murky water. The earthy, putrid scent of the bog assaulted her senses.

"We can't go back the way we came." She considered their options, looking forward not back now, and saw a hollow tree that had fallen across the embankment and over the water to the other side of the swamp. "But we could crawl through the log."

Hawk put his arms around her to anchor her in place, trapping her against his body, the intimacy of his gesture catching her off guard. He lifted his chin. The back of his head sank deeper into the mud as he shifted, his neck arching upward so he could see what she saw lying just beyond them in the darkness. He made a face. "Crisos."

"What?" she demanded.

"You think I'll fit in that?"

She sized up the opening, then the man beneath her. The entrance wasn't huge, and it would be a tight fit, but she was certain he could do it. Although if he didn't want to take a chance . . .

"You could always walk over the top of it rather than go through," she suggested. "But there might be things for us to collect inside it and we need the energy."

He gave a curt shake of his head. "I think we should stay as close together as possible. Who knows where we'll end up when we reach the other side." He gave her a light slap on her mud-crusted buttocks. "Climb over me."

River began the awkward process of shimmying over his body, crawling like a new recruit on the first day of boot camp. Except this wasn't basic training and she wasn't crawling through a mud pit anymore. She was crawling over a man—a stranger who was holding her hips, attempting to steady her in a gesture far more personal than she should like.

Her hands skimmed smooth, hard, mud-slickened muscle, and although she was agile, adept at conquering almost any obstacle, she still had to command herself to keep her focus. The hurdle beneath her shifted, clearly as disconcerted as she.

Hang on, River.

She did not want to fall back into that rat-infested water. Taking care not to hit his face with her boots, she widened her knees as she crawled the last few inches over his body. Hawk turned his head to avoid the mud and debris dripping from her clothes.

Once past him, she climbed onto her hands and knees and glanced over her shoulder. With stealthy movements Hawk rolled onto his stomach, taking care not to fall off the narrow ledge. He nodded to her. "Let's go."

"Just a second." River groped around until she found her rucksack. It was soaking wet and smelled bad. She made a face as she slung it over her head and around her neck.

"What's the deal with the bag?" Hawk said. "Get rid of it."

"I can't. We need it to carry anything we collect," she explained. "Everything counts in the game, no matter how small or insignificant it might seem."

With Hawk tight on her heels River inched forward, the rucksack bumping against her chest, then paused at the dark opening of the hollow log to take a minute to prepare herself. Before entering she thought about the Soul Man, or Dark Lord as Hawk called him, and wondered what, if anything, he was going to throw at them next.

Her hand automatically went to her side where she fingered the hilt of her sword. Whatever it was, she was going to be ready this time. He could count on that.

CHAPTER EIGHT

♦

Nick hung up the phone, deciding the hell with Kaye. He could check up on what River was doing in the morning as easily as that night. She was too smart to let her vitals get out of control. She pushed the envelope when he was there only because she knew he'd watch out for her.

Besides, the disturbing phone call aside, he was still pissed with her that she'd lied to him and gone back to work on the game alone. That was the whole reason for Kaye's phone call.

It was time that Nick stopped protecting her. Doing so was drawing too much attention to himself, and Nick hadn't made it this far in life by dancing naked on tabletops. He didn't do serious danger. He didn't need Bane sniffing around or Crazy Kaye calling him at all hours for nonexistent updates. He'd expected easy cash from this assignment, not an ulcer. Or a bullet between his eyes.

He heated a frozen pizza and ate it in front of the television, then fell asleep during a stupid remake of *America's Funniest Home Videos*.

Now there was a whole dying television genre that should never have been revived.

When he awoke, morning sun was seeping through his apartment's living room window. He wished he could say he'd slept well, but it was hard to sleep with a werewolf in town and a nut job riding his ass.

He checked his watch and it was still early, so he took a shower before eating breakfast and made sure he left the apartment a few minutes after his normal time. He didn't want River to think he was rushing to check on her, and he knew she'd never be late for work. She had freakish stamina and a one-track mind. That was what made her so much fun in bed.

He was going to miss the sex.

There was an abandoned subway station three blocks down from his apartment building. The infrastructure of the old days had been one of the first things to crumble during the war when population numbers could no longer sustain mass-transit costs. The larger cities, where the majority of the war's survivors had settled, were slowly rebuilding, but here in the outlying areas mass transit would be a long time coming.

Nick found it difficult to imagine that at one time people could fly to Europe or the United States and back in the same day. Now only the obscenely rich could afford such a trip, and even they would have to plan it in terms of weeks, not days. Visas to other countries were hard to come by. Borders were no longer open.

Telecommunications. The next best thing to being there. That was where investors were sinking their money these days. Telecommunications and technology of any kind. The Rivers of the world were going to make the Amos Kayes filthy stinking rich.

The wind was still brisk and Nick rolled up his jacket collar around his ears. A subway ride wouldn't be such a big deal for a downhill trip, although it would be nice for the trip back up the steep mountain streets. Subway tunnels, however, made great shortcuts, protected from the weather as they were—if one was brave enough to try.

Unfortunately they also made great shelters for the less-than-human, and Nick wasn't all that averse to fresh air and exercise.

He bought a coffee from a Tim Hortons not far from the compound. A lot of franchises had gone out of business during the last days of the war, unable to compete after the drastic drop in the world's population, but Tim Hortons' business remained steadier than ever.

Maybe Nick should open a Tim Hortons somewhere.

He took a swig of his medium double-double as he opened the door to the compound and flashed his pass at the security guard.

Those passes were a constant source of amusement to the team. They swapped them like playing cards, making bets as to who would get tagged first for using someone else's. Nick checked the photo. Today he had Marsha's.

The security guard grunted as Nick walked by, his eyes focused on the small television set.

"Huh. Did you hear three people got killed in town last night?" The security guard gave an exaggerated, full-body shiver. "The news report says one guy had all the blood drained from his body. Bet it was vampires."

Vampires, trolls . . . *werewolves* . . . Nick gave a little body shiver of his own, but his was heartfelt. Bane had been busy.

He wanted to ask if River was in, but decided not to drag the security guard away from his morning CNN. Besides, wanting to ask that question made him feel clingy. Like he was River's bitch or something. He needed to regrow a pair.

He was in a totally foul mood by the time he reached the short end of the ell in the hallway and took a right into the gaming room. He opened the door, half expecting the team to be waiting for him and complaining that he hadn't brought coffee for everyone, but the room was silent. The light was on, but the screensaver on the monitor facing him was running clips from an old turn-of-the-twenty-first-century cartoon he liked to make Johnny watch.

His footsteps sounded far too loud as he walked into the room.

"Hello?" he called out.

Nothing but the hum of the computer and the fluorescent lights overhead. This was creepier than hell.

He crossed to the computer monitor and saw River, crumpled on the gaming platform, her black hair splashed across her white face and her helmet lying at her fingertips.

Jesus, Mary, and Joseph. All the blood rushed to Nick's head and he swore he saw stars. He dropped the coffee cup on the desk and ran to River's side.

Her com-link was still strapped on her wrist and her vitals were registering normal. Nick frowned. She'd removed her helmet, and removing either the helmet or the com-link should have disengaged her from the game. She needed both in order to play.

He checked her over again, straightening her limbs in an effort to make her more comfortable. She seemed unharmed. It was as if she were sound asleep, except her skin was too pale for his liking.

What the hell had happened to her?

He reached for the com-link, thinking to remove it from her arm, then decided to check the computer first to see what level she'd been in. It was possible she'd encountered a problem in the game and mentally hadn't been able to deal with it. He didn't want to yank her out only to have her go into shock.

Nick crossed to the computer, keeping a worried eye on her as he punched in his password and brought up the screen.

For a moment he forgot about River's body lying behind him as he stared in amazement at the monitor. She was in the game, and she wasn't alone. She was also in a level completely foreign to him.

How had a swamp gotten mixed into the jungle?

Nick slumped into the chair in front of the monitor and watched as River and Sever crawled through the swamp, mud and slime dripping from their clothes.

It really was time for Nick to end his relationship with her. He was sitting here actually jealous of the way a computer-generated character was watching her ass.

Not only that, but he'd spent a rough few hours worrying about her because of Bane and Kaye, while she was living it up with a cartoon character.

He spun away from the monitor to look at her physical form lying on the gaming platform. His eyes narrowed, then widened in shock. How was she playing the game without her helmet?

He had to pull her from the game before the others arrived. He didn't want anyone else to see this. There would be time enough later to worry about what it meant.

Footsteps rang in the hallway and Nick started to sweat. There wasn't time to pull her safely out. Thinking fast, he darted over to her body and tugged the gaming helmet back onto her head.

The security guard opened the door a crack. "Everything okay in here?"

No, everything was not okay, and the lazy bastard would know that if he had actually made his rounds through the night like he was supposed to.

"Fine." Nick was breathing too hard and he was sure his voice sounded odd, but he was out of the line of vision of the doorway and the security guard seemed satisfied.

"You have a visitor. An Amos Kaye. Want me to sign him in?"

Nick's hands started to shake and his mouth went dry. Having Kaye actually show up in person wasn't good. Especially not with River catatonic like this. "Sure."

The door closed and the footsteps retreated.

Nick held River for a moment, reassured by the soft rise and fall of her chest and the steady beat of her heart, and wondered what he was supposed to do now.

He left her curled up on her side with his jacket rolled up beneath her head and dashed back to the computer seconds before Kaye walked in.

Kaye wasn't exactly an intimidating-looking

man. Not at first glance. He was midsixties, bald-headed with a trim gray goatee, and of average height. Only the oddly colorless eyes gave away the crazy factor. Nick hated having those eyes pinned on him.

Kaye sized up the situation in the room, noting River lying on the platform. He then looked at the monitor.

"How is it possible," he asked, "that she can be unconscious and yet still play the game?"

Kaye was crazy, but also exceedingly bright. And observant. Nick thanked God he'd thought to put the helmet back on River's head.

"The helmet taps into her prefrontal cortex. As long as there's brain activity, she can play. That's one of the marketing points of the game," Nick explained. "It can be used by people with varying levels of paralysis, including sufferers of Lou Gehrig's disease, and it's as if they're as able-bodied as you or me." He frowned. Although playing from an unconscious state might make for a rather interesting game experience. Perhaps that explained the swamp/jungle snafu.

Kaye leaned forward to examine the activity on the monitor more closely. "Very impressive."

Nick didn't want Kaye taking too active an interest in the game. God only knew what the creepy little freak would want to add to it, and River had already made it more complicated than the average gamer could handle. No one else on the team would even touch it. The real lawsuits were going to come from all the people who lost their minds trying to play, not from the potential heart attacks and brain aneurysms.

Not his problem.

"Why are you here?" Nick asked, spinning his chair around to face the other man and effectively blocking the screen.

Kaye straightened. "Bane had difficulty following some instructions he was given. I'm here to protect an investment."

His freaky eyes slid to River, and Nick went cold. What had Bane been up to?

Who were the three people he'd killed in the night?

Nick glanced at the clock on the wall, and suddenly he knew. He should have known it all along. He just hadn't wanted to admit it. Bane had wiped out the other three members of the team.

Nick wondered who might be next.

"If you're trying to protect an investment," he said, "shouldn't that protection extend to the game's developers?"

Those colorless eyes sparkled with amusement. *Jesus.* "The game isn't the investment I'm interested in protecting. I thought it was time to meet her." He nodded at River. "Can you bring her around?"

Nick had no idea how to do so, but he did know that he wasn't interested in introducing River to Kaye. Not ever, but especially not right now.

"She's been playing too long," Nick said, reluctant to tell Kaye too much but wanting desperately to buy River more time. "There's a fine line between realities that makes pulling her from the game risky at this point. It's better to let her come out of it on her own."

"Can you communicate with her when she plays?"

"Through the com-link on her wrist. We thought it was better to have external communication come from a different source than the helmet. It helps the player make the distinction between what's real and what's not."

"Fascinating." Kaye was silent for a few minutes, clearly considering what he'd been told. Nick was the health expert on the team, but Kaye was a bona fide doctor. Nick could only bullshit him so far. "How long do you think she can stay in the game?"

Nick had absolutely no frigging clue. "As long as her brain stays active."

"Fascinating," Kaye repeated, that crazy light back in his eyes. "Without food or water that might be three days, more or less." He looked again at the monitor. "Leave her in the game. If she doesn't pull out on her own, I want to see what happens when her body starts to shut down."

♦ ♦

As Hawk watched River forge ahead it struck him, unwanted, that she was the kind of woman any Guardian would feel the need to protect. There was something about her, although he couldn't quite put his finger on it. She might be smart, strong, and competent, and could come close to kicking his ass with a weapon, but she brought something out in him that had been buried for a long time. Under the circumstances he wasn't certain that was good thing.

But no matter how much he wanted to protect her, he knew she was capable of handling just about anything thrown at her.

Except for maybe a giant rat. For a woman who seemed fearless, or at least liked to present that image to the world, he wondered where that particular fear had originated. The fact that she had fears at all made her seem all the more real to him, and for the first time in a long time, he didn't feel quite so alone. A reminder that he missed being with someone. He missed his wife.

His daughter, he couldn't bear thinking about.

He pushed the past aside and began to wonder more about River. An overwhelming urge to know everything about her pulled at him, from what made her tick to her desperate need to create and conquer this virtual game of hers, so much so that she'd bartered with her soul. His need for the information was strictly for survival. If they were going to get out of this alive he needed to gather intelligence, to understand her past, her abilities, why the Dark Lord was so damn desperate for her soul, and who the gamer named Nick on the other end of their com-link really was and what he meant to her. Hawk needed a lot more information than he currently possessed in order to be able to trust her.

Once they exited the hollow log she let out a breath and visibly relaxed, a clear indication that she was back in her territory. Hawk held his own breath, exercising his right to reserve judgment for the time being as he stole a glance around to familiarize himself with the new data. The moonlight spilled over them, a halo of light in the dark night, and Hawk couldn't deny that he found beauty in the untouched, overgrown, primitive surroundings. It reminded him of home, although on his home world there was nothing primitive about the beautiful landscape. The Guardians had created a haven for themselves by using all the technology at their disposal.

The Dark Lord's virtual prison was nothing

compared to the genuine technological marvel of the Guardian world.

"Now, we hunt," River said to him. "Then we can summon the Wizard."

Shrouded in darkness, River took one step forward, pushed through the thick foliage and heavy shrubbery, and immediately stumbled over the root-choked weeds that veiled the jungle floor. Keeping pace, Hawk captured her waist and anchored her to him before she fell. After seeing the way she'd maneuvered through the jungle earlier, with such speed and agility, he knew exhaustion must be pulling at her, causing her to misstep.

She turned to him and as gratitude passed over her face he noted the telltale bruising of fatigue below her big blue eyes. "Thanks," she murmured. "Again." With a twist of her shoulder, she made a move to go, but he refused to release her from the circle of his arms.

As he held her tight, watching dark lashes flashing against her pale skin, he diligently worked to ignore the way her body pressed against his, and the way his own body responded to her closeness.

"You need a break before you go any further." The illusion would work wonders for her, and one tiny mistake or even the smallest miscalculation could be enough to make or break them. The Dark Lord would use any little weakness to his advantage.

Her eyes met his, and behind that sea of blue she telegraphed a silent message as her hand crept down her side, her movements slow, calculated. His body tensed instinctively in response, wondering what the hell she was doing, what she was trying to tell him.

"River . . . ?"

In the span of a second, she drew her sword and drove it past his shoulder, neatly planting the sharp tip of the blade into the head of an encroaching snake and nailing it to the towering tree behind Hawk's head.

Hawk turned so fast it left his head spinning. Damn, she was quick. Even when tired. She had the lightning reflexes of a Fae.

"See? I'm fine," she said.

It was a lie and they both knew it. Clearly she wasn't about to show any signs of weakness to him, and while he found that admirable, he knew she needed rest. He changed tactics as a seed of understanding blossomed inside him, giving him a good sense of her personality.

Since the next few hours were going to be crucial, he decided to take one for the team. "You might be fine, but I'm hungry. And by the looks of things, you just nailed dinner."

She took a tiny step back, and her stomach chose that moment to grumble.

"Dinner?" She arched a dubious brow, brushing a dangling branch from her mud-caked cheek with the back of her hand. "We don't need to eat it in order to collect its energy for the game. Since none of this is real, how can eating a computer-generated snake possibly fill my very real, incredibly empty stomach?"

Hawk turned and pulled the sword from the snake's head. He handed the weapon back to her, stretched the reptile out to its full length, and examined her kill. "Mind over matter. Everything's real as long as you believe it's real."

She crinkled her nose, and he could feel her skepticism melt as her gaze scanned the long, meaty snake draped over his arm. "I've never eaten snake before."

"It tastes like chicken."

Intrigued, her lids widened, and her eyes snapped up to meet his. "Really?"

Despite himself he let loose a laugh, shocked that the ability to do so had suddenly come back to him. He rolled a shoulder. "If you want it to, yes."

River shot him a look of amusement and laughed with him, the silky sound catching him off guard and rattling him right to the core. He couldn't remember the last time he'd heard laughter. Genuine laughter. Like the sound his daughter used to make when he'd chase her through their garden, catch her in his arms, and spin her around in circles until they both collapsed in a heap of giggles.

River licked her bottom lip, rubbing her stomach in mock anticipation. "Forget about chicken. Mine is going to taste like a big juicy burger dripping in onions and barbecue sauce."

The sound of River's voice reeled his mind back to the present, the smile falling from his face with the same swiftness it had appeared. Annoyed with himself for his own weakness, he worked to refocus his thoughts, perturbed that old memories had begun to emerge from dark corners and rise to the surface. Not only did he not want to deal with those memories, or revisit his losses, he didn't want the Dark Lord catching wind of them. Fuck knew what he'd do with the information, or how he'd use it against him if given the chance.

River was studying him, and he shifted, suddenly uncomfortable, partly from his thoughts, and partly from the way his filthy fatigues clung to his body like a molting second skin. He looked past her slight frame.

"What?" she asked, astute enough to pick up on his rapid mood change. "Do you have an aversion to burgers or something?"

"Yeah, something like that." He tossed the snake over his shoulder and pushed past her, his body brushing hers aside as he went. Heavy moisture from the overhead trees gathered into big fat droplets and dripped onto his already wet clothes. It gave him something else to focus on and he said, "We need to build a fire to cook. And we need to get these clothes dry."

River disagreed. "Not a good idea. The smoke will attract animals."

He should have thought of that. He was a smart guy, analytical. Years of training had taught him to think everything through. It was ingrained into his personality. So why was he all of a sudden making mistakes? He caught River's uneasy glance. He clenched his jaw and forced himself to refocus, drawing coldness back inside him.

Before he could ask if she liked her meat raw, a soft rustling to the left of their booted feet interrupted him and a noise, not at all unlike a contented cat's purr, rose from the dense foliage.

River's eyes flashed with a mixture of excitement and relief and she dropped to one knee, but Hawk grabbed her arm to haul her back, half expecting to see a jungle cat pounce.

She held her hand up, palm out. "It's okay," she assured him. "It looks like our luck is starting to change."

Yeah, well, he didn't believe in luck, destiny, or fate, and never left anything to chance. Hoping for the best but prepared for the worst, he bent his head for a better look.

That had to be one of the ugliest creatures he'd ever seen. And he'd seen a lot.

"What is it?"

"It's a Tabinese," she said.

"A what?"

"Tabinese. Part tabby cat and part Pekingese."

River pulled the mutant animal from the bushes and stood, cradling it in her arms. As it stretched out long, retractable claws its large green eyes stared up at Hawk, a flat pug face suggesting it had run into one too many of those impenetrable green walls. Literally.

River picked twigs and leaves from its ratty orange fur, matted together and plastered against its skin, and explained. "I built these into the program. They're a safeguard that temporarily gives us an advantage. When you discover one you can use its energy to create a bubble, and you're camouflaged inside. You can see and hear out, but no one can see or hear you in return."

Hawk considered that information. If it was her creation, something from her game, intuitive intelligence told him it should shield them from the watching Dark Lord as well.

Which would give Hawk a perfect opportunity to pump her for more information without an audience.

River tapped her cat/dog on the nose. "Just like a watchdog, this little guy will warn us when danger is near."

"It's the ugliest fucking thing I've ever seen."

She gave him a hurt glare. "Be nice."

"What'd you have to make it so ugly for?"

"When I was a little girl, I had a tabby cat and a Pekingese dog. They're both long gone now, so I guess this is a way for me to remember them both. Besides, it's a defensive mechanism. Who's going to attack anything so ugl—Uh, objectionable?"

Hawk wasn't convinced she'd done it a favor. "It looks like something out there wasn't following your line of reasoning." He touched the animal's hind quarter and it whined. Hawk pulled his hand away, a dark stain that could only be blood smearing his fingertips.

River lifted the animal to examine it. "Damn it all."

Hawk brushed his hand over his sword and looked around. "It could be a trap."

"It's not a trap."

"Put it down, River. I think we should kill it."

She turned slightly to protect it and he wasn't prepared for the emotion in her voice or the way it unearthed something inside him—something better left buried.

"We're not killing it. It's hurt."

He blew a heavy sigh and ran an impatient hand through his hair, aware that the animal was far more important to her than it should be. "I'm not so sure about this."

She stood her ground and met his gaze with an unwavering one of her own, a pink tinge staining her cheeks. "Well, I am. I know what I'm doing."

He trusted that she knew what she was doing. After all, she'd proven herself adept and shown him that she had great survival skills. But this mutated animal wasn't a long-lost pet. While he respected the fact that she disliked backing down, he wanted to remind her that they were dealing with life and death here.

But he knew when a battle was lost. The desperation that passed over her face as her fingers brushed the animal's coat told him she'd dealt with enough already this evening, not to mention the way it put a knot in his gut.

The cat/dog buried its face in her neck, its purr cutting through the dark quiet around them, easing the mounting tension. "So it looks like we can have that fire after all," she said brightly, lightening the mood, the subject closed as far as she was concerned. "The bubble will shield us."

He removed his hand from his sword. When had he gotten so bad at dealing with people and their emotions?

Restless and edgy now, he grudgingly conceded. "I guess your Pekihuahua might come in handy."

Relief washed off her.

"It's not half Pekingese and Chihuahua, it a Tabinese, Hawk. Get it right," she scolded him, but the tone of her voice made it clear she knew he'd skewed the name on purpose. Maybe she even understood why. "Come on, we have limited time."

River used the energy from the animal to create the camouflage bubble, then they walked through the thick jungle growth until it thinned and revealed a dark skyline sprinkled with stars. Once in the clearing they both worked together to find dry leaves and sticks.

Twenty minutes later Hawk had a fire going, and while River examined the cat/dog's wounds, he took his knife from the sheath and skinned the snake. Then he went to work on making a lean-to from the kindling lying around, one for over the fire and one to dry their soiled clothes on.

Once that was done he used his knowledge of the forest and ducked back into the dense woods in search of a water vine. A few minutes later he came back with a Blue Creek Belize and a few stems of Jippa Jappa for added nourishment.

"What do you have there?" River asked, threading her fingers through her hair to push it off her face as she gave his findings a good long inspection.

"Here, drink this." He dropped everything in front of the fire and offered her the vine. She opened her mouth and drank the sweet liquid. A few droplets dripped down her chin, and her pet licked greedily at those. Hawk slicked another vine and held it over the animal's mouth.

River wiped her lips with the heel of her hand, but only managed to smear the mud on her face. "Mmm, delicious." She grinned at him. "Tastes like Red Bull."

That was one he'd never heard of, but whatever Red Bull was, it must be pretty good judging by the look on her face.

As she drank the juice with obvious enjoyment, Hawk said, "We need to get out of these wet clothes." He removed his coat and pants, laid them over the makeshift clothesline near the flames, and ripped off a piece of his T-shirt. He sliced another vine and wet the cotton. "Here."

River used it to wash her face and hands, then climbed to her feet to remove her soiled gear, taking obvious care to keep her underclothing on, although Hawk wasn't certain a thin white undershirt and a scrap of red thong could be classed as clothing of any kind.

He ripped another piece of his shirt and went to work on bandaging the Tabinese.

The animal gave a loud purr and brushed a

scratchy tongue over Hawk's arm. River dropped down beside him and said, "He likes you."

"What's not to like?"

Feet planted and knees bent, she collapsed onto the ground. Once again her silky laughter curled around him. "You look like you've done that before."

He ignored the comment, and too much of a guy to be immune to the sight of her barely clad body, he concentrated on bandaging the animal. Once complete, he settled it on her stomach.

As he then tossed the gutted snake over the fire, River stared up at the stars and gave a heavy sigh. When a strange, longing look came over her face, he threw a few more branches onto the flames and asked, "What are you thinking about?"

"My childhood home," she said dreamily. "I grew up on a farm, and used to count the stars at night."

Since she'd opened the door he decided to let himself in. "Did you have any siblings?" he asked, carefully easing her into a personal conversation.

"My mother couldn't have children." Then, as if she'd said too much, she tried to retract her words. "What I mean is—"

Hawk immediately knew they'd touched on a sensitive subject. "You were adopted?"

A long pause fell as her guarded gaze moved over his face, and then she said, "My dad found me abandoned by a river not far from our house. That's how I got my name."

Hawk got a sense she was telling him something very personal. A peculiar urge to tell her something in return pulled at him. Instead he offered, "It's a nice name." Strong, deep, and unpredictable. Like her.

She gave him a half smile, but he detected bitterness in her tone when she said, "Tell that to the girls at Trinity School."

Protective instincts kicked into gear, catching him as much by surprise as they did her. "If given the chance I will."

"Thanks, but not necessary. I haven't seen those girls in more than ten years. Besides, they're probably all fat by now. Wouldn't that be great?" She smiled impishly, telling him a lot about how she must have been as a young girl. That sudden urge to defend her made him feel foolish now. He'd bet she'd more than held her own against a few insignificant teenagers. The truth was they'd probably been jealous of her.

She placed her Tabinese beside her, rolled, and turned her back on him, and undoubtedly on the direction of their conversation. He took a moment to do the math, putting her at around twenty-eight years of age. She would have been born at the tail end of a major world war on earth, if he remembered his history correctly. He usually did.

"Do you know who your birth parents are? Have you ever gone looking for them?"

"No." That one word and the way she delivered it informed him that the topic was no longer up for discussion. But he also picked up on a lingering regret behind it. River might feel more comfortable with herself if she knew who she really was.

He moved to another subject for the time being. "Tell me more about your adoptive parents."

She turned back to him and met his glance, her blue eyes bright in the firelight. "My *parents,*" she gently corrected him. "There's nothing really to tell."

"You don't like talking about them?"

"They're just not something I'm used to talking about, that's all." A pained expression crossed her face. "I grew up in a small town and went to a one-room school. Everyone knew I was adopted. There was no need to talk about it. And believe me, I was enough of a misfit as it was. I didn't need to hammer the point home to anyone."

Interesting. "What makes you think you were a misfit?"

She threw her arms up in the air as if it should be obvious to him, then rested them on her Tabinese as it snuggled back onto her stomach. "I'm a gamer. In school the girls were into hair, and makeup, and guys, and I was into role-playing games and computers. All the girls thought I was a weirdo. And the boys, well, the boys never gave me a second thought."

Calling her a misfit was somewhat inaccurate. She would simply have outshone the other girls. As the firelight spilled over her smooth, pale skin, and smoke billowed upward to outline the shape of the bubble around them, he pitched his voice low and asked, "Why are you telling me this?"

She pulled a face. "I don't know. Maybe I'm just hoping that it will trigger something we can use. Something that can tell us how I tapped into the Soul Man's world and why he would want me."

He took note of the purring animal. "Did you draw a lot from your childhood when you were creating this game?"

She thought about that. "Yes, I guess I did. Mostly from dreams."

"You must have had some pretty weird dreams."

Her cheek dimpled. "I did. Still do, in fact."

With the Ferals, the wichtlein, and the Uultur they'd experienced already, he hated to imagine what the next level held for them.

Hawk peeled a Jippa Jappa and took a bite from the shoot. As he chewed, he passed it to River. She bit into it and moaned with delight, and in that instant it occurred to him that there was something a little too intimate in the way they were sharing food. River handed the shoot back and Hawk grabbed a stick to test the meat, deciding it was done.

Her tongue brushed over her bottom lip and she gestured toward the plant. "How did you know that was edible?"

"It was part of my training to learn how to survive on other worlds. And when you've been around as much as I have, you learn things." Hawk speared the snake and removed it from the flames. The scent of charred meat made his stomach grumble.

"Where all have you been?"

He didn't know her well enough to trust her, but despite that he found himself wanting to talk about his life and his losses.

He chalked it up to being too long without real people to talk to. What a kick in the ass it would be if the Dark Lord had finally managed to break him.

And to break him with kindness.

"Lots of places. Too many to count." He redirected the conversation. "Have you always had such fast reflexes?"

"Always."

As the meat cooled, he probed. "And you've always been good with technology?"

She nodded as if it was nothing out of the ordinary, even though Hawk knew it had to be. There was something about her unusual abilities that the Dark Lord wanted.

She rolled onto her side, planting her elbow and resting her head in her palm. "Tell me more about being a Guardian."

She listened with interest as he went on to explain his technologically driven world and his role in it. He saw no reason not to tell her. He wasn't revealing anything the Dark Lord didn't already know, in case he had somehow managed to tap into their conversation despite River's bubble.

Or, in case River wasn't as harmless as she seemed.

Hawk tested the meat, ripping off a piece and tossing it into his mouth. The succulent scent attracted the attention of insects, swarming around his head. Hawk swatted a few away.

"Careful," River warned. Her cheek dimpled again. "I planted a few viruses in the program. Malaria is one of them."

The jungle was a paradise for insects, which could prove to be more of an enemy than the Ferals or Uultur put together. The last thing they needed was a bout of malaria.

"Malaria's not a virus," Hawk pointed out. "It's parasitic, caused by protozoan infection."

She yawned. "In computer programs, they're all

viruses. Don't swat at the flies. You just bring on more." She eyed the meat. "Is that good?"

"Yeah, it's good. Big, juicy burger good." He held it out to her and she took a bite on faith. The power of suggestion was an amazing thing.

"Mmm."

Silence fell over them as they ate, both lost in their own thoughts.

Hawk suddenly noticed her fixation on the fire and the way her eyelids drooped, then snapped open. He shot a glance toward the Jippa Jappa plant. His reasons for gathering it had been twofold—one for nourishment, and one to distract River if need be. The palm-shaped leaves could be used to weave baskets, and if it came down to it, teaching her how to intertwine the leaves would be something to help occupy her mind and keep her awake.

Hawk glanced upward. Thick clouds had been moving in for a while now, gradually veiling the sparkling tapestry of stars overhead. A storm was coming.

His skin prickled and the cacophony of night noises fell silent.

"What's out there?" River asked, her voice barely a whisper. Her Tabinese's hackles rose in warning and it let out a barklike cry. River stiffened. "Are you ready to summon the Wizard?" Tension weighted her words.

"Why?" Hawk asked.

The scent of wet fur filled the air, answering his question.

"We only had a little bit of time inside the bubble!" Far more alert than she'd been just minutes ago, she jumped to her feet and grabbed for her clothes. "You'd better get dressed. The Ferals are coming."

CHAPTER NINE

No sooner had they pulled their half-dried clothes on than Ferals closed in on them.

Frothy fangs and stark white teeth flashed as the bubble burst and they approached the flames, drawn like moths to the light. Thick beefy paws carried them closer, snapping twigs along the way.

Hawk did a quick count and knew they were out-numbered. River pressed her back to his, and while part of him wanted to tell her to run and to shield her from the attack, he also knew he needed her with him.

In a second the hounds were on them, sharp inci-sors nipping at their bodies. He heard an *oomph* and felt River drop to the ground behind him.

Hawk turned, catching her in a tangled mass of fur and claws as two more attacked. He drove his sword into the beast that had her pinned to the ground and did a roundhouse kick to the other, sending it flying backward and temporarily stunning it.

River climbed out from underneath the dead Feral and in the moment he took to scan her body for injuries, her eyes flared hot. This time he understood her unspoken signal. Hawk ducked and she swung her sword, driving it into the belly of the beast that had gone up on its haunches and was about to sink its teeth into Hawk's shoulders.

Hawk grabbed her hand and hauled her upright, and together they moved in a circle, fighting off their attackers. Hawk's com-link dinged with each kill, and in no time at all, with both of them understanding the silent signals, a pack of Ferals lay dead at their feet.

His chest rose and fell with his labored breathing, and he twisted around to scan the woods.

"They're gone," River whispered. "And our energy has tripled."

"We need to move."

A cry caught their attention and Hawk turned in the direction of the sound. He spotted River's Tabinese lying before the fire with its entrails spilling out. He winced and stepped in front of River to block her line of sight, but she pushed past him.

"River, don't—" But he knew it was already too late.

He moved in behind her and captured her shoulders, knowing what he had to do, but not necessarily liking it. "Why don't you snuff this fire out while I pack our things?"

She nodded, understanding what he was really about to do, and started gathering mud and dirt to smother the flames.

Hawk pressed his sword against the Tabinese's throat and sliced it quickly, putting it out of its misery.

He heard River draw a breath and turned to her. She was trying to be brave, he saw, but exhaustion was getting to her. She bit her lip and he watched as she struggled for composure, pity seeping unwillingly under his skin. If there was one thing he couldn't stand it was to see a woman cry.

Awkwardly gathering her into his arms, he tried to remember how to comfort. "It's not real, River." She needed to grasp that. "When you're tired, everything feels more real."

Something about the way she sagged against him sent a riot of emotions rocketing through him. Once again, unwelcome memories of his wife, and worse, his daughter, rushed to the forefront. Crisos. He didn't want to feel. Feeling scared the shit out of him because nothing good ever came from it.

"You have that look on your face again," River said.

He dipped his head to see her. "What look?"

"Like something scared the shit out of you. You had it back at the bog, when we were on the ledge."

"I thought those hounds were going to kill you," he admitted.

She laughed a little at that. "You were worried about me?"

The innocent way she looked at him, with a trace of barely controlled panic buried deep in her eyes, reminded him of Vienna and every other beaten soul the Dark Lord was torturing. River didn't deserve this. No one deserved this. And one simple mistake could end up costing her her life.

He slipped his hand around her head and drew her face to his chest. "Yeah, I was worried about you."

♦ ♦

Nick wondered for a second if he'd crapped his pants. He checked. Nope. Still clean.

Thank God Kaye had gotten bored and left during that period of silence when River found her stupid half-dog, half-cat creature thing and hid inside its bubble.

Why had she hidden, and more important, what had she hidden from? That was what didn't make sense to Nick. She had to realize by now that something was wrong with the game. Things were seriously out of place, and she was fanatic about quality. She should be jumping up and down, screaming into her com-link, and trying everything she could think of to get the team's attention.

And he should be doing everything he could to get her out. Trouble was there was nothing he could do to help her right now, not with Kaye calling the shots.

Of course, River getting killed off by Ferals might get her out of the game on her own and then Nick wouldn't have to interfere.

It might also leave her a drooling vegetable. He didn't know if Kaye considered a drooling vegetable a protected asset or not, but he did know that if anything happened to River, he was going to take the fall for it.

He sat back in his chair, studying the screen and the readings from her com-link. Her heart rate had been all over the board during that fight sequence, but it was back to normal now. He frowned, not believing the readings. In fact, her heart rate was better than before the fight. She seemed to be drawing energy from the game, and he didn't see how that was physically possible.

He finally had to admit that perhaps Kaye wasn't as crazy as he'd thought. Okay, he was every bit as crazy, but maybe he wasn't completely wrong.

Nick might possibly be the one who was wrong.

River was beautiful, frighteningly smart, and possessed almost superhuman stamina and reflexes. He hadn't wanted to examine those characteristics too closely while they were sleeping together because it might have interfered with his fun. Now that there was no way they could continue that particular aspect of their relationship, Nick was forced to admit that perhaps he might have unconsciously overlooked some of the more obvious signs.

That didn't mean he thought River had magic. More than likely she was a result of one of Kaye's twisted bioengineered experiments that had gone north instead of south, like Bane and all the werewolves of the world, and Kaye was trying to reclaim her.

It also meant that River was probably far too good for Nick, and had been all along, and he had no idea how he could possibly protect her from all the shit that was going to happen when he couldn't even figure out how to save himself.

The jangle of the gaming room phone, which almost never rang, nearly launched him off his chair. He cut River a look, some idiot part of him actually worried that the ringing phone might disturb her.

"Could I speak with River Weston?" a nasal, bored-sounding voice inquired.

"She's not in this morning." Nick figured that wasn't a lie, not that a lie would bother him anyway, but the bored guy on the phone sounded like a cop. Cops were chronically bored.

"Would Nick Sutton be in, then?"

There was now no doubt in Nick's mind that the rest of the team was dead, and he and River had been tagged as "persons of interest."

What was it with werewolves? Why did they have to be such homicidal maniacs?

Nick considered saying he was out, too, but then thought better of it. Sooner or later the cops would want to stop by to check out the team's background, and with River in her current state, Nick couldn't imagine a worse time than right now.

"Speaking," he said.

"Mr. Sutton." There was a crackle on the line as if the guy was shuffling papers around. "My name is Constable Jim Peters. Would you mind if I stopped by for a few moments to speak with you?"

Yes, Nick would.

"Actually," he said, looking at the clock on the wall, "I was just about to run out on some errands.

I'd be happy to drop by the police station and save you the trip."

He set a time, then hung up the receiver.

He hated leaving River alone but he didn't see what choice he had, and reminded himself that she'd been alone all night and seemed none the worse for it.

On the monitor in front of him Sever was holding River in his arms, and River was looking far too content. Nick threw his empty coffee cup into the garbage can with unnecessary force.

She was fine for the moment.

He locked the game room behind him when he left. The security guard would never enter anyway, no more than sticking his head in, but Nick didn't want Kaye coming back while he was gone and the dumbass security guard letting him in.

A quay ran along the river, cutting through the town's central downtown. Two hundred years ago early settlers had used the river to bring trade goods into the mountains. Thirty years ago, almost 150,000 people had lived here. Now, ten thousand inhabitants would be a generous estimate.

Nick's boots clicked on the wooden boardwalk as he strode along the riverfront. Some office towers remained empty, with boarded-up windows, while others had reopened for business over the past few years.

The country stood on the leading edge of economic recovery, with a competitive future in world technological trade. Nick had always been optimistic about what the future held for his tech-savvy generation, but now he had some serious questions about its morality.

He'd never worried about morality before. In the postwar era people were all about self-preservation, which was the biggest reason Kaye's monsters went mostly ignored. They'd served their purpose to help bring about the end of the war. And as long as he wasn't their target Nick was as willing as anyone to turn a blind eye to their continued existence. No one wanted to admit what they were: a weapon that had seriously turned on the very society they'd been intended to protect.

People were equally as scared as hell of the government, and with very good reason.

So where did River fit into the picture? Nick didn't believe that Kaye was interested in using her for the betterment of mankind. Not unless he was enhancing it by genetically altering it, and Nick wasn't sure anyone sane could consider what Kaye did "enhancement."

The police station was at the far end of the quay and up three streets. It seemed everything was uphill in this town.

Nick entered the station, gave his name at the

desk, and while he waited for Constable Peters to sign him in, he wondered how far his somewhat sketchy personal moral code would carry him when it came to protecting River.

◆ ◆

Constable James Peters hated his job, hated his coworkers, hated his life, and pretty much hated everything.

He also hated the case that had been dumped into his lap. He guessed he knew now who the department scapegoat must be.

As he wove his way through the warren of drab, dirty cubicle dividers to the front desk, he asked himself why anyone would implicate a woman in such an ugly murder.

He had photos of River Weston and quite frankly, he didn't see how she could have ripped the ass off a guy. The accompanying description of her said she stood about five foot two. He wasn't quite sure how she could have snapped the neck of a woman who stood five ten either.

This whole mess stank, and he wished like hell it had landed on someone else's desk.

When he reached the front desk he immediately disliked Nick Sutton. Since he immediately disliked almost everyone, that didn't trigger any alarms.

But Sutton had a smartass, arrogant look about

him—not to mention being taller, younger, thinner, and better looking than Jim—that made him want to give him a very hard time with this interview.

Someone was protecting Sutton, at least for the moment, and that added to Jim's dislike. He didn't doubt that whoever it was, he'd eventually turn on Sutton, too, but for right now they'd only sold out the Weston girl. Jim didn't know why, and he didn't want to know.

The problem was that Jim knew that the province's premier was a major investor in the game that the dead people, Weston, and Sutton were all working on, and the premier did want to know. And Jim was every bit as afraid of the government as most sensible people in the country. Probably more, at the moment.

The younger, taller, better-looking man stuck out his hand and introduced himself. "Nick Sutton."

Jim awkwardly accepted the handshake after only a fraction of a second's hesitation. The younger generation had no trouble with the courtesy, but Jim remembered all too well the fear of touching and the incessant hand washing from the days of the war.

He couldn't help it. He reached for the hand sanitizer fixed to the wall by the front desk, the smell of vinegar tickling his nose.

There was one of the greatest jokes ever on mankind. Millions of people dead, billions of dollars spent on research for a cure, and plain old household vinegar proved to be the best preventative of all.

"Follow me," Jim said, rubbing his rough, freckled hands together.

Sutton followed him through the maze to a small, glassed-in room at the back they used to interview witnesses.

Jim moved a stack of magazines off a chair and cleared someone's crossword puzzle from the conference table. He gestured to the now-empty chair. "Have a seat."

As they discussed the start to the hockey season, he studied Sutton. The younger man sounded relaxed. Too relaxed, considering his team hadn't shown up for work and he'd been called in for police questioning. Fine lines around his eyes and too-rapid blinking told Jim that he wasn't as relaxed as he wanted him to believe.

The officer slapped a thick folder onto the table. Dust drifted into the air. "Weren't you curious at all when three of your team members didn't show up for work this morning?"

"Not especially." Sutton shrugged. "Maybe a little. But we were all drinking last night." He shifted in his chair, his expression reflecting concern now. "Why? Has something happened to them?"

Now wasn't that interesting? By Jim's calculation there were four team members unaccounted for.

He ignored Sutton's question and opened the folder in front of him. "Witnesses say that River Weston left the bar ahead of everyone else. Do you know where she went?"

"I assume she went home."

Hmm. Jim kept his face carefully blank. He could almost see the wheels spinning in Sutton's head. "Let's assume she didn't. Where would she go?"

"She'd go back to the compound to work on the game. But she wasn't there when I came in this morning," Sutton added.

The security guard had seen her enter, but he hadn't seen her leave. Jim supposed it was possible that Weston had left while the guard was on rounds, but Jim knew Tom Dover personally and he'd be willing to bet that Tom hadn't moved his lazy butt from his chair all night—unless it had been for a quick trip to the can. But even then, surely he would have heard her leave.

He noticed that Sutton didn't ask if something had happened to Weston. Since Jim knew for a fact that a lot had happened to the other three gamers, he figured Sutton should be showing more concern. Particularly since reports indicated that he and Weston were boinking.

Or unless Sutton knew for certain that nothing had happened to her.

Right there, Jim would have bumped Sutton to the top of his suspect list if someone hadn't already provided the arrogant piece of crap with a rock-solid alibi. And, too, Sutton seemed 100 percent human— although "seeming" wasn't exactly a guarantee.

Whoever had done this to these people hadn't been human. This was the second part of the case that Jim really, really didn't want to be involved with.

That left River Weston as the possible freak, which was exactly what the informant had said. That River Weston wasn't human.

If she wasn't human, did Sutton know he'd been sleeping with a freak?

Jim looked at the picture of Weston again. She was a beautiful girl. Fresh-faced. Somewhat serious, if the picture was anything to go by, and with intelligent eyes. Not at all like the creepy, colorless eyes of the general who'd fingered her.

But if a general said she was a possible freak, then as far as Jim was concerned she was guilty as charged. This was the third part of the case he didn't intend to argue about. Jim had seen some disturbing shit in his long career and he didn't need to see any more.

The catch-22 for Jim was the premier's involvement. The premier wasn't going to like it that the money he'd been spending was about to disappear into an enormous sinkhole, one probably created by the military. There wasn't much a premier could do to a general, but a premier could make Jim's already pathetic life a living nightmare. The military wasn't the only one with monsters on a chain.

"If she didn't go home, and she wasn't at the compound when you showed up this morning, where else might she be?" Jim asked.

Sutton leaned forward, his hands clasped loosely between his knees. "Why don't you tell me what this is about?"

Arrogant son of a bitch. Jim flipped through the folder of graphic crime-scene photos until he came to his favorite. He pushed it across the table toward Sutton, interested to see what his reaction would be.

Sutton looked at the photo in silence for a few moments, paled, then slowly shifted to an unhealthy shade of green.

Jim grabbed a wastebasket and shoved it under Sutton's face. He'd seen that color enough times to know what was coming.

Sutton threw up until the dry heaves started. He sat back in his chair, his face slowly losing the green pallor, and Jim handed him a wad of paper towels to wipe his face on. The photo was pretty bad.

"Can I get you something to drink?" Jim asked. "Juice? Coffee?"

"Water," Sutton rasped.

Jim got him his water, stuck the rank wastebasket outside the door, and sat down at the table again. He didn't ask any more questions. He simply waited.

Sutton wasn't as relaxed now. In fact, he looked as if he might crawl out of his skin.

"I had nothing to do with that," Sutton said. His eyes went everywhere but the photos, darting back and forth like a trapped rat's.

He might not have, but he knew who did.

"No one thinks you did," Jim answered. "You were seen entering your apartment building long before the murders. Your neighbor said you were on the phone, and that he could hear you moving around your apartment. Nosy neighbors are convenient sometimes, aren't they?" He put the photos back into the folder and closed it. "I want to know where River Weston might be."

A look of stunned incredulity made Sutton's face sag. "You can't possibly think that River had anything to do with this."

"I don't," Jim admitted. "But it doesn't matter what I think. Someone more important than me thinks she did."

♦ ♦

River pressed her cheek into Hawk's chest, and for a few panicky heartbeats seriously worried that her mind might have been pushed past its limits.

Battle fatigue and sleep deprivation were the only explanation for her falling apart over the death of a character in a game that had no true life other than what she'd programmed into it.

The trouble was that her Tabinese was a character that wasn't intended to die. It stayed behind when the player progressed to a new level.

Never mind that it also symbolized her childhood—she didn't need any psychoanalysis right now. Her mind was a little too fragile for that.

She pulled free from the warmth of Hawk's arms. She appreciated his effort to offer comfort because she doubted that it came easy for him, but her mind was her problem. He had enough troubles of his own. As long as she still had her ability to reason, she could move forward.

But what were they moving forward into? Somehow, someone had altered her game. *Her* game. And now he was making it personal. That gave her something to focus on and brought out the competitor in her. She was good. She was going to win this game.

She dug deep and drew a rejuvenating breath, something she'd done more than once during the long, grinding nights she'd spent at the lab when her body was eager to shut down but the rest of her wasn't quite ready to call it quits.

Like sucking water through a straw, she pulled

energy from the pit of her stomach and visualized it moving through her veins. As her muscles filled with rich, revitalized blood, both her spirit and her strength punched up like magic. Her nerve endings tingled. Her skin hydrated. Her blood sugars stabilized.

She felt very much alive. She was more than simply a virtual character in a game.

And not just any game. This particular one had a few features the Soul Man wouldn't be expecting either.

Steadier now, and calmer, she shot a glance around them. Morning light filtered through the sagging clouds, moisture heavy in the air as the storm threatened overhead.

"I'm about ready to get out of this jungle," she said. "How about you?"

Hawk examined her, his dark eyes moving over her face and slowly filling with suspicion at her sudden change in mood. "You okay?"

"Of course I am," she said, not wanting to admit that for a moment she'd been wondering the same thing herself. "Why?"

"You seem . . . different."

"Different?" She stole a look at her clothes and then held out her hands, turning them over for a closer examination, hoping Hawk's mind was okay and he wasn't suddenly seeing her as the enemy. "How?"

"I don't know. I guess maybe most people would have collapsed from exhaustion by now, yet you seem to have new strength all of a sudden." He shook his head, clearly confused. "I really don't know what's keeping you going."

"It's a trick I learned growing up," she confessed, embarrassed at having to explain one more thing about her that made her different from most people but wanting to reassure him. They couldn't afford to waffle like this between trust and distrust of each other. Mentally, it wasn't healthy. "I'd want to stay up all night playing games, and my parents would want me in bed. I'd go to bed, get up again once they were asleep, but then I'd have to keep my energy up so they wouldn't figure it out. I did the same thing just now."

He angled his head, his glossy black eyes scrutinizing her. "How long can you keep that up?"

"I'm not really sure." These days she tried to stay on the same schedule as the rest of the team, as difficult as that was sometimes. She wasn't always successful, which explained her current predicament. "I don't keep track. I do know that when I crash, I crash hard," she admitted.

She watched him watching her, weighing her words, wondering if she was telling him the truth.

"Does this energy you tap into come from inside you?" he asked.

He believed her, she saw with relief. Then she frowned.

If he believed her, why did he sound so worried?

Disappointment in him curled through her insides. "Don't worry," she said. "It comes from my physical body. I don't take it from either you or the game credits we earn."

Surprise lit his eyes. "That never crossed my mind."

Maybe not, but something had and he wasn't going to tell her what it was. At least he hadn't thought she was stealing from him. That indicated some level of trust on his part, didn't it?

She wondered if she could pass some of her energy over to him. She'd never tried to give it to anyone else before, but reached out to touch his arm, just to see.

He jumped as if she'd Tasered him and leapt away. Shocked incredulity washed over his face as he rubbed his arm.

River clutched her hands to her chest. "I wasn't trying to hurt you."

"You didn't hurt me. You surprised me. Save your energy for yourself," he advised her, still rubbing his arm.

She was trying to help here. What in the world was his problem? "The more energy we both have, the more likely we are to make it through the game," River pointed out.

"Don't use your energy for anything in this program," he practically shouted at her. "You never know who might be watching!" He turned away, changing the subject. "How do we get out of here?"

He was scaring her and River didn't like it, but she didn't know what to do about it either. The question in her mind shifted from whether he trusted her to did she trust him?

He noticed her silence, correctly interpreted it, and ran a hand down his face, blowing out a heavy breath. "I'm sorry, River," he said, sounding somewhat calmer. "You haven't done anything wrong. You've just surprised me, that's all." He gave a rusty little laugh. "I thought I was beyond being surprised by anything anymore. Well." He rocked awkwardly from one foot to the other, like a little boy acknowledging bad behavior and waiting for punishment. "Let's try this again. How do we get to the Wizard?"

"The entrance is ahead a few hundred yards."

He stepped forward, gnarled tree roots snapping beneath his heavy boots. He stopped, turned back to her, and took her face in his hands, bringing his mouth to her ear as if not wishing to be overheard.

"I meant it," he whispered to her. His voice was fierce, despite a new gentleness she'd seen his eyes, and River shivered. "Don't use your energy in the game. Not for anything."

What was that all about?

She didn't have the time to gather her startled thoughts and ask before he turned away.

Moving quickly, Hawk pushed ahead by using his sword to cut a path. River brought up the rear, keeping half of her attention on the trail behind them and the other half on checking for escape routes in case they needed one in a hurry.

She glanced at the morning sky, then at her comlink as they walked. Nick or someone else on the team should have been contacting her by now. A feeling that something was wrong—even more wrong than it was already—crept up her spine. She knew what was happening on her end. She had no idea what was going on at theirs.

They reached the edge of a clearing. At the far side of that clearing there should be a doorway. That doorway should lead to the Wizard.

A second later Hawk stopped dead in his tracks. River knew by the way his body tensed, by the way his fingers curled into fists, and by the dry sounds coming from low in his throat that something else was seriously wrong.

CHAPTER TEN

♦

Nick stood on the sidewalk in front of the police station, wondering what in the hell he was supposed to do now. He should be glad that Kaye hadn't sold him out instead of River, but he had no idea why Kaye had provided him with an alibi. The neighbor hadn't heard shit, other than Nick slamming the door on the way in.

He wished he could get the taste of vomit out of his throat. He'd known what werewolves were capable of doing. He'd just never seen the actual evidence before.

What Bane had done to Tanner was something Nick hoped never to see again. Or worse, to experience firsthand.

Nick decided that Kaye's real reason for being here was to clean up after Bane. And he was using River as the mop.

The sky overhead had shifted to gray and the threat of rain hung in the air. He didn't dare go back to the compound to check on River just yet. Stocky, redheaded, freckle-faced Constable Peters was no idiot.

He couldn't go all the way back to his apartment

either. As soon as he could, he was going back to River. The thought of Kaye getting to her first made him want to throw up all over again, and his stomach was too empty now for that.

He thought he might head to Andy's and see if she was open. She might have heard something about what went on last night. Nick didn't think he wanted to know any more than he already did, but at the same time he couldn't afford not to.

He passed bits of crime-scene tape fluttering in the wind. Other than that, the street had been hosed down and all other traces were gone.

Andy's was open for business as usual. Nick pushed through the heavy doors just as the sky opened up and rain pounded against the glazed front windows.

Andy was standing behind the bar, wiping down the counter, eyes on the high-definition television screen on the other side of the room. CNN was blasting an updated report on the three dead gamers. Pictures of all five of them flashed across the screen.

It wouldn't be long before Nick found himself famous.

That wasn't good. It would make it difficult for him to disappear.

"Nick," Andy called out when she saw him. She threw the cloth under the counter and scooted around the bar to intercept him. "Where's River? Is she okay?"

Andy was one of those rare women who aged well. She also had a certain warm quality about her that made people want to be near her. Nick thought she was hot as hell and told her so. Frequently.

He couldn't muster up the energy to flirt with her today. He also couldn't find the energy to lie. Lying to Andy took way too much effort at the best of times, and besides, he always felt like he'd wasted it when he did.

"River's fine," he said, keeping his voice low, not wanting the few other people in the place to hear him and report his words back to Peters.

Andy took his cue. "Thank God," she whispered under her breath. She didn't ask him again where River was, which Nick greatly appreciated. "Let me bring you today's special, on the house." She sized him up. "And a double Red draft. You look like you could use it."

Nick took a seat at a corner booth at the back of the bar. He had no idea how he was supposed to get out of the whole fucked-up situation. Not with his picture plastered on the news.

Amos Kaye slid into the booth across from him.

Jesus *Christ*. Nick waited to see if his heart would start beating again. "Where the hell did you come from?"

"How did the little Fae make out in her game? Did she ever reappear?"

"Yeah," Nick said. "And she's still alive, thanks for asking." He leaned back in his seat and tried to look the crazy fuck in the eye. "Why are you following me?"

"I told you. I'm protecting my assets."

"By turning them in to the *police*?" Nick asked, not able to keep the *Are you insane?* tone out of his voice.

Kaye clasped his hands and rested them on the table, leaning onto his forearms. "I turned her in to keep you from doing so."

Why on earth would Nick turn River in?

It took Nick a few seconds to puzzle that out. And then everything Kaye had done made more sense to him. With River out of it the way she was, Kaye thought it possible that Nick might panic and call an ambulance, or, if he waited too long and River didn't make it, call the police to try to save his own ass. Now that Nick was in effect harboring River, Kaye had just made sure he couldn't exercise either of those options. He'd also managed to deflect local police attention away from Bane. A two-for-one deal.

Coldness crept over Nick and he wished Andy would hurry up with the beer. He really needed that drink.

"You are one scary bastard," Nick said.

Kaye smiled as if pleased with the compliment.

Andy showed up then, sliding Nick's beer in front of him. She looked at Kaye, her normal friendliness absent.

"Can I get you anything?" she asked him, polite but not welcoming.

"Thanks, I'm good," Kaye said, smiling at her in a way that made the hair on Nick's arms lift.

Andy shot Nick a look that told him she was not at all impressed by the company he kept. She gave the wooden tabletop a quick swipe, dropped a knife and fork on it, then walked away, her back stiff.

Nick wasn't surprised by her attitude. Andy was a fairly good judge of character and Kaye gave off "psycho" vibes like bad body odor.

Nick had to get away from him. That might mean running for the rest of his life. He eyed the television screen. CNN had moved on to other news topics. He wondered how long they'd be broadcasting his picture.

"What exactly do you want from me?" Nick asked, playing with the knife. "And when I get it for you, can I get the hell out of this boring piece-of-shit town?"

"I want you to keep the Fae in that game as long as possible to see how far she can make it. I want you to report to me on everything that she does, and how her physical body reacts to what her mind is doing."

Kaye pushed away from the table and got to his feet as if preparing to leave. Before he did, he planted his palms on the table and leaned over Nick.

"The second she returns to her body, *if* she returns to her body, I want to know about it. And I expect you to keep her alive until I come to get her."

♦ ♦

Hawk drew in slow, steady breaths and tried to collect himself.

River was right behind him, and whatever game the sick Dark Lord was playing now, Hawk had to protect her at all costs. He'd have to figure out how a Fae had found herself in such a situation later.

"Who is she?" River whispered. She tried to move into the clearing with him, but Hawk blocked her with his body, keeping her behind him and shielded as best as possible by the jungle overgrowth.

Having to explain Vienna to a Fae was almost as bad as having to explain her to his wife.

"She's dead," Hawk said tersely. "She's a tortured soul who has no will or mind of her own." And Hawk felt so fucking sorry for her right now he could have wept. "That means she's dangerous, because the Dark Lord is controlling her."

"You know her," River said, and Hawk caught an undercurrent of sympathy in the statement. Her hand crept to his, giving it a quick squeeze of comfort before releasing it so he'd have both his hands free if he needed them.

River might be Fae, but she thought like a fighter.

Naked and shivering, bare feet coated with mud, Vienna reached out to Hawk with her right hand, her left hand clasped behind her back. Long, unkempt hair spilled over her stark white shoulders. Dark purple scars marred her ashen flesh.

"Help me, Hawk." The dark despair in Vienna's voice cut him. Hawk pinched the bridge of his nose and gave a quick shake of his head.

"She's not real, River," he said, trying to convince them both of that even though he knew it wasn't necessarily true. Vienna's suffering was real enough. Her mind and body might be long gone, but the Dark Lord's torturing of her soul could go on for all eternity.

He could never allow this to happen to River.

Vienna took a step toward them, and Hawk held his hand up to warn her away.

"Don't come any closer, Vienna. I don't want to have to hurt you."

Tears glistened in her eyes. "Please, Hawk. Don't

make me go back to him. Let me stay here with you." Her full lips curved provocatively. "I'll be *very* good."

"What's going on?" River asked. Hawk heard the little bleep on her com-link that warned him her blood pressure had just shot up.

His jaw clenched. "It's a trap."

If Hawk had been paying more attention to River and less to Vienna, he might have been able to prevent what happened next.

Then again, maybe not. River's reflexes were lightning fast.

In a blur of motion and with surprising strength she pushed past him, her sword in her hand, charging across the clearing with the obvious intent of doing what she believed Hawk didn't have the guts for.

That was when Hawk realized he should have been paying more attention to the hand Vienna held behind her back.

Panic gave him added speed of his own. He raced after River, and with his longer legs managed to cut her off before Vienna had time to fully release the detonator.

He hit River hard with his shoulder, sending her much lighter body soaring across the clearing. She landed with an audible thud on the spongy ground, and Hawk hurled himself on top of her less than a second before the bomb went off. Dirt and debris, and what could only be bits of Vienna, showered around them.

Crisos . . .

The ringing in his ears was going to take some time to clear.

River angled her head to the side and groaned. A sick, apprehensive knot twisted his insides and he wondered how badly he'd hurt her. Everything had happened too fast. It was going to take a few seconds for his brain to catch up.

He tried to roll off her, to give her some room to breathe, but his mind wasn't ready to cooperate. He needed to get over the shell shock first.

River wriggled her way free and sat up beside him.

"Wow," she breathed, her eyes going wide. "You need to do something about yourself."

"That bad?" Hawk said, wondering what damage she saw when she looked at him.

"Yes, it's that bad," she confirmed. She attempted to straighten his body, tugging on his leg and arm.

"Give me a second," Hawk complained. "I need to pull myself together." He felt a little better when she laughed at the bad joke.

Her eyes stopped below his right knee, and Hawk lifted his head to see what was causing the sick expression on her face.

His torn pant leg exposed a gaping wound. Like a filleted fish, red slabs of flesh peeled away in layers and exposed the sharp edges of a broken shin bone.

"You need to heal this," she said.

"I need to heal my back first." Hawk knew that was where he'd taken much of the force of the explosion, and at the moment his limbs weren't working very well even aside from the broken leg.

He'd suffered considerable damage this time, he knew, and it scared him. It meant the Dark Lord had almost finished him, and if the Dark Lord did manage to claim him River would be left on her own. He knew she had no other Guardian to protect her because none would ever have allowed her to play such a dangerous game, and against such an opponent.

But protecting Fae wasn't what Hawk had been trained for. The psychology tests had labeled him too quick to react, and the tests were right. He might have killed her the first time he laid eyes on her. As it was it made him physically ill to think he'd actually struck her.

If he ever got the chance, he was going to rip the immortal's black heart from his dried out body and serve it to him on a dirty plate. Now that was something worth programming into the Dark Lord's prison.

Right now, he needed to get River out of this

game. Hawk's mind raced through the possibilities even as he discarded them. Fae could jump—transport themselves at will—but it was dangerous at the best of times and took years of training, even for the most skilled. And even supposing River could jump back to her world, it merely provided a temporary solution and led to a larger problem. River would then have no Guardian at all to watch over her. Something could happen to River at any time, anywhere, and if it did, her soul was the Dark Lord's.

Hawk wondered again how they could use the glitch in the prison program to their advantage. He was missing something.

Something important.

"So who was she?" River asked again, curiosity lighting her eyes.

This was not a conversation Hawk intended to have with a woman, particularly a Fae. Neither he nor Vienna had been willing participants in acts that had only been meant to humiliate and destroy. He didn't want to think about Vienna, already back in the Dark Lord's lair and having to face his disappointment at her failure, anymore. Given a choice between saving River or Vienna, River won hands down, but it didn't make it any easier to know that the Dark Lord was right now torturing Vienna because of him.

It worried him, too, that the Dark Lord had some-how known Vienna would make him hesitate. The Dark Lord understood him far better than Hawk liked.

"Let's just find your damn Wizard," he said, and River wisely let the subject of Vienna drop.

Gritting his teeth, Hawk propped himself up on one elbow, his other hand going to the open wound on his leg. He placed his palm over the laceration, and with fierce concentration he drew a deep breath to center himself. Precious seconds turned into min-utes as he willed the gash to close.

"Come on, Hawk. Concentrate." River tried to smile, but Hawk could see how worried she was. "You're not taking the easy way out and leaving me here all alone."

The hell he'd be leaving her alone anywhere. His mind was made up on that. He'd keep her with him as long as he safely could and hope they got out of the game together. She was a Fae all alone in the universe, and that had to be linked in some way to the dwindling number of Fae souls. Getting her out of the game without him would be a last resort.

"I am concentrating," he growled.

She tapped her com-link and the worry in her eyes deepened. "We're running out of time for this level. If we don't get moving, we'll be timed out and end up back at the beginning of the primitive world."

As if that wasn't enough to top off the perfect beginning to an otherwise perfectly shitty day, the clouds opened up and cold buckets of rain splashed down on them.

The rain probably lasted no longer than five minutes, but it was long enough to make Hawk wish he'd gone commando. Wet clothes, especially wet underwear, weren't comfortable.

When it stopped River wiped the rain from her face, blinking droplets of water off her long lashes. "That's it. I've had enough. We're getting out of here," she said.

The energy pouring from her arm into his skin when she touched him made him forget his wet, clinging clothes. It made him forget everything, or at least dulled it to a faint memory. For the first time since before he'd lost his family, he felt at peace.

Within seconds his body was whole again.

He sat up, testing his various parts, and found everything worked as good as new. Maybe better. She needed to learn a little restraint. Uncontrolled magic could create a whole shitload of problems.

"I thought I told you not to use magic in this game," Hawk said evenly, wanting to be angry with her but not yet able to summon the emotion. "Not for any reason."

River gaped at him, her mouth slightly open, then she started to laugh. "Magic?" she said. *"Magic?"*

He refused to feel stupid so he clung to stubborn instead. "What else could it be?"

"Do you know what a software-defined radio system is?" River asked.

"Of course." He was mildly insulted by the question. Very simply put, it was a radio that could send and receive waveforms while running different types of software.

"The game is initiated by the player's brain waves," River explained, as if addressing a class of the newest and dimmest academy resources. "The software I designed receives the signals from the brain, interprets them, then passes them on to other software in the program. That software interprets the second set of signals, alters them, and passes them on, again and again, and so you get software running software. The gamer's brain starts the chain of events, but each signal is interpreted in a different way, depending on the software receiving it. It's deliberately random so the player never has the same gaming experience twice, but there are still elements of the game that can be controlled.

"You showed me one way to heal myself in the game," she continued. "By sending the right signals, I can heal you a different way. I pull energy from my physical body, then simply introduce it as new code in the program over a secure frequency." She lifted her dripping shirt away from her skin and shook it, trying to get rid of the excess moisture. "It's the secure frequency that's causing me the most problems," she confessed, clearly frustrated. She made a face. "It's not dependable. It's more than likely how the Soul Man tapped into the game."

Hawk wondered if her "secure frequency" was based on true technology as she believed, or if it was more firmly rooted in Fae magic. Either way, she'd created something that was so far beyond her world's ethical intelligence it made him sweat to think about what might happen if the wrong people got their hands on it.

Or what might happen if the Dark Lord got his hands on *her*. Her Fae magic was tied to her soul. If the Dark Lord controlled her soul, he controlled her magic as well.

And River's magic was clearly something out of the ordinary. Worse, she had no knowledge or understanding of it. He had no idea how he was supposed to protect her.

Letting the game time out wasn't going to help him figure it out.

The clearing had turned into a massive, muddy crater. Across the crater, behind River's back, was the door where Vienna had stood. The blast hadn't harmed it. That could be good or bad.

He tilted his chin and said, "I take it that's the entrance to the safe house? What are we going to find when we enter?"

"What we find inside depends on what we collected in the primitive world," River said, glancing over her shoulder at the safe house, then again at her com-link. "That door's not as close as you think it is, so we have to get moving." She held up her sword, a bright smile on her lips. "But at least we have enough energy left to summon the Wizard when we get there."

She started to laugh again.

"What?" Hawk demanded, helping her to her feet.

She shook her head. "Magic is part of your reality, not mine. The only magic I can use is what I program."

Hawk slicked his wet hair off his forehead. "Tell that to the Dark Lord," he advised. "He's part of your world's history, not mine."

◆ ◆

Death was something Vienna no longer needed to worry herself over. Her soul was the Dark Lord's for eternity.

He did wish, however, that she had more spirit left in her.

She crouched in the corner like a whipped puppy, despite the fact that he was not at all displeased with her performance in the game. She'd gotten him useful information.

River was indeed a Fae, the Guardian had a weakness the Dark Lord could somehow exploit, and all was right in his universe again. Time might no longer be on his side, but it wasn't on theirs either.

He'd been planning his escape from the moment of his incarceration. He'd been planning his revenge for equally as long. The Guardians had left him his seeing stones as a kindness, but to the Dark Lord, kindness equaled weakness. Through the seeing stones he'd been able to find lost souls like his Vienna. He'd also found the Fae, River. The Fae with their earth magic were little more than farmers compared to an immortal and the high magic he held, but River's earth magic would be more than enough to get him out of this prison.

Now he had to make it as difficult as possible for River and the Guardian to reach those safe houses, instead forcing them directly to him, and he was going to have to take a few more risks in order to do so. Those safe houses were the one area of River's game that he couldn't seem to tap into no matter how hard he tried. Smashing them was impossible. It was very frustrating.

He didn't like it either that River and the Guardian were now offering each other support. That would have to be addressed.

They both had weaknesses. Catching them by surprise was the key.

◆ ◆

"What were you thinking when you programmed *this*?"

They stood in a light mist of rain on the edge of a moving pedway that led to the base of a leaf-shrouded bluff some fifty feet across a crocodile-clogged ravine. A living, moving carpet of green covered the pedway. Loud croaking filled the air.

"That if people are going to pay for a challenge, they should get their money's worth," River replied. She hadn't planned for getting stuck in the game. Next time, she would.

Hawk furrowed his brow in thought. "What are we supposed to do?"

She pointed. "There's an opening at the top of the bluff and we have to lower ourselves in."

He eyed the pedway, doubt in his eyes. "Do we get points for squashing those frogs on the way?"

"Of course not. We don't cross that way. It's too obvious. We go over it," she said, bending down to place her hand on an exposed tree root. Thirty feet above the ground, from the top of the tree, a stalk shot outward, twisting and turning as it spanned the frog-littered pedway and embedded itself into the bluff beyond.

His eyes snapped up to examine the speedy growth, then he turned back to her. He watched her for a long, thoughtful moment, until the strange look on his face started to irritate her.

"Another trick you wrote into your program?" he asked.

"Yes." She wished he'd forget the crazy idea that she had magic. The suggestion made her uncomfortable. Technology was what River understood best. Sequences, codes, and probabilities. All of those could be controlled.

She patted the tree trunk, redirecting the conversation. "Time to climb. We go up, then over. Oh, and watch out for poisonous snakes."

Hawk made no move to follow. Instead, he stood with his feet firmly planted on the ground, shoulder width apart, his head tipped back as he looked upward. "You couldn't have made those frogs worth points so we could cross the pedway?"

"That would be too easy. And predictable." River wrapped her legs around the slender trunk and began to shimmy upward to the lower limbs of the tree. She swung onto one sturdy branch, hooking a knee over, and began to climb. She looked down, noticing that Hawk still hadn't moved. "Aren't you coming?"

He ruffled his hair with a rough hand and avoided her eyes. "I'm not good with heights."

Was this why he hadn't wanted to go over the hollow log earlier in the game? The fine lines around his dark eyes deepened, and her heart softened. She got the sense that it took a great deal of effort for him to admit to any weakness.

So the badass warrior was afraid of heights. It was no big deal. He wasn't computer-generated. He was a living, breathing being capable of a broad range of emotions, fear included. And that made him seem very human to her.

"I'll talk you through it," she assured him.

He wrapped his hands around the trunk and gave the tree a careful shake. "Are you sure this will even hold me?"

"It supported Sever." When he continued to hesitate she said, "Trust me, Hawk. I'll get you through this. It's the fastest route and we don't have much time."

He adjusted the sword at his side and started to climb. "The damn Wizard had better have some answers."

The fact that he trusted her made it all the more important to help get him through this. River reached the top of the tree and tested the wirelike stalk with her foot before stepping onto it.

She held her arms out to the sides for balance and concentrated on the task ahead. "Let me go first. It's not meant to hold both of us at the same time."

"At least get down on your hands and knees!" Hawk barked sharply. "Otherwise we find a safer way across. Or we let the game time out and we start over."

"I'm good at this," River assured him, totally confident. "The faster I cross, the more time you'll have."

She didn't give him any more opportunity to argue. Using careful, measured steps she sailed across the stalk like a tightrope walker, and when she reached the other side she turned to face Hawk, triumphant. "Your turn."

Hawk stepped onto the stalk, which bowed a bit under his weight. The creaking made him visibly cringe, and when he looked down to take in the hungry crocodiles at the bottom of the ravine far below, River tensed at his expression.

"Look at me Hawk, and listen to me. Don't try to cross the same way I did. Sit down and shimmy your way across."

He was bigger than Sever, and suddenly he seemed too large and too awkward to maneuver such a slender stalk. The soft mist of rain made it slippery. She held her breath, afraid, certain that if he fell, this time he wouldn't recover from it.

Hawk lifted his chin to focus on her. Intense dark

eyes locked on hers and she could read the determination in them. With slow, easy movements he lowered himself and wrapped his arms and legs around the stalk, inching forward. He reached the halfway point and River started to breathe again.

"You're doing just fine," she called. She started to laugh, relief making her giddy. She'd underestimated him. He was going to make it. "But you look ridiculous."

An answering grin broke across his face. "Do I earn any points for the loss of dignity?"

Not in the game, but he'd earned major points with her for being able to laugh at himself in spite of his fear. The light on his face took her breath away. She'd thought him grim. He was anything but, and she was as impressed as hell.

River was about to respond with something smart when a dark shadow filled the sky. An Uultur soared over the treetops, setting its sights on Hawk dangling midway over the deep ravine. She'd been so absorbed in his crossing that she'd failed to keep an eye out for approaching danger.

Hawk noticed the Uultur at the same time she did. He looked up, breaking his concentration, and he slipped sideways on the rain-slickened stalk. River let out a small, horrified cry and started forward, but there was nothing she could do to help.

A loud curse echoed off the ravine walls as he caught himself midair. His large hands clutched the thin stalk in a death grip as he dangled over the chasm. Hungry crocodiles, drawn by the prospect of a meal, swarmed below him in a tangled mass of snapping jaws and thrashing tails.

The Uultur swooped down, inches from Hawk's fingers, and there was nothing he could do to protect himself.

Cheating by inserting new code would take too long and was too unpredictable. River, her hands shaking and her mind reeling, took up her sword and cashed in a collection of energy, striking a boulder with the sword's blade and grabbing the bow and arrow stashed underneath. Alarm bells dinged on her com-link and she swore under her breath.

Hawk swung his legs around the stalk and tried to strike the persistent Uultur with his fist. Then, hand over hand, he grappled his way across the ravine far faster than was safe.

As the Uultur came back again, River positioned the bow and arrow and took aim. The bird let out a loud, shrieking cry as it dropped to the bottom of the ravine, an arrow through its breast. Seconds later, the crunch of jaws on bone filled the air as the crocodiles finished it off.

That could have been Hawk.

River shuddered uncontrollably as Hawk closed the distance between them. A few moments later he planted his feet on the ground, and then he had her in his arms.

"It's okay, it's okay," he said over and over, his cheek on her hair and his hand rubbing her back until her shaking stopped. She wrapped her arms around his waist and held on tight, relieved beyond measure that he'd made it. When faced with danger to herself, she had no problem. It was a totally different story when the danger was to someone she cared about.

"Why couldn't you have moved that fast from the very start?" she demanded, her voice muffled against his chest.

She felt him exhale, and she inched back to look up at him. She didn't miss the blaze of his eyes as his hands stroked her curves, then stilled on the small of her back.

His warrior face softened, and in that instant she became very much aware of his blatant masculinity, the way her breasts pressed into his chest, and the intimate way his hands anchored her body to his.

He dipped his head and his warm breath wafted over her face when he said, "I needed the right incentive." He kissed her forehead and closed his eyes. "That was close."

"Too close," she agreed, a knot tightening in her

stomach as she acknowledged to herself how nice it felt to be held by him and how awful it would be if a moment like this never happened again.

Although they didn't really have time for this right now.

Reality inched its way back into her brain and she eased away, and Hawk's forehead creased as he took note of her blinking com-link. "Shouldn't someone be helping you out by now?"

She frowned and lowered her gaze to the com-link. "Something has to be wrong at home. Nick would be having a fit right now if he knew what was happening."

Nick would be having a fit, all right. He made jokes about Sever all the time, but River knew that deep down he was really jealous. She'd thought that funny until now.

Now, Nick had every reason to be jealous even if he didn't know it. Hawk was no fictional character she'd dreamt up, and she found him far more attractive than Nick would like.

Was that why Nick wasn't helping her? Because he was jealous of Sever?

No way. River didn't believe that. Nick wasn't planning a future with her any more than she was with him. He could be possessive, but only because he wasn't quite ready to move on just yet. Something must have happened to him. She hoped it wasn't because of her. Had the Soul Man somehow managed to hurt Nick and the others?

Hawk slipped his finger under her chin and lifted until her eyes met his, correctly reading her thoughts. "I can't think of any way the Dark Lord can get into your world, not even through your game. Not yet. If something's happened to your friends, it isn't your fault."

"If I hadn't made a stupid wish—"

"You didn't know. If anyone is to blame for all this, it's the Guardians for creating a virtual prison and not maintaining it."

Regardless, her feelings of responsibility weren't about to be so easily dismissed.

"If anything happens to the others because of me, I don't know if I can live with that," she confessed.

"Nothing is going to happen to them, River."

She hoped he was right, but something inside her told her he was wrong. Call it woman's intuition. "I need to get back to them."

"We'll get you back."

The slight beat before Hawk's response didn't go unnoticed by River. Neither did the way his eyes slid from hers when he spoke. He didn't want her to leave the game. Why not?

If she did, what would happen to him? How could she go back home and leave him trapped with a monster in a virtual prison? It could take months before she found the right combination of code to free him, if ever. The game might be hers but the prison wasn't, and if Hawk was right, it had been created by people with far more technical skill than she possessed.

She could try introducing new code to corrupt the program, but what would then happen to Hawk and the other souls he wanted to protect?

Defeating the Soul Man had to be the key.

She swallowed hard and pushed past Hawk. "Come on. We'll have to keep our time with the Wizard limited if we want to hold on to enough energy to enter into the next level."

"Why? I thought we had plenty of energy."

"I had to cash some of it in to get the bow and arrow."

Hawk didn't seem pleased by her choice. "If you'd saved your energy, then you might have been able to get all the information you needed from the Wizard to get home."

"And leave you here for dead? Forget that," she said. "We're going to beat the Soul Man."

Hawk caught her face in his hands, taking her by surprise with his sudden intensity.

"Listen carefully," he said, any traces of softness in him vanishing in an instant. "Nothing is more important than getting you to safety. That means we have to beat this game by whatever means, but no matter what, you leave the Dark Lord to me. As long as he has a claim on your soul you aren't safe. No taking unnecessary risks. Everything is about keeping you safe, and that's an order. Do you understand me?"

He was ordering her to keep herself safe at the expense of all others?

Rage, white-hot then ice-cold, slid through River's veins and blazed from her fingertips. The air around them charged with it, so thick with her angry energy that her hair lifted on it as if on a breeze. Thick ropes of flowering vine sprouted from the ground in response, twisting and winding around their feet with lightning speed. In seconds they were ankle deep.

"An *order*?" she demanded. "You're *ordering me* to keep myself safe? I couldn't very well let the damn bird eat you then, could I? I might need to use you as bait if something worse comes along."

Hawk lifted one foot from the tangle of vines. His mouth kicked up at the corners, but the odd mixture of frustration and awe that flashed across his face didn't go unnoticed by her despite her near-blinding anger.

"As long as we understand each other," he said.

CHAPTER ELEVEN

♦

Once Kaye had left the bar, Andy slid into the seat across from Nick.

"You have to find yourself better friends."

Her amazing green eyes, by far the best of her many great, although mature, features, regarded Nick with something like pity.

He didn't like that.

"He's not even close to the bottom of the barrel," Nick replied. "Although I wouldn't exactly call him a friend." He dug into the plate of steak and baked potato that Andy had placed in front of him, although it might have been rubber for all the interest he had in it. He took a swig of beer to wash down a mouthful past the raw lump in his throat.

"Do me a favor and keep him away from River."

Nick choked on his beer. "Why would you think he'd have anything to do with River?"

"Because he's a stranger, and at the moment, everyone's interested in River."

Andy was too clever by far. Could there not be at least one other dumbass moron in this town besides himself? He was starting to feel outnumbered.

Andy's gaze softened. "Everything's going to

work out okay," she said, covering his hand with both of hers.

"Tell that to Tanner, Marsha, and Johnny."

"They'll get their justice." Andy squeezed his fingers. "You can't blame an animal for being an animal. But you can blame the one who sets it loose."

Terror seized Nick's insides and threatened to bleed his bowels dry. She knew far too much about something, and Nick didn't want to be associated with anyone who knew anything about whatever it was. He withdrew his hand from her grasp. "I don't know what you're talking about," he said.

Andy folded her hands in her lap. "We both know River's in trouble," she said quietly.

He doubted if Andy really knew the half of it, but if she did, then Nick was in far more trouble himself than he'd thought. It meant he didn't know anything at all about Andy, and who or what she was. It also meant there was nowhere in this town where he'd be safe. River either, for that matter. And was it really River's safety Andy was interested in?

He leaned forward. "I don't know anything of the kind. But I do know that River's a big girl. She can take care of herself."

"She's a big girl," Andy agreed, "and she's also special. I think we both know that."

Was he the only person who knew River who'd

been blind to what she was? Okay, he still didn't know what she was. But he might as well hop on the bandwagon and assume she was a freak of some kind. And he'd yet to meet a freak that wasn't deadly or damaged in some way.

Nick's brain started to spin, sorting through the possibilities. Perhaps Bane hadn't been responsible for what happened to Tanner and the other two. Maybe it had been River all along. Maybe she'd killed them and then gone back to the compound.

And maybe the tooth fairy blew baby breath out her ass. River was probably a freak, true enough. She thrived a little too well on thrills to be normal. But she was about as deadly as dust bunnies. She'd catch spiders and set them free.

Which left damaged.

She needed to be protected. From Kaye, from Bane, and even from Andy until Nick could be certain of who their friends were. In short, Nick planned to trust no one. He was all River could count on right now, and that probably wasn't saying much. He knew his limits.

"I know she's a good fuck," Nick said crudely. "And even that is starting to get old."

Andy didn't flinch. Instead, she smiled. Nick had the oddest sense of something brushing his thoughts, as if examining what made him tick, and it gave him the creeps.

"You're a better person than you think," she said.

Nick pushed his plate of unfinished food away, unable to stomach even one more mouthful. He snatched up his jacket off the cracked-vinyl-covered bench. "We both know what kind of person I am."

He bolted for the door, drawing stares from the few other people in the room, driven by a need to be with River right now more than anything because nothing was right, no one was what he seemed, and she only had a selfish bastard to look out for her interests. That didn't say much for her odds of survival.

He broke into a run when he hit the street.

◆ ◆

The beeping of River's com-link prompted them both into action.

"If we don't get into the safe house within the next minute," she said, "we'll have to start this level again."

Beyond the bluff of the ravine where they stood tangled in vine was a hill flanked by jungle, but Hawk got the sense that the jungle really served as a wall. This was the end of the level.

Hawk tested the tangled vines they were going to have to wade through in order to reach the door to the safe house. They were springy and sturdy, and probably far easier to walk on than the jungle floor.

The hell she didn't have magic. Or a temper. He was going to have to help her learn to control both, or there'd be shit to pay on Earth.

"Think you can keep up?" he challenged her, knowing she would, and started to run. The vines acted as a springboard, adding speed and height to his stride.

They reached the safe house in seconds.

River rammed her sword into the base of the hill, then pulled it out. A ping, and then the door to the safe house lifted, leaving a big gaping hole in the side of the hill. River and Hawk stepped inside, and as the door behind them sealed they were presented with two more doors. Hawk guessed one would summon the Wizard and the other would lead to the next level.

River lifted the console next to one of the doors and pushed the blade of her sword into the slot. Like a debit machine, the computer read the amount of credits she'd accumulated in the outside world. As the door hissed opened and the Wizard came into view, a countdown began, the depletion of her credits already under way.

"We need to save enough credits to enter the next level," River said to him. She did a quick count under her breath, then pulled the sword from the slot.

The sight of the woman with the mystical green eyes on the other side of the door startled the hell out

of Hawk as much as it seemed to put River at ease.
A beautiful, rich blue silk robe billowed around
her ankles and she pressed her hands together, her
ancient, knowledgeable eyes cutting from River to
Hawk and back to River again.

Hawk leaned in and pressed his lips to River's
ear. She gave a slight shiver in response. "Your
Wizard is a woman?"

"Of course." River tipped her head sideways to
give him a *What did you expect?* look. "The Wizard is all knowing. Why would I make her anything
other than a woman?"

"Of course," he echoed, shaking his head. "I don't
know what I was thinking."

The Wizard might make River relax, but Hawk
didn't share the feeling. Too many things had
changed in the game from what River had programmed for him to lower his guard. The troll demon in the last safe house sprang immediately to
mind. He kept his hand close to his sword, ready
to defend River if the Wizard posed any threat to
her whatsoever.

"Hello, my little lost soul." The Wizard's gaze
left River and panned to Hawk. "I see some things
aren't quite as they should be."

"No, they're not." River got right to the point.
"There's some sort of glitch in the program and now
I can't get out of it."

"River, my little one, it is your program. Born by you, and buried by you. And to die is to be reborn."

"She's not making any sense," Hawk said, shifting restlessly. He hated cryptic, mystic shit. "Am I missing something here?"

"She doesn't give direct answers, Hawk. We have to figure out her riddles."

"Great."

Something didn't seem right to him. Hawk moved closer to the Wizard and inhaled, then stiffened. His voice dropped in warning as he took a protective step in front of River and said quietly, "We need to go."

River shushed him. "Our credits are getting low." Hawk heard the panic in her voice as she continued to seek guidance from the Wizard, despite his warning. "Define buried," she said to her.

"To die is to be reborn and it is in mortality that we find the answers we are seeking."

Hawk grabbed River's elbow and tugged. "Now, River."

Impatient, she twisted around and cast him a sidelong glance. "Hawk, wait a minute."

"You don't understand," he said, unwilling to say too much in front of the so-called Wizard.

"Dammit, we're out of time."

The door slammed shut and River slipped her

sword back into its sheath. She rounded on Hawk. "What the hell were you doing?"

"Your Wizard isn't what you think she is." It made Hawk antsy simply being on the other side of a locked door from her.

River's body tensed. "What are you talking about?"

"She's using magic," Hawk explained. "It's the exact same magic used by the Dark Lord. I can smell it all over her."

Blue eyes filled with doubt blinked up at Hawk. "This magic," she asked. "What exactly does it smell like?"

"It's peppery, and burns the sinus cavity when inhaled. It's subtle, but trust me." He fought off a cold shiver. "If you ever smelled it, you'd never forget it."

It was a scent that seeped from the walls of his prison cell and grew stronger when the Dark Lord used his magic to inflict pain on Hawk. Now, just the slightest whiff of it was enough to remind Hawk of the bastard's cruelties, and the extent he would go to in order to break a soul. Without conscious thought his hand closed over River's shoulder and he squeezed, silently vowing never to let him get his hands on her.

"Peppery, like sage?" She looked down, as if in thought, and Hawk got the uncomfortable sense that she was as familiar with the scent as he was.

He didn't like that.

"I suppose," he said.

"Magic should smell the same no matter who's using it, shouldn't it? Magic's just magic, right?"

"I don't know," Hawk confessed. The magic of the Dark Lord was different from the magic of the Fae, but what if it wasn't the magic itself that was different, but the way in which it was used? The times he'd caught traces of Fae magic on his wife's skin after she'd traveled with them hadn't been unpleasant, even though now that he thought about it, its smell was very similar to the Dark Lord's magic. The same, only different. "I don't like this. Why are we smelling magic at all? Magic can't be programmed, and if this Wizard is just a character in your game, why would she have magic?"

For that matter, why didn't he smell magic when River used it? And that she used it, there was no doubt in his mind. She just didn't seem to be aware of it. Maybe the smell of it was associated with her mortal body. He didn't like that idea either. What if she used magic in her game, and someone recognized the smell on her physical form for what it was?

"I'm not sure why she has magic, or even if she really does." River pressed the heel of her palm to her forehead, frustration crossing her face. "Everything is messed up, Hawk. It has to be another wrinkle in the game."

"I agree, but what's causing those wrinkles?" Hawk knew of only one Dark Lord left in the universe. If the magic wasn't coming from him, then who the hell was it coming from, and how did its user know about this game?

And was that user friend or foe?

He thought of the arrow that had saved River at the start of the game, so conceded the former was a possibility, but he wasn't counting on that. He'd smelled Dark Lord magic, not that of the Fae. There really was a difference between the two.

"Maybe the answer lies in what the Wizard told us," River suggested.

"That mystical shit? Born or buried?" Hawk didn't bother trying to hide his skepticism. He didn't trust anything about her Wizard.

"Let's move on to the next world," River said. "Maybe we'll see something there that will trigger the answer."

A few minutes later, after River cashed in the last of their credits, they found themselves standing on the sidewalk in a small town.

Hawk did a quick assessment of his clothes and weaponry. No longer were they dressed in fatigues in order to camouflage themselves in a jungle. Now they wore jeans and T-shirts, light windbreakers to protect them from the elements, and running shoes, better to blend in to a modern-day city from River's world. He patted his side and was pleased to find a gun instead of a sword.

He drew the weapon and turned the .40mm Glock over in his hand to examine it. He unloaded the chamber and studied the silver bullets. Interesting choice of ammunition she'd made.

He reloaded, keeping a watchful eye on River as she, too, checked her ammunition. The lush curve of her ass and the way her jeans hugged her thighs pulled an instant and inappropriate reaction from him.

Almost everything he'd heard about Fae women appeared to be true. River was perhaps even more beautiful than claimed, although granted, she wasn't as gentle and delicate as he'd been led to believe. When it came to virtual worlds she could hold her own as well as any man, and better than most.

But there was a reason why Guardians and Fae normally traveled in same-sex pairs. Mixing of the two races was unwelcome by both. The chance of losing a host for a Fae soul through a half-breed birth was considered too great a risk to take.

He pulled his eyes from temptation and scanned the street for danger instead, doing a quick analysis of their environment.

Day had morphed into night, although streams of soft yellow light from the streetlamps provided sufficient light for him to see the hilly landscape and the deserted streets. Matching town houses with microscopic lawns were lined up like obedient soldiers. Hawk guessed they were on the outskirts of big-city living, in the suburbs. Off in the distance a dog barked and the sound carried in the eerily quiet night. He could tell it was a war-torn city, although things were slowly beginning to rebuild. Scorched, empty lots dotted the trim rows of houses like missing teeth, and several rooftops bore the scars of falling shrapnel. At some point in the recent past, this place had been bombed.

"This is your world?" he asked.

"What's left of it. It's a little run-down still, but technological advancements are going to stimulate the economy and help us rebuild," River said, sounding both defensive and proud. "That's where our future lies, Hawk. Technology. And since I'm good at it . . ." She paused, furrowing her brow in thought. "Do you think that's why the Soul Man wants me? To fix the error in his program?"

No. Hawk's Guardian soul could give the Dark Lord everything he needed to repair his program. But the magic of a Fae combined with that of the Dark Lord could help him escape his prison altogether. That was the scariest prospect imaginable, and Hawk didn't want her knowing about it. There was no way he'd ever let the Dark Lord touch a Fae's soul. He'd sacrifice his own first.

"Probably," Hawk lied.

The light tread of their rubber-soled footsteps was the only sound to be heard as they walked the deserted streets and made their way to the downtown core, where there were a few run-down buildings, large compounds, and small eateries.

"Born and buried," River repeated as they passed a pub with the name Andy's over the door. "People are born in a hospital and buried in a cemetery."

"Not necessarily," Hawk disagreed. The scowl she shot him was so dark he laughed.

"You aren't helping."

"Sorry. But you pointed out yourself that making frogs worth points and a pedway that could be crossed were too predictable for a game. Don't you think that hospitals and cemeteries are a little too predictable as well?" He caught movement in one of the shadows, then relaxed when it turned out to be nothing more than a common street rat. He hoped River hadn't seen it, given her love of them. "What do you have written into your program that could double as places to be born or buried?"

"I don't know. But there have to be rules in the game," River pointed out. "Without them you could be born or buried anywhere. The Wizard had to be referring to specific places, because otherwise, it's not a real clue."

Perhaps that had been the Wizard's goal—to send

them off in the wrong direction in order to waste their time and make them have to start over.

He didn't say that to her, however.

She talked to herself and Hawk listened while continuing to scan the streets. So this was what earth looked like. No Guardian had dared step foot on the planet since the combined council of the Fae and the Guardians had judged it beyond salvation. The last Guardian to try to help the self-destructive planet had never made it home. Neither had the Fae he'd escorted, a loss that was mourned to this day.

That had been one of the rare matchings between a Fae and a Guardian of opposite sexes, if he recalled correctly, but Fae women outnumbered their men, and their magic was stronger. It had been considered too dangerous an assignment for two women, so a male Guardian had been selected.

A male Guardian and a female Fae had traveled to River's world together—never to be heard from again.

Hawk paused to do a quick mental tally.

River was good with technology.

River had magic.

And Hawk had to be the dumbest person in the history of his entire race.

Something had obviously happened to her birth parents. Something that prevented their souls from returning home. That was why she had no one to protect her, and had no idea what or who she was.

And what she was, was a half-breed.

The product of a union that never, ever should have happened. His insides clenched and for a brief moment he had no idea how he felt about that. Then revulsion and anger hit, not for River, but for the Guardian who must have been her father. Hawk couldn't imagine taking advantage of his position as a caretaker of a Fae and her soul in such a way.

"What's wrong?" River asked, and Hawk realized he'd stopped under the tattered canvas awning of a boarded-up doorway. She had her weapon in her hand and was anxiously peering up and down the empty street, thinking he'd sensed danger. The night was cold and she was shivering in the light wind.

"Nothing. I'm just thinking." He pulled her automatically against him so that his body shielded her from the cold and the wind as best he could. Half-breed or not, River had magic and therefore possessed a Fae soul.

Fae souls were reborn. *To die is to be reborn.*

Perhaps there was something to the Wizard's mystic crap after all. Where in this world had River been born, again?

He opened his mouth to ask, but River was following her own train of thought.

"Buried belowground," she was saying to herself. "It has to be belowground. What's belowground?" Her eyes shot to his, the excitement in their depths leaping like sparks from an open fire. "The subway. It's belowground and I wrote it into my program."

He nodded, quickly deciding to see where that led them before exploring his own theory. "That's something definitely buried under a city."

"There's a station not too far from here." River turned a corner and darted forward, Hawk careful to stay close to her.

"Shouldn't we be collecting something to earn us credits for the next level?" he asked. Broken strips of yellow and black crime-scene tape fluttered from a telephone pole and a nearby stair railing. River slowed her steps to examine them, a frown on her lovely face.

"I don't remember these being part of the game," she said, ignoring his question. "I can't imagine what purpose they'd add."

"A distraction?" Hawk guessed. "Or a warning of some kind?" His neck hairs were standing up now and he didn't bother to point out the dark, telltale stains on the sidewalk.

"Maybe." She shook herself and released the piece of tape she'd taken in her hand. "And yes," she said, answering his earlier question. "We should be gathering information as well as energy in this level. There are demons we'll have to fight to gain energy, but the Ferals are werewolves now. They'll be disguised as people. If we let them get too close to us they turn into wolves and we can be killed, but we can't kill them until they turn into wolves in case they're innocents. We lose energy for killing innocents. Plus, innocents are the ones we gather the information from. Some of them will give us the questions we'll need to ask the Wizard. Of course," she added, "we'd earn double energy for killing Weres in their human form."

That explained the silver bullets. He almost hated to ask. "What about the demons? Do they look like people, too?"

"No, they look like wichtlein, only much, much larger. We kill them by fighting them." River cast him a sidelong look that contained more than a hint of mischief. "They get a bit more complicated in the next level."

Hawk's experience with demons was limited to the Dark Lord's prison. If hers were based on those, then fighting them was going to be complicated enough already.

They rounded another corner and there on the street in front of them was the stairwell leading to the underground subway.

They approached it with caution, Hawk in front

with River positioned safely behind him. Without warning, a head appeared out of the darkness.

Hawk never hesitated. He took aim and fired. The head exploded all over the stairwell.

"Nice going," River said, eying the damage. "There's one less person to give us information." She checked her com-link. "And so much for our energy. The next thing you kill had better be worth something. You do realize, don't you, that there are going to be more innocents than werewolves? Otherwise gamers could just kill their way to the next level."

"I knew that," Hawk said. He tucked his gun back into his waistband.

River touched a panel on the outer side of the stairwell wall. A small door slid back. She reached inside and pulled out a flashlight.

They cautiously descended the crumbling concrete stairs, deeper and deeper into the darkness. Hawk blinked, trying to see into the shadows beyond the flashlight's narrow beam. So far, so good. He placed one hand on the wall to steady himself.

"Don't touch the walls!" River warned him, her voice low. "They're crawling with spiders."

Hawk jerked his hand back. "Let me guess. Malaria again?"

"Common cold. But it's a nasty one. It could

develop into viral pneumonia before we finish the level."

He swept the flashlight beam from side to side, making certain nothing was coming up the stairs while they were going down. "You really expect people to *pay* to play this game?"

"It can always be written out of the program," she said, sounding a little defensive. "Nick thought the virus was a stupid idea, too. I don't know why I put it in."

Hawk wondered where this mysterious Nick had gotten to. He'd far sooner keep River with him at this point, but still, Nick was supposed to be watching over her body when she played the game.

River's physical well-being was becoming more and more of a concern for Hawk as time passed. River couldn't keep this up forever, regardless of whether or not she had magic. Hawk hoped like hell this Nick was as trustworthy as River seemed to think.

There might be another way to get River out of the game if, or when, it became necessary. She could jump if she had to. But River was half Guardian and Hawk didn't know how that might affect her ability, or even if she had the ability at all. If she did, and she jumped, without the proper training, where might she end up?

The possibilities left him cold. Jumping wasn't a solution.

They reached the bottom of the stairs and plunged into the tunnel leading to the subway platform and tracks.

◆ ◆

Nick was going to kill her.

If she didn't get herself killed first, that was. When had River ever been in the subway tunnels?

That she had been in them in real life was unquestionable. Nick had been in them, too, and her level of detail was far beyond coincidence, right down to the long, jagged crack in one concrete wall.

He leaned over the monitor, his hands clenching the edge of the desk, his knuckles turning white as he watched River and Sever dive into the tunnel leading to the tracks. Did she know the tracks still ran an electrical current in real life? Was there a danger of her being electrocuted?

Of course there was. River wouldn't do anything by halves.

He wished he could hear what she and Sever were talking about, but the game wasn't programmed for a viewer's entertainment. The monitor was really just a safety measure.

Dumbass that he was, he was the one who'd suggested turning the Ferals into werewolves in this level. At the time he'd thought it funny to put real-life monsters into a virtual game and mess with Kaye a little.

River and Sever would have little trouble dealing with the werewolves, though, although she might want to stop Sever from blowing the head off everything that moved. The demons she'd come up with on her own were mean fuckers, far more so than the werewolves, and she needed to gather more energy if she intended to fight any. On the other hand, each blow she struck to a demon would shrink it and give her additional strength. The werewolves, she had to kill outright.

Nick held his breath as River and Sever walked to the edge of the platform above the tracks. As they reached the edge, lights embedded in the walls flickered on, illuminating the entire tunnel. River took the flashlight from Sever and tucked it into the back of her jeans.

Smart girl, Nick thought approvingly. The flashlight might be needed up ahead. At the very least, it was an additional weapon.

Sever caught Nick's attention. There was something odd about him, and Nick leaned closer to the monitor screen, trying to puzzle out what it might be. River had programmed the character to be protective, so that wasn't out of the ordinary, but as Sever scanned the platform while keeping one hand on his gun and the other firmly planted on the small of River's back, Nick couldn't help but think there was something just a bit too human about the way he watched over her. Sever's programming was more reactive than proactive, so it didn't seem right for him to be watching out for danger the way he was.

Nick had warned River about her brilliant idea to have software programming software. If it had altered Sever, even for the good, it could as easily turn him into an enemy.

At the moment though, it proved to be a very good thing. One of the shadows shifted, morphing into a stout red demon with thick legs and no neck, its head thrusting forward from its shoulders. It hulked forward, its eyes on River, as Sever whipped out the Glock. *There*. That was a clear flaw in Sever's programming, and just what Nick had warned her about. Sever was supposed to hit it with his fist, not waste silver bullets by shooting at it. Nick closed his eyes, not sure he wanted to see the upcoming carnage. His fingers inched indecisively toward the com-link, then pulled back, torn between saving River and protecting himself.

Once he touched that com-link he'd be making his choice. Then there would be no turning back.

CHAPTER TWELVE

♦

River knocked Hawk's gun arm with her shoulder, ruining his aim, and spun into action. Before he could stop her she'd lashed out with one fist and struck the demon solidly in its rock-solid chest.

The monster staggered, then flickered and diminished in size. River finished it off with a kick that sent it flying over the edge of the platform onto the tracks below. A satisfying sizzle rang in her ears as the electricity coursing through the rails in the tracks did just what it was supposed to.

Hawk had that angry, intense look in his eyes that she'd learned meant he was about to start giving her orders again.

"They aren't as tough as they look," River said, cutting him off before he could get started. She waved her arm with the com-link attached under his nose. "And see? We just got ourselves enough energy for you to shoot another innocent."

"For the record," Hawk said, slipping the gun back into his waistband, "shooting innocents isn't what Guardians do best." He glanced over the side of the platform as the demon's lifeless body twitched on the rails for a few more seconds, then flickered out of existence. "Now there goes something I hope the Dark Lord is totally pissed at."

River didn't bother asking if her demon was something else she'd lifted from the Dark Lord's prison because it probably was. It seemed she wasn't as creative as she'd thought, and she didn't like that. It made her question herself and her abilities, and River had spent her whole life doing that. Gaming was something she'd been entirely sure of. Or at least it had been.

"What's wrong, slugger?" Hawk asked, picking up on her change of mood. He crooked an arm around her neck and tugged her against him, rubbing the top of her head with his knuckles. "You just kicked a demon's ass."

River turned her face into the crease between his shoulder and his chest, resting her forehead against him and sliding her arm around his waist.

"My game is ruined." She felt the deep rumble of silent laughter building in his chest beneath her cheek. "It's not funny."

Hawk took her chin in his fingertips and tilted her face so she was forced to look up at him. She focused on the tip of his nose—broken at least once in the past—so she could concentrate on not bursting into tears. She was being overly emotional because she was tired, she knew, and she didn't like that either. River wasn't good with weakness.

"Look at me," he said. His dark eyes, normally hard and ice-cold, were warm and soft. "We're in this together, remember. Tell me why this game is so important to you."

She chewed on her upper lip, torn between wanting to tell him and not wanting to talk about it. His interest seemed sincere, though, as did his concern, and that was what made up her mind for her.

"The virus that kicked off the war didn't die out entirely after the war was over," River said. "Viruses mutate, and that makes them hard to stamp out. My mother picked up a mutation that hid in her immune system for a long time before anyone realized what was wrong with her." Even now, more than ten years after her death, River found this difficult to talk about. "We watched my mother, who took mixed martial-arts classes so she could protect her family, and was the strongest, most independent woman I knew, turn into a quadriplegic who needed twenty-four-hour-a-day care. The loss of independence was what killed her."

Understanding, then appreciation, gleamed in Hawk's eyes. "So this game was really going to be your way to give life back to people who've lost all hope." Another emotion, deeper than understanding, reached out from him to her and touched her soul with a breathtaking ferocity. "You are truly a bringer of life and hope, River. Don't ever let anyone tell you anything different. Your world may not be ready for your kind of game, but believe me, there are other worlds in the universe that most definitely are."

River's facial muscles ached with the strain of trying to keep her tears in check. Without conscious thought, but with gratitude for his understanding the primary motive, she rose on the tips of her toes and kissed the full, firm line of his lips.

She felt him freeze, no doubt surprised by her spontaneous action, but she had no time for embarrassment before his mouth began to move over hers in a response so full of passion and unleashed need it turned her bones to pulp and melted her into his arms.

Never in her life had she been kissed like this, setting her soul on fire with a hunger that threatened to consume them both. She felt her soul reach out to wrap around him, and search for an answering response from his own.

And, as if from a very great, far-off distance, she got the response her soul was looking for.

"Sweet mother of God," Hawk breathed against her lips. A mixture of shock and awe blazed on his face as he lifted his head to stare down at her. "I felt that. I felt you touch my soul."

She'd felt it, too, and it scared her half to death.

"It was just a kiss," River said. "Maybe you're finally going crazy." She hadn't meant her words to sound so hopeful but they did, and that made him laugh again.

"I'm not going crazy," he replied. He dragged his fingers through his hair, spiking it, and his laughter died. "But you have my deepest apologies. I should never have kissed you."

"It was just a kiss," she repeated, a little insulted, "not an attempt on my life. And also for the record, since we're keeping track of things, I was the one who kissed you."

His eyelids dropped, hiding what he was thinking from her. "But I was the one who knew better."

She wanted this conversation, this entire incident, over and done with and forgotten about forever. She hadn't liked that connection she'd made with him because now she knew his soul was tired. The time it had spent with the Dark Lord, coupled with the time it had spent tied by sheer will of consciousness to a body in a far-off place, was weakening it.

She wanted to believe him invincible, able to look after himself if she had to leave him alone in the game until she could find a way to get him out. Now she was afraid for him. Hawk's soul and body needed to be reunited. Soon.

And she didn't want him to know that. She didn't

want them both to be afraid. They needed to be strong.

"Believe me, I'll definitely know better from now on as well," she said.

Hawk took her face in his hands and brushed his thumbs across her cheeks in a soft, tender gesture. "You misunderstand me. It's forbidden for Guardians to interact too . . . deeply . . . with someone they are meant to protect." Regret filled his eyes and his voice lowered as he spoke again, this time mostly to himself. "Now I know why."

Even though Sever's character had been created to watch her back, River didn't care for being cast in the role of damsel in distress. Not with anyone, but especially not with Hawk. If they were in this game together, then they were in it as equals.

She took hold of his wrists and gently extricated herself from his touch. "I can take care of myself."

Hawk took a step back, pulling free of her hands and drawing his gun in one single, fluid motion, and fired a shot past her head.

River, throwing up her arms in an instinctive, protective gesture, whirled around. What at first appeared to be a human body lying on the platform in a spreading pool of blood slowly morphed into a werewolf.

The echo of gunfire down the long subway tunnel faded away, leaving silence behind.

"You can't keep randomly firing at things," River finally said when she found her voice. "You're lucky that was a werewolf and not an innocent."

"Luck had nothing to do with it," Hawk replied. "Most people don't smell like wet dogs."

She tried to remember if Tanner had attached a smell to the werewolves. "I'll have to do something about that," she said. "The level's no good if the werewolves can be picked out from the innocents so easily."

"The level's good from where I stand." Hawk pointed at her com-link. "Check out the energy we just earned."

River was torn between thankfulness for the energy and disappointment in the game.

Hawk correctly interpreted the conflict he must have read on her face. "Be grateful, River," he advised, the corner of his mouth kicking up a notch. "You can fix the smell later when you fix your Wizard."

Stung, River took exception to that. "There's nothing wrong with my Wizard!"

"Not if you can interpret her mystical crap," he agreed. "Speaking of which, we should probably get moving. Where do we go from here?"

They had two choices: left or right. The passage behind them leading back to the street above was now closed.

River pointed to a man leaning against the wall near one of the benches, about half the platform away. "I'll ask him."

Hawk drew his gun. "Let me ask."

"You can't ask him at gunpoint," River said. "If he's a werewolf, he'll lie to you."

"And if you don't ask him at gunpoint, he might try to kill you."

River shot him a smile. "That's why the game is so fun." She patted Hawk's arm. "Relax. We have enough stored energy to move faster than him if he's a werewolf," she assured him. "If I don't kill him, I'm sure you will." River's reflexes were the fastest of the two of them and they both knew it, but she could see that he didn't like it.

She had to get close to the man in order to ask the question. She could actually feel Hawk's eyes drilling into her back and the twitch of his fingers as he held his hand ready to draw his gun.

"Excuse me," River said politely to the man when she was an arm's length away. "I'm lost. Can you tell me where I should be going?"

The man pointed to the left and the energy stored in her com-link dropped. River turned in triumph to Hawk, ready to say *I told you so,* when a huge rat scurried out from beneath the bench and ran across her foot.

River shrieked and totally lost it. She grabbed her

gun and fired off three rapid shots before Hawk was at her side and prying the gun from her fingers.

"From now on," he said, holding the hot barrel away so that it wouldn't burn either one of them, "I do all the shooting. Your aim is terrible."

She was shaking from head to toe, dancing and slapping frantically at her denim-clad thighs in an effort to rid herself of the crawling sensation of rats creeping up her legs. She knew it wasn't real, and that the rat was long gone, but the sensation refused to go away. "You don't understand. I never programmed rats into the game. I hate them."

"I can see that." Hawk's mouth went tight. "And yet this is the third time a rat has appeared."

"Third?"

He ignored her outburst, his mind obviously working through something else. "So. It seems the Dark Lord has discovered a weakness in both of us."

River's was rats. Hawk's was . . . Vienna?

There had to be more to his than that, River decided, as she seized on the question as a way to regain control of herself. What was it about Vienna that made Hawk weak?

He took her hand. "Let's get moving. If we see any more rats, try to remember they aren't real."

River shuddered. "That's easy enough for you to say."

He squeezed her fingers in sympathy. "I know. Believe me, I know that very well."

♦ ♦

The Dark Lord rarely wasted much time thinking about the past. When one was an immortal, there was a lot of past to be sifted through.

Therefore when he wanted to remember something in greater detail, he turned to his seeing stones. He could project his thoughts into the stones, and there they would form the images he wanted to see.

He'd watched these particular memories unfold for probably the thousandth time, although this time he watched them with a different purpose in mind. Never before had escape been so close at hand, and he wanted to memorize every detail of his capture and imprisonment so he could ensure it never happened to him again.

The Guardians responsible were long dead, their souls well beyond his reach, although torturing the one soul he'd managed to capture was not without its satisfaction. Fae souls, however, were another matter entirely. Fae souls were reborn. The ones who'd played a part in his downfall would still exist. Once he was free, the Dark Lord would find them. Then the games would truly begin.

The Dark Lord smiled to himself, and the souls hovering around him fluttered backward in terror.

River Weston was an open book. The Dark Lord could read her as easily as a child's primer. No one had taught her how to hide her thoughts and he could browse through them at leisure.

Picking random thoughts from the Guardian had been more difficult. The man had few weaknesses, other than the one thing that had brought him here in the first place, and he'd guarded that secret so closely the Dark Lord had not been able to pick the thoughts free. Vienna had been a lucky guess on his part.

But the Dark Lord didn't want the Guardian to discover that he was sifting through River's thoughts. Not yet, because he wasn't certain how he was going to use the knowledge he gained from her.

It certainly helped to know what she expected to find as she moved through the game, however. The randomness she'd inserted into her programming had proven to be an interesting twist. Being able to transmit his own signals to her game's receivers made throwing in obstacles as easy as breathing.

The danger in doing so was that it introduced randomness to his program as well. Transmissions went both ways. Each time he initiated a change to her program, an error occurred in his own. That was what was causing his program to falter. He hadn't been able to find a solution for that from her thoughts because she simply didn't have one.

But she was getting closer and closer to the final level, and he was gaining greater control with far fewer risks. At any time now he could start tapping into her magic. She only needed to be pushed into using it.

The Dark Lord closed his eyes and drew a deep, satisfied breath as he remembered the magnificent touch of her magic. He'd never felt more alive than he did when she summoned the lightning as she entered his sanctuary. The energy released ignited his own.

He opened his eyes, leaning forward over the crucible of seeing stones again so he could check on their progress in the game.

River had no idea how to harness her talents. That ignorance would be her downfall. The code he had given her would make her game work. It simply wouldn't work the way she'd expected it to.

◆ ◆

"So much for your innocents answering questions honestly," Hawk said, staring at the brick wall barricading the tunnel at the final terminal.

Now he knew why it had been so easy for them to move forward. It was unlikely it would be as easy to backtrack, since River had programmed that as a near impossibility. At least the tracks gave them a measure of protection. When they walked between them, werewolves and demons alike couldn't seem to cross. Each time they'd tried, they'd been electrocuted.

He and River had wasted a lot of time by walking this far. He doubted if they could recover it.

River tilted her head back, exposing the smooth skin of her throat, her midnight hair sweeping between her shoulder blades as she examined the tunnel ceiling. "He was honest," she said. "I didn't ask him the right question."

Try as hard as he might, Hawk couldn't keep his eyes off her. Her Fae soul had touched his, and now he understood full well why her father had made the choice he did. Hawk would never again be able to look at her or stand at her side without this strange mixture of want and need, this physical awareness of her, welling inside him and clouding his thoughts.

The dangers in such a distraction weren't lost on him. He wished he could turn back time. He thanked God she didn't seem to be having the same drawn-out reaction to him, even though he knew she'd been as stunned by the touch of their souls as he had been, because he'd felt it. He could only hope this strange, unwanted reaction on his part was temporary, too.

Except it wasn't as unwanted as it should be. He'd known how precious a Fae soul could be. It had only

been since his imprisonment that he'd fully understood how precious all souls should be. That light
brush of her soul on his had made him feel whole
again. Connected. He wanted that. He wanted it
badly.

But he wanted River's safety more. That meant
he had to stop thinking like an oversexed teenager.

"We have to go up?" Hawk guessed, following her
gaze upward. A ladder on the wall led to a narrow
shelf along the tunnel roof that disappeared beyond
the bricked-up wall. The opening it passed through
was barely big enough for him. He'd have to tear
away some of the bricks in order to fit through. He
wondered what that would do to the small amount of
energy they had left. He also noticed the wall where
the ladder hung was crawling with spiders. "What
are the chances we can get past the barricade without being infected by those spiders?"

"Slim to none," River said without hesitation. "But
if we can make it to the next level before the virus
takes full effect, the virus will disappear."

It was risky. She'd programmed the virus to mutate. Even though they could convince themselves it
wasn't real and that they weren't really sick, it would
likely keep rebounding on them. That was going to
slow them down even more, along with any other
nasty little surprises the program and the Dark Lord
happened to throw at them.

Good-bye, sanity.

"Demons can be taken down by striking them?" Hawk asked.

"Three times," River said. "Unless you electrocute them, but that doesn't earn us any points."

"Okay." Hawk leapt over the tracks and vaulted onto the terminal platform and rushed a startled oncoming demon. He struck it once in the chest, then in the head. He finished it off by jumping on its minimized form, and it shimmered out of existence.

Hawk reached off the platform for River's hand so he could pull her up to join him.

"Impressive," she said.

She didn't sound impressed and Hawk tried not to smile, willing to bet she was annoyed that her demon hadn't been more difficult for him to beat. She might have a Fae's nurturing soul, but she had Guardian pride in her, too.

He tried to decide how best to get them through that small hole and past the barricade, and still be able to keep an eye on her. He'd be damned if he let her go first only for him to get stuck and not be able to follow and protect her. He wasn't about to feed her to werewolves either by leaving her on the platform below while he tore out some of the bricks above.

He compromised by going first and testing the

ladder, then helping her up with him. They both climbed onto the narrow shelf along the ceiling. Hawk tried not to look down.

"You can brush away spiders while I make this hole big enough to crawl through," he said to her. He hoped like hell no rats appeared on the shelf with them. He couldn't predict how River would react, but he was willing to bet it wouldn't be well.

Tearing a hole proved easier than he'd anticipated and in no time, they were through.

He poked his head into the faint gray light of predawn.

The tunnel vanished on this side of the barricade. In its place was an overgrown road, more like an old logging trail. The ledge they were on came out at ground level.

"Huh," Hawk said. He looked behind him at River. "What was some of that crap your Wizard was spouting, again?"

"Something has to die to be reborn?" she suggested, pushing at his legs, wanting to see.

"And it is in mortality that we find the answers we are seeking." He drew a slow breath and asked, "Is there an old lab or factory of some kind in your program?"

"No."

He moved ahead so she could join him. "There is now."

A mixture of surprise and apprehension washed over her face. She hopped down from the ledge, her feet landing in a puddle and splashing dirty water over their jeans as she turned in the direction he was looking.

The road narrowed in the near distance, becoming a weed-choked gravel path. Tall trees grew randomly, low-slung branches dangling from their gray, weathered trunks.

The complicated ventilation system on the roof of the building was a good indicator of what it had been. Hawk didn't care for the idea of what might have died and been reborn here. If it was buried, it was probably best if it stayed that way.

"Do you know what this place is?" he asked.

"It's not from my game," River said.

They had to go forward since they couldn't go back. The subway tunnel behind them was gone, replaced by a now-familiar wall of tightly intertwined vegetation.

As they carefully negotiated the narrow path, Hawk breathed in the familiar, peppery scent of sage and his uneasiness tripled. "Is the Wizard responsible for this?"

River frowned, and he could see a similar unease on her face. "I'm not sure."

The air grew heavy, almost suffocating, a layer of fog hanging over the low building before them like a wet woolen blanket. The entire place was protected by a sagging iron fence, rusted and jagged and reaching for the sky, daring the brave to climb over. Thick ferns, waist deep in places, carpeted the ground between the forest and the fence in abundance.

Hawk waded through the ferns and reached out to test the strength of the fence, but when he did, little electrical jolts ran up his arm and sent him flying backward. "What the hell?" He fisted his hand and tried to shake off the vibrations.

River, who'd followed him, touched his throbbing arm. "Is it electric?"

"No." The tingling in his hand became more tolerable. "Someone is using magic here."

River's eyes widened. "I can smell it."

He eyed the fence. "But is someone trying to keep something in, or everyone else out?"

She walked toward the barrier and palmed the air.

"What are you doing?" he asked, staying close to her.

"I'm looking for a weak spot."

Hawk watched her carefully as she walked the protective perimeter, her fingers wiggling, testing the air. She pinched her eyes in concentration, and dragged the scent of sage into her lungs.

As she searched for a way in, a noise behind

Hawk brought his head around. The hairs on his nape tingled and he spun around to peer into the forest, but couldn't pinpoint the exact location of any danger.

"Here," River said, stopping at a spot near the back of the building. "I think I found an opening."

Hawk hadn't been paying too much attention to what was on the other side of the fence, being more focused on whatever was stalking them from the forest. So he had to look twice for it to register that at the back of the building, inside the fence, was what appeared to be a graveyard. It didn't have nice, tidy granite headstones. Each mound of dirt was marked with a wooden picket.

Hawk stepped up behind River, protecting her, unsure whether they'd be safer where they were or on the other side of that fence. "How did you find that?" he asked.

"The energy feels different here."

He felt it now, too. "Look out."

When River stepped to the side, Hawk kicked at the rusting fence. The posts had weakened, probably not buried deep enough in the soil to begin with, and it didn't take long for him to knock a section of it down. One post swayed backward, another forward, and the chain links folded to rest on the ground enough so that they could walk overtop. His hand closed over the butt of his gun, and he shot one last look behind him before he stepped across the makeshift portal, River following close behind. He felt her shiver.

"This place gives me the creeps," she said, tucking her hands beneath her arms and hugging herself. "Do you think it came from my world or the Soul Man's?"

"We got in without using any points, so my guess is that it's not part of your game. It's real. I'm just not sure in whose reality." Hawk examined the grave markers, all numbered but not named. "But I'm fairly certain that whatever is buried here was never meant to be discovered."

"If this place doesn't use points, then it won't earn us any. So why did the Wizard lead us here?"

Hawk had some serious issues with this Wizard of hers. If they somehow earned enough energy to summon her again, this time he was doing the questioning, not River.

A growl came from behind them, and both Hawk and River turned in time to see a swish of black in the gloomy light.

Crisos. That thing was bigger than any were they'd encountered yet.

The were pounced. Seconds before it would have pinned River beneath its big, beefy claws she sidestepped it, moving with lightning speed. The animal landed in a crouch a few feet away, then slowly circled to face them. A frothy mouth peeled back to reveal razor-sharp fangs, and the sight of that snarl pulled an instinctive response from Hawk. Thankful for a chamber full of silver bullets, Hawk pointed his Glock and peeled off a shot, catching the hound between the eyes. The pungent smell of sulfur reached his nostrils as the animal's body dropped to the ground not far from River. Spasms shook its legs a few times, then it lay still.

Hawk gave her a quick once-over. "You okay?"

"I'm fine." She looked at her com-link. "That thing was worth a lot of credits."

She leaned against a tree and gave a sweeping glance over the graveyard. Hawk knew she didn't like him hovering over her so he left her alone, although he stayed close in case she needed him for support. She was badly shaken and he wasn't convinced the were was entirely responsible for that.

As the dead were began to decompose over one of the unmarked graves, River looked up at Hawk and said with absolute certainty, "This is where they bury the monsters under the bed."

"What?" He wasn't certain he'd followed her line of thought, but whatever she was thinking, it was disturbing her. Tears streamed unchecked down her cheeks and she made no effort to hide them. Hawk suspected she didn't even know they were falling, and that scared him.

"I can feel them," she whispered. "Their souls. They're here."

"Whose souls?" Hawk asked, his spine turning to ice at the horror creeping over her face.

"There were these conspiracy theories being thrown around about the government creating fairy-tale monsters, then disposing of them when they became difficult to control. I never believed the stories." She rubbed her arms, cocking her head to one side as if listening to something, and swiped at her tears with the back of one hand. "Until now."

"Crisos."

"I know."

If that were true, her world was even more corrupt than the Guardians suspected. Hawk walked farther until he came across a mound with no markings. He replayed the Wizard's words in his mind.

To die is to be reborn . . .

Hawk jumped back just as a demon burst from a nearby grave. Then another one, even closer. And another. Spitting fire, they were little like the ones he was supposed to be able to strike three times.

He had no intention of trying. These weren't buried demons. These were traps, planted here to protect what was buried beneath the ground. "Shit. River, look out!"

Fear for her safety seized him and in three quick leaps he was beside her, grabbing her hand and forcing her to run with him. He didn't wait to see if she could cross back through the downed fence on her own. There wasn't time. He scooped her up under her arms and swung her like a child so that her feet never touched the ground. Then she was through the fence and he was behind her, urging her on.

"Head for the forest," he shouted at her. It was the only way he could think of to outrun whatever those demon-things were. They were big and awkward, and couldn't maneuver through the trees as easily as he and River could.

An explosion ripped the ground near his feet.

Although it seemed they could blast any trees in their way into extinction.

River was fighting him now, trying to turn back, to run in the wrong direction. He grabbed her around the waist, lifted her higher, and threw her over his shoulder. She was small, but she was putting up a hard struggle.

"What's wrong with you?" he shouted at her. Another blast drove him to his knees and he dropped her in a bed of ferns. She rolled to the ground, then came up on her feet and would have escaped if

Hawk hadn't grabbed one of her ankles. She fell harder this time, and he threw himself on top of her to protect her from the sprays of rock and dirt.

"My parents!" she panted, her blue eyes wild with angry determination. "I felt them back there. I can't leave them!"

CHAPTER THIRTEEN

♦

Sweat beaded unnoticed at Nick's temples as he stared hard at the monitor, not wanting to believe what he was seeing but not able to explain it away.

River had found Amos Kaye's playground. There it was in the game, and if Kaye ever found out she'd somehow managed to replicate it he'd kill her, and Nick, too, because he'd never believe that Nick hadn't told her about it.

Nick had only been there once, and once was more than enough. It had been one of those shadowy midnight blindfolded deals, just like in the movies. Very high drama. Nick had thought it totally overplayed until he'd seen what Kaye had been hiding there. Then he'd been more than grateful for the blindfold and wished he'd been allowed to keep it the whole time. That was when he'd first realized he'd gotten into something way over his head. And that was how he knew the conspiracy theories River made such fun of were fact, not fiction.

Nick had no idea how River could have found that lab, but there she was, with Sever, nosing around in its graveyard. She'd never get inside the building. The bioengineered watchdogs Kaye had planted would guarantee that.

Sure enough, Nick watched as Sever grabbed River's hand and dragged her back through the fence with those watchdogs firing full blast. Nick frowned, blinking the sleep from his eyes, leaning closer to the monitor. But what was River trying to do?

For Christ's sake. He gripped the desk top. She was trying to get back into the graveyard. Why?

Nick's fingers twitched toward the com-link controls, torn between fear of Kaye and fear for River. Before he could make up his mind, Sever tackled River to the ground to stop her. Nick leaned back in relief. It was about time that dumb fuck character earned his keep. Sever was a waste of 3-D graphics and Nick trusted him and his capabilities about as much as he trusted Bane. Or anyone, for that matter.

For some reason the watchdogs weren't pursuing River and Sever beyond the fence, but were continuing to fire and their weapons had serious range. Sever needed to get off his stupid ass and get them moving.

A small noise behind Nick made him spin around, chills shooting straight to his bladder, and he half expected Bane to leap out at him from a corner and do to him what he'd done to Tanner, the poor bastard.

There was nothing behind him except River, or at least what was left of her, curled up as comfortably as Nick was able to make her. She'd been in the game now for more than twenty-four hours, and although she'd been showing unbelievable stamina and the occasional boost in energy, her vitals were becoming increasingly erratic. He'd repositioned her periodically and she'd made no physical movements of her own.

His eyes narrowed. Had she moved? Was that how he'd left her last? He couldn't be certain. He didn't have her stamina, or the ability to boost his energy level. He was dead tired. The only thing keeping him going was a fear of being dead, period.

An alarm went off, nearly scaring the shit out of him, and before he could recover, River's whole body stiffened, her back arching, her mouth widening in a gaping rictus. Choking noises rattled from her throat.

Nick grabbed the external defibrillator from the wall near the gaming platform, ripped open River's shirt, and slapped the paddles to her exposed chest.

He shocked her three times before her heart rate stabilized.

There was a knock on the door and Nick heard it crack open.

"Everything all right in here?" the security guard called out.

"Fine!" Nick called back, praying the guard wouldn't suddenly develop a sense of responsibility and decide to investigate. "I was just testing some of the game's security systems."

There were a few seconds of silence, as if the guard was actually considering coming in, then the door clicked shut.

Nick rocked back on his heels, tears welling and spilling over onto his cheeks. He swiped angrily at his face with the heels of his hands, mad at River, mad at himself, and most of all mad at the game, irrational as that anger was.

Nick darted across the room and back into the chair in front of the monitor, furiously pounding on the keyboard with trembling fingers. River and Sever needed to get away from that lab before Kaye returned and caught them there. Sever shooting like a maniac and wasting all their credits wasn't helping matters. Focusing his anger at the game on Sever helped somewhat.

Nick wasn't as good at coding as River, and she'd likely want to kill him for screwing with her program, but she'd have to take a number on that. He wasn't nearly as afraid of her as he was for her. She'd become more important to him than he'd realized. Or wanted. And that made him angrier still.

He hit the com-link button. "Listen up, asshole," he said into it. On the screen, he watched Sever's head come around. River, he noted, was conscious, but barely. At least she wasn't trying to get back into the graveyard anymore. "I've planted a door to the next safe house off to your right. You don't have enough credits to get to the next level, and you don't have enough to talk to the Wizard. You don't have much time either. Get River inside before the door disappears, then drag your ass back into the level and get enough credits to move on."

Sever's eyes shifted to look almost directly at him from the screen. If Nick didn't know it wasn't possible, he'd almost believe Sever could see him. It gave him the willies.

So did the cold, intelligent expression on Sever's face. "Who is this?" he demanded.

Nick cut off communication, not bothering to answer, and slouched back in his chair to think. He watched the screen, his tiredness forgotten for the moment as his brain spun like a hamster on a wheel. Planting new code had been dangerous. Not because Kaye might find out, although the idea of him doing so made Nick want to hurl, but because of the random elements to the game. Already, too much had been altered. He'd never liked the idea of software programming software, and Sever was a case in point. That was no more the Sever River had created than Nick was the Easter Bunny.

But had Sever been altered because of something River had done, or was software now in control of the game?

♦ ♦

Hawk nursed a pair of sore nuts, glad that well-aimed knee of hers hadn't been able to do permanent damage to his real boys.

He didn't waste time trying to ask River in her current state if the voice on the other end of that com-link belonged to the mysterious Nick. It did.

The bastard had cut off communication again, though. Hawk didn't know what that indicated, but it didn't take a degree in quantum physics to guess that it didn't mean anything good. Either Nick couldn't get River out of the game, or he wouldn't. It didn't make any real difference which it might be. It did mean that Hawk didn't trust him.

River's glazed eyes, more Fae-like now than ever, had taken on an emptiness that reminded Hawk far too much of Vienna and he tried not to think about the uncomfortable comparison. Tousled black strands of her hair contrasted starkly against too-pale cheeks. She was struggling, mentally and physically, to come to terms with everything that had happened over the last few hours, and it made Hawk's guts ache to watch her. The Dark Lord had his fingers wrapped tightly around both their souls. Was River finally weakening? Was the Dark Lord beginning to claim her?

He needed to get her to safety. Hawk didn't like the idea of using the safe house Nick had offered them but he had no other choice, because Nick was right. They didn't have enough energy left to move on and Hawk was very much afraid that River might never survive another round in this level. She'd thought she felt her parents' presence back in that graveyard, and Hawk doubted she meant her adoptive ones.

Something terrible had happened to her birth parents. They would never have abandoned her otherwise. And whatever had happened to them was linked to that graveyard. But he needed to help her understand that even though she thought she'd felt her parents' souls trapped in it, that particular graveyard didn't really exist.

It existed somewhere in reality though, and somewhere a Fae soul and a Guardian's were trapped in it. And Hawk couldn't do anything to save them while the Dark Lord had a grip on his soul.

But he could still save River.

"On your feet, Fae," he commanded, burying all sympathetic feelings for her and assuming the position of a Guardian charged with protecting a Fae's soul. He pulled her hand into his and tugged.

She hadn't been raised Fae, or been trained to obey the orders of a Guardian without question, and yet the Fae half of her must have recognized and accepted his authority because she did as he said. Still, he had to drag her in the direction of the safe house through dense clusters of low-hanging branches that scratched deeply at exposed skin and drew blood. Their sneakers and light clothing weren't meant for dodging demons armed with grenade launchers in this kind of environment. They'd been meant for wandering city streets and fighting werewolves and demons.

Another explosion rocked the ground and Hawk hauled River to him, protecting her body with his as clumps of dirt and chunks of trees spewed around them. He looked ahead, wondering if Nick had lied about that safe house door. He spotted a beaten gravel path through the towering trees. Since time was not on their side, and they couldn't backtrack thanks to the limitations River had set and that the game seemed to have permanently adopted, they had no choice but to follow the path and hope for the best. His fingers tightened over River's and they ran hard until the gravel beneath their feet turned into black pavement. The soft soles of their shoes slapped against hard ground as he scanned the city streets, and he prayed he had enough credits left to get them inside the safe house.

Off in the distance the sign for Andy's flickered like a homing beacon, and Hawk was suddenly afraid they'd come full circle to the beginning of the level again. He looked up and down the street, wondering which way they should go now. River pulled her hand from his.

"That's the safe house," she said, pointing at Andy's and sounding more like her normal self. Relief rushed through his body. "But we'll have to make a run for it. We don't have enough energy left to fight anything off if we're attacked."

The dank scent of wet dog fur stung his nostrils, and with senses on high alert he shot a glance around, daring a werewolf to come at him. Energy or not, he'd kick its ass. With pleasure.

The street remained silent.

River looked past his shoulder in the direction they'd just come from and the fleeting sadness in her eyes made him look as well. A thick wall of green blocked the path behind them.

Hawk circled his arms around her waist to anchor her body to his. She tipped her chin, her lips parting slightly. He was glad to see a little life back in her eyes, although it still wasn't enough to totally ease his concern.

"Sorry about that shot with the knee I gave you," she said. "I wasn't thinking clearly."

He knew how hard this must be for her. He'd suffered one hell of a loss himself, and he hated to think that maybe his wife and daughter's souls were suffering out there somewhere, too. But River was strong. He'd help her deal with this.

"That's okay," he replied. "The boys aren't real anyway. But a word of warning. My new ones are now titanium. You might want to remember that for next time."

That earned him a small laugh.

"We're out of credits," River said, her voice thready and low. She rubbed her head. "I have a pounding headache, and I'm so thirsty I'd even drink water from that swamp right about now."

Here was yet another worry. Dehydration was most likely affecting her physical body. He glanced at his com-link. "Hang in there. I still have enough credits to get us into the safe house."

"But we don't have enough—"

The scent of wet dog grew stronger and Hawk pressed a finger to her lips, cutting off her words. His skin prickled and he slipped her hand into his, tugging her into a full run.

A moment later they found themselves on the

front steps of Andy's. Hawk examined the doorway. "How do we get in?"

"Use the barrel of your gun."

Then Hawk spotted the doorbell. He lifted an ornate cover and studied the intricate panel for a moment before pressing the polymer muzzle of his pistol over the switch, completing the circuit. Instead of a sound chiming in the background, the heavy front door slowly inched open.

He pushed the door all the way open and hurried River inside. Unfortunately, no door to the Wizard or the next world presented itself.

A bleep on his com-link told him they were running out of time and no doubt would have to start at the beginning of the modern world again, unless he took Nick's advice to drag his ass back into the level and go on a killing spree. He wasn't opposed to the that, although he hadn't much cared for the *dragging his ass* directive.

But first he needed to make certain River would be safe if he left her here.

The inside of the pub looked much like what he'd expected. Bar stools lined the counter where a computer-generated bartender stood motionless, ready to be keyed into action to take an order or lend a shoulder to cry on.

The bartender's too-green eyes locked on both River and Hawk the second they entered. Hawk inhaled and pulled the peppery scent of sage into his lungs. *Magic*.

The bartender and the Wizard were one and the same.

Alarm bells dinged in Hawk's head. There was something about that woman that just wasn't right, and yet River had pulled her from her real world. Maybe he should be as worried about her real world as he was about this one.

He turned his attention to the plush, cracked-vinyl booths lining the walls, and the rows of heavy wooden tables strategically positioned in the center of the wide-planked floor to make the best use of space.

As the door behind them clicked shut he felt River relax slightly, her fatigued body sagging against his. She obviously felt comfortable in this place, and for that he was thankful even though he didn't for a moment think she was safe here. But he needed her relaxed and rested in order for her mind to handle the next level, and this was as good a place as any.

"I smell magic," Hawk said to River.

"You smell Andy's," she corrected him, sounding more like herself. She was no longer complaining of a headache or thirst either, he noticed. "It's not magic. It smells like this in the real world. I love it."

He didn't bother arguing with her. He did smell magic. And he did not love it. To him it screamed *danger*! If he'd had any other option he would have thrown River over his shoulder and made a run for it.

But their previous run through the trees had been hard on her, and equally as dangerous. He took in her stained clothes, the thin gashes on her face and hands, and the way she wobbled as she tried to hold herself upright.

She needed energy, and he didn't think she could tap into it herself this time. There had to be a limit as to how many times she could pull that off before it caught up with her.

But if she couldn't get energy for herself, how did he get it for her?

He brushed his thumb over a dried streak of red on her cheek. "We need to get you cleaned up." He tried to lighten the mood. "You didn't happen to put a shower in this place, did you?"

Her eyes lit up. "Andy has an apartment in the back."

His gaze locked with the bartender's. For a second it felt to him as if she were trying to read his soul and he didn't like the sensation. His soul was strictly off-limits. The Dark Lord, River, and now the Wizard . . . Too many people were trying to stake a claim to it.

He set his jaw and gestured with a nod toward the counter. "Isn't that the Wizard?"

River gave a slight smile, the warmth in her eyes genuine. "Not here in the safe house. That's Andy. She owns the place."

Andy stood stock-still and Hawk wondered what they had to do to get her to talk. So far the only movement she'd made had been with her eyes. Maybe it was because they had no credits left.

Deciding it best to leave her exactly as she was until River was in a better state of mind, he sidestepped the counter and with River in tow, walked the long corridor behind the bar to Andy's apartment.

Once inside the small area off the back of the pub, Hawk took in his surroundings. Andy had a thing for rich blues and deep purples. He noted a small galley kitchen, tiny sitting area with a pull-out sofa, primitive television, and a back room that he assumed was the bathroom. The air felt cooler in here than in the pub area. He turned his attention to River. She had her arms wrapped around her chest, hugging herself in an attempt to ward off a shiver.

He was doing a shit job of looking after her. If she were a male Fae he might not worry about it quite so much, but she wasn't, and he did.

"Come here." Hawk pulled her to him and ran his

hands up and down her arms, the friction generating temporary warmth.

He inched back to look at her and noticed the slight droop in her lids, and the fine lines around her eyes. He needed to get her mental state back on track. To do that, he needed to improve her physical condition.

"Shower?" he questioned.

She nodded toward the small room off the galley kitchen. Hawk didn't like the idea of her being out of his sight. He also didn't like the idea of them being locked in a tiny room with no way to escape. He didn't trust Andy no matter how much River did.

He planted a hand on the small of River's back and nudged her down the narrow hall to the bathroom. It was close quarters but functional, with a sink, shower, and toilet. He rooted through the contents of a wall cupboard. Along with the usual female toiletries, one shelf held thick towels.

Now this was attention to detail. He frowned. Way too much attention to detail. He grabbed a towel and a container of shampoo.

River watched him, waiting, as though she didn't know what to do next and was too tired to really care. While he couldn't say he'd enjoyed getting kneed in the nuts, River kicking ass was far preferable to the automaton she was right now. He wanted her alive, not half dead.

He wanted her, period. And that was never going to happen. Her father had fucked up. No way was Hawk making the same mistake. He had to get her out of the game, save her soul from the Dark Lord, then somehow he had to get her home. To her real home, not that piece-of-shit planet she'd found herself stuck on for the past almost thirty years. River needed to learn how important she and her magic really were. Whole worlds depended on the Fae.

Unfortunately, River was beyond undressing herself.

Hawk turned on the water and let it come up to temperature as he sank against the counter, pulled her between his thighs, and went to work on unzipping her windbreaker. He gently peeled it from her body to reveal a light blue T-shirt beneath.

He could do this. This wasn't any different than undressing his daughter at bath time when she was little. The memories of a soft, soapy, slippery little body and all the giggles and squeals as he'd poured water over her curly head made him want to smile and cry at the same time. He blinked them away.

He gave a soft command. "Lift your arms for me, River."

River leaned into him and put her arms over her head. Hawk proceeded to remove her shirt, all the while trying to ignore male urges at the sight of the perfect, near-naked woman before him. Okay, so this wasn't quite the same as undressing a toddler.

He bit down on the inside of his cheek to suppress a groan, and even as he bullied himself for having inappropriate, wayward thoughts his eyes dropped lower to her skintight jeans. Getting those off wasn't going to be easy.

Working to summon all his control, he made short work of the button and zipper and dropped to the floor before her in an effort to help her slide them off. He reached her ankles, then tapped one leg. Understanding his command she lifted her leg and he swiftly removed the pants leg. When he gestured for her to lift the other one, her hands pressed against his shoulders as she shifted, using his body for balance while he rid her of the rest of her clothes, save for her underthings.

Hawk cleared his throat a second time and stood. As he loomed over her, he became acutely aware of their close proximity as well as her lacy bra and underwear and the responses her near nakedness pulled from his body.

He briefly pinched his eyes shut and struggled with an all-consuming need racing through his blood, and the overwhelming urge to bury himself in her body and stay there for eternity. Crisos. If kissing her had touched his soul, then what would greater intimacy do to him? For the first time he felt real pity for her father. If the attraction to her mother had been like this, the poor bastard never stood a chance.

He needed to go, to run, to get as far away from temptation as possible before he did something he would regret forever. He inched back, twisted around, and stepped toward the door, needing desperately to clear his head for both their sakes.

"I'll be right outside." He tossed the words over his shoulder.

An odd sound rose from her throat and he made the mistake of turning to look. He met with expressive eyes full of worry and . . . *want*.

They exchanged a long, heated look and he swiped his hand over his jaw, fighting the urge to take her into his arms and kiss away her every concern while he satisfied both their needs. Sex after stress was just about the most relaxing thing imaginable.

The last thing he wanted to do was walk away from her, especially when she looked so completely irresistible, and if it were simply a matter of physical attraction he didn't think it would stop him at this point. This was a virtual reality and there was no danger of a pregnancy. He was man enough to interpret that as an exception to a rule, particularly when she clearly wanted him as much as he wanted her.

What stopped him was what had happened with

that kiss. That hadn't been bending rules. That had been smashing them, tearing them apart, and dancing on the remains. He could pretend that the physical contact wasn't real because they were in a virtual world, but the emotional connection between them would be there in any reality.

She reached for him and her touch shot straight through his flesh, caressing his soul and breathing new life into his very existence. Oh, God, he wanted, no, *needed* her in a way he'd never needed before. This was nothing like what he'd had with his wife, and he'd loved his wife to the point that her death had nearly destroyed him.

"Hawk." That one word and its soft, sensual delivery melted his resolve.

He drew her against him and with much more harshness than intended demanded, "What do you want?"

She parted her lips, the invitation in her actions shattering what little shred of decency he had left. He'd been trapped in the Dark Lord's prison for far too long, and before that, he'd been an emotional wreck for months. He needed the touch, the intimacy, and the connection River offered him that went well beyond the physical. What could be the real harm in reminding them both that they were still alive, and still had so much to live for?

Yes, he needed to be strong for her. For himself,

too. But the second she pressed her body against his and placed her palm on his cheek, every reason he had for keeping his distance suddenly lost all significance. He leaned into her and put his mouth so close to hers he could taste her honeyed sweetness. His shaky hands fisted at his sides.

If he did this, he had to be prepared to face the consequences of his actions for both of them, because somehow, someday, this union, this melding of souls, could come back to haunt them. Once they made love, there would be no turning back.

"Hawk," she whispered again, her voice trembling with emotion. "I don't want you to leave. I want you with me." Their breath mingled, and the urgency in her voice made all the consequences in the universe insignificant by comparison.

Hawk took a deep breath and made one last effort to walk away before it was too late. "I know, River. Believe me, I know. But—"

She slid her palm down his arm and caught hold of his hand. As she backed up toward the steamy water she tugged him with her, her intentions impossible to misinterpret.

Hawk, fully dressed, followed her into the spray. River urgently yanked on his clothes. Hawk cupped her hands and placed them at her sides, needing to slow things down almost as much as he needed to hurry them up.

He tossed off his jacket and shirt, but his wet pants proved to be more of a challenge. River's warm, exploring hands continued to touch him all over, caressing his body in an erotic way as the needlelike spray prickled his skin. He swept his gaze down the length of her as he leaned against the porcelain stall and struggled out of the wet jeans clinging stubbornly to his thighs.

Once naked, he put his full attention on River and the way her hungry eyes fixed on his body. With shaky hands he tore the scrap of material from her hips, circled her silky curves and released her bra, allowing her gorgeous breasts to spill free from the constricting material.

Hawk pulled in a sharp breath as her pert nipples darkened and hardened under his visual caress. As equal measures of lust, want, and need ambushed him, a low tortured growl sounded deep in his throat and he stepped closer, desperate to feel skin on skin, flesh on flesh.

He grabbed a fistful of her hair and packaged her against him. When she gave a violent shiver and brushed her warm mouth over his skin, he let loose a moan of want. As her intimate touch drove every sane thought from his mind, passion overwhelmed him, and his shaky legs made standing damn near impossible. He inched one knee between her legs and widened them, then gave a slight tug on her

hair, poising her lips open for him as her heat
reached out to him. He looked at her, really looked
at her, as his heart pounded in his chest. A tremor
raced through him and it was all he could do to
maintain some small shred of control. He forced
himself to be calm.

But when she licked her bottom lip, moistening
and preparing it for him, he growled, no longer able
to ignore the heat arcing between them. His mouth
crashed down on hers. Hard. He kissed her long
and deep, releasing months of pent-up need.

And there it was again. The connection. But this
time he was more prepared.

She trembled, and he pulled her impossibly
tighter, meshing their bodies as one. His fingers
burned as he raced his hands over her skin, mold-
ing and shaping the perfect curves of her body.
Hawk knew what they were doing was wrong, and
against everything he'd ever been taught, but he no
longer cared that he didn't have the strength to
stop it.

"Please . . ." she murmured, her voice soft, coax-
ing, and with an underlying impatience that made
him smile.

His mouth moved to her neck, and he buried
himself in the soft, silky hollow. "River," he whispered against her flesh, "tell me what you want."
He needed to hear her say it. Needed to hear her

vocalize what it was she was feeling, to say exactly what she wanted.

"I want *you.*"

Her sweet scent curled around him and his heart nearly stopped. He swallowed hard, bombarded by thoughts that brightened and healed his dark, damaged mental corners. He held his breath, his mind racing out of control.

He swallowed, not expecting the impact those three simple words would have on him. It had been so long since he'd been connected to anyone, or felt anything other than pain and suffering. To be wanted by River—a *Fae*—was an honor he didn't deserve but was going to take.

There would indeed be consequences.

He buried his face in her hair and drew her scent deep into his lungs. He splayed his hands over her body, and using the soft pad of his fingertips he shaped her curves, brushing over the soft contours of her breasts, stopping long enough to caress her rosy nipples as they beckoned his mouth.

"Baby . . ." he murmured into her hair, then dipped his head to draw one pert nub into his mouth. As he closed his mouth around her perfect, hard nipple, River threw her head back and moaned, her fingers raking through his hair and holding him to her body. Her back arched and she pressed against his invading leg, rubbing herself along the length of his hard thigh. Her warm, scented moisture saturated the small room and nearly drove him mad with need.

He tilted his head forward to see her and the heat in her eyes licked him from head to toe. He needed to be inside her. Now.

Hawk grabbed the soap from the shower ledge and soaped up his hands. River's body convulsed when he raced his palms over her flesh and washed the grime of the graveyard from her body. He then turned the soap on himself and pulled her under the spray with him to bask in the hot, sudsy water. After cleansing their bodies, he drew her to him and positioned his mouth near her ear. He pressed himself against her stomach and he felt her shiver when he whispered, "I want you beneath me, River."

"The sofa," came her breathless reply.

Hawk turned off the spray and grabbed a towel. He bent forward and patted down her naked body. The seductive feel of her hair sweeping against his shoulders made him quake and the arousing imagine of River sprawled out on the mattress, her hair wild and untamed, spilling over the bed sheets as he buried himself inside her, sent heat rushing through his body and prompted him into action. He knotted the damp towel around his waist and gathered her hand in his.

Desire reflected from her eyes as he ushered her to the main room where he pulled out the sofa into a makeshift bed.

He turned to her and his heart nearly stopped at the sight of her standing there before him. He reached out and found her fingers trembling. He brushed his lips over hers, a barely there kiss, and she stepped into him. He could feel the rapid beat of her heart matching his own.

"Are you okay?" he asked in a soft voice.

She nodded. "Yes," she whispered. She placed a fist over her chest. "It's just that this doesn't feel like a game to me, Hawk."

Warmth streaked through him and he felt a flash of possessiveness. Feeling very ill-equipped to deal with the powerful emotion, he closed his hand over hers and squeezed, the pull between them too powerful to deny. "It's real."

"Hawk." His eyes moved over her face, assessing her as he brushed a loose strand of hair from her cheek. Her breath hitched, and her body molded against his as she said, "I need you to kiss me."

Hawk cupped her face and lightly did so. She responded with a needy sigh. The sound weaved its way through his veins, turning darkness into light. He took a quick glance at the window and smiled. As though mimicking his emotions, rays of sunshine lit the walls with a hazy orange glow.

Hawk backed River up until her knees hit the bed. Then he gave a light shove and watched her sprawl across the mattress, her every movement sensual, her desire-drugged eyes never leaving his as her body opened for him.

He pulled in a breath, and for the longest time he just stood there watching her, reveling in her sweet, familiar smell, the feminine curves, the slick valley between her legs, and the way her hungry eyes raced over his body with undisguised want. His muscles tightened and bunched as he moved in beside her, using his weight to press down on her, pinning her to the mattress and caging her between his chest and the bed.

The fresh scent of soap reached his nostrils and when he flicked his tongue out to taste the hollow of her neck his senses exploded like a round of gunfire.

"Mmm," he murmured, and nudged her chin up with his own for a better, more thorough taste of her flesh.

"More," she demanded, desperation lacing her voice as she writhed beneath him, her actions expressing her want and need.

Ignoring the burn in his body, he climbed over her and with excruciating slowness pressed his lips to her skin, taking his time to taste and savor every inch of her glorious flesh, despite her protests.

His mouth moved from her neck to her breasts where he tasted her perfect mounds, drawing her nipples in to lick, suckle, and nibble until their cries of pleasure merged. Once his mouth had had its fill he moved lower, trailing his tongue over her stomach, stopping to dip into her belly button before continuing a downward path. When he reached her apex, he shot her a glance. River went up on her elbows, and their gazes collided. He watched her throat work as she swallowed.

Her pink tongue snaked out to moisten her lips and longing colored her voice when she said, "I need you to kiss me." But this time he knew exactly where she wanted his mouth.

When she widened her legs to grant him entrance, he dipped his head and closed his mouth over her warm sex. Her hips came off the bed, and she grabbed the bed sheets and fisted them in her hands. Seeing her so aroused nearly became his undoing.

"Hawk," she cried out, her eyes alive with anticipation.

He watched her give herself over to the pleasure he was offering her. With that he inserted a finger and lightly brushed over the sensitive bundles of nerves inside. He felt her body clench, close, and pulse around his fingers and he suspected she was close to erupting, but he wasn't quite ready to bring her over just yet. He wanted to be inside her for that.

The sound of her voice bombarded him with hunger, and he turned his attention back to her sex, lightly stroking his tongue over her while slipping another finger inside. The dual assault pushed her to the precipice. He greedily pulled her into his mouth and worked his finger in and out of her slick entrance.

Moments before she tumbled over, he climbed over her and positioned himself at her entrance. She bucked forward and he breached her scorching entrance. Hawk stilled his movements, and went up on one elbow to brush her damp hair from her face. The way she looked up at him made his whole body tremble.

"River . . ." he murmured, unable to voice what he was feeling, but needing her to understand the importance of what they were doing.

"Now, Hawk."

As her sex clenched around him he thrust forward, pushing himself all the way up inside her. He held her smoldering glance and in that instant, his world shifted.

Her hand cupped his cheek and he knew he was in trouble. The intimacy in what they were doing combined with the look in her eyes was more than he could bear. Then suddenly, he could feel her energy move through him, touching, healing, soothing, and taking him beyond anything he'd ever known.

Her nurturing soul wrapped around his like a blanket of warmth, melting the last lingering traces of ice.

He let himself go, giving her a part of himself that he'd never released before. And for the first time, he caught the faint, peppery scent of sage on River's skin, warm and enticing and exactly as he'd expect Fae magic to be.

As though feeling something inside him give, River began trembling and panting and palming his muscles as her burning mouth pressed hungrily against his flesh. She pitched forward, demanding his undivided attention. His blood pressure soared and tension rose in him as her breath scorched his body.

He began pumping, pounding into her with a need so fierce it was as exhilarating as it was frightening. Her cheeks flushed with color, the scratches on her fine skin sealed shut, and somewhere in the back of his mind he understood that this was a good thing, and that something in the intimacies they were sharing had helped release her magic and increase her ability to heal. Was the council aware that a Guardian's physical touch helped give new life to a Fae soul?

His thoughts moved in a new direction when River moaned in bliss.

He swiped his tongue across her lips, then drifted

in for a deep, soul-searching kiss. He wanted to slow down, to take his time with her and do this right—he really did—but he couldn't control himself with her. The need was too strong.

"So good," she murmured, wrapping her arms and legs around him to hold him tight.

Hawk felt her muscles spasm, then felt her release. He drove deeper and stilled, and his hands gripped her shoulders as he let himself go. He held her tight and absorbed her tremors as he completely depleted himself, his soul never having felt more at peace.

Once their bodies stopped trembling, he lowered himself beside her. He grabbed the sheets and covered their damp, naked bodies. When he cast River a glance he couldn't even begin to describe how the smile of contentment on her flawless face made him feel. He held his hands out to check his own wounds—not a scar to be found. Just who had healed whom?

She nestled against him and he ran his fingers over her flesh. As he reveled in the feel of her next to him, he tried desperately not to think about the ramifications of their actions.

CHAPTER **FOURTEEN**

♦

River shifted into a more comfortable position on the makeshift bed, angling her naked body so she could take pleasure in the sight of the man lying next to her. She made a small sound of contentment and without conscious thought, reached out and traced the pattern of Hawk's firm jaw line, trailing her fingers lower to enjoy the feel of well-defined muscles beneath her palm. His skin felt warm, smooth, soft.

Real.

Late-afternoon light spilled across the bed, bathing their bare bodies in a soft glow and taking the chill from the air. Even though she hadn't slept for several days, River had never felt more alive in her life. Amazingly enough she'd just found another way to boost her personal energy levels, and she had to say, she liked it even better than Red Bull. Hawk seemed to be the key, because this had never happened before. Not in quite the same way.

But while her energy level had recovered, the fine lines crinkling Hawk's eyes hadn't been missed by her. Nor had the weariness lingering in the depths of his unsettling gaze. Hawk's body and mind were tired.

Drained.

Running on empty.

And it was dangerous. Hawk ran the risk of losing his grasp on reality.

But Hawk wasn't just exhausted from being trapped and tortured by the Soul Man. He'd been damaged long before he'd ever been captured in the virtual prison. While they were making love she'd touched his soul and unearthed things he worked hard to keep buried. River had felt his pain as if it was her own, and as she registered the depth of the losses he'd had in his world, she finally understood who he was, what made him tick, and why he sometimes seemed so grim. She'd grazed his memories, never intending to invade his privacy, but she'd been caught off guard by them. The emotions that went with them had been unavoidable for her, and she'd recognized the deep pain of loss because she'd felt it herself.

He slanted his head, and when he met her glance the surprised tenderness in his gaze filled her with warmth and even more energy. Hawk had shown a gentleness with her that she hadn't expected, and after everything he'd been through, in his world and in this one, it gave her a newfound respect for him.

She blinked up at him, her heart aching. Her fingers touched his face as she whispered, "I'm so sorry, Hawk."

A look of confusion crossed his face, but only lasted briefly before understanding dawned. He'd touched her soul as well. He cleared his throat as he pulled her tighter against him, as though her touch helped ground him in this virtual world.

"I lost my wife and daughter a long time ago."

He'd had a wife and daughter. People he'd loved. She trailed her fingers over his heart. "Not that long ago that it doesn't still hurt."

Hawk's arms tightened around her. "It's not a good idea for me to be talking or thinking about it, River. Not here. If the Dark Lord gets too much information about us, you never know what he'll do with it."

"We're in the safe house," River reminded him.

"I know." He grew quiet for a moment, thoughtful. "My whole life changed in the span of a single second. I miss them, River. Like mad." He pressed one fist over his heart, beside where her hand rested. "But when you touched my soul it dulled the pain, and I'm not sure I'm ready for that. If I don't feel the pain, it means I've let them go."

"I understand." She did. Letting go was the hardest part and Hawk was an intense man. He'd let them go when he was ready, and on his own terms.

He tilted his head back to look at the ceiling and blew out a breath. "You really are special."

She thought about the way his touch had breathed

new life into her own soul. "You're pretty special, too," she pointed out.

"In what way?"

She caught the teasing warmth in his tone. He wasn't ready to let go, but he was willing to be distracted, and that was an important step.

"You make me feel like a brand-new woman." She threw her leg over him and felt the way his length thickened beneath her thigh. She gave a lazy, cat-like stretch, hardly able to believe this was the same man she'd met just a few short days ago. "I must say, I'm glad I made Sever so anatomically correct, but if this were real life, I'd be sore in some awkward places."

Smiling eyes met hers. "Lack of sleep must be getting to you. Your game is wrong. I'm far better than anatomically correct."

Laughter bubbled up inside her. She drew energy from deep within her core, and holding her hand steady over Hawk's heart, she expelled it, wanting to help him the way he'd helped her. In his current exhausted state it was only a matter of time before he accepted craziness as reality.

When she touched him, Hawk gave a little start. He closed his hand over hers and squeezed. In a drowsy voice still filled with desire, he cautioned, "What did I tell you, River?"

She patted his chest. "You told me never to use

magic in the game because I don't know who might be watching. But if someone was watching us now, magic's not what I'd be worrying about them seeing."

His body tensed. In the span of a second his expression changed, turning serious. He shifted and sat up straight, pressing his back against the cushions of the pullout sofa. His brow furrowed and River could almost hear his mind racing.

She sat up, too, drawing the sheets over her breasts. She shot a glance around, half expecting a were to pounce, then checked her com-link. Nothing was wrong that she could tell.

"What is it?" she asked, alarmed.

"So now you believe me? That you have magic?"

She didn't know what she believed anymore, other than that her world would never be the same again. "I felt my parents back there. My birth parents." She lifted one bare shoulder. "I'm well past the point of denying that something isn't quite right. That there's more going on than I understand."

His tension eased. He took her hand and gave a comforting squeeze. "Tell me exactly what happened back there in that graveyard."

River stared at the wall for a moment before she could find the right words to answer. "I felt them reach out to me, move inside my body and touch my soul like they were trying to tell me something."

River swallowed, her throat dry and very painful. "I felt magic, Hawk. It was the same feeling I get when I summon my own energy." She shrugged her shoulders, unable to explain. "Only different."

She'd left her parents back in that awful place filled with buried monsters, held there by magic. She'd done nothing to help them.

Hawk was watching her closely, reading her emotions as easily as she'd read his. He laced his fingers with hers, his hand warm and reassuring.

"Your parents weren't in that graveyard because that graveyard wasn't real, so you can't possibly have abandoned them." He squeezed her fingers. "They wouldn't want to see you dead. I have a feeling they went to a great deal of trouble in keeping you alive. But they're out there somewhere, in someplace similar, and we're going to find them. I promise you that." His voice grew grim. "If there's one thing I've learned over the past months, it's that souls should be free."

She believed him. It made her feel better about walking away from her parents, although no less frantic.

"Do you think that's why the Wizard led us to that graveyard?" she asked. "To find them?"

His face closed, the way it always did when the Wizard came up. "I don't know," he said. Then he changed the subject. "Do you now understand what you are, River?" Dark, intense eyes locked on hers. "And how important you and the rest of the Fae are to this universe?"

She rolled her shoulder, trying to ease the sudden tension in her neck as she acknowledged the possibility that she was Fae. "I'm different," she said. "I've always known that. But no matter what I am, I'm no more important than anyone else. Neither are you, and neither are the Fae. I don't believe one person or race is better or worse than another. We all have our place."

"Perhaps. But your place is slightly different." He got quiet for a moment, and she could tell he was trying to choose his words carefully. "Some thirty years ago, a Fae and a Guardian were sent to Earth for the first time since the Dark Lords ruled. It was hoped Earth could be saved from self-destructing. No one has heard from them since, and no Fae or Guardian has ever been back."

Understanding dawned. "So you're suggesting the Fae and the Guardian were my parents?"

"I don't think there can be any other explanation." He tapped her com-link before resting his knuckles over the center of her chest. "You have Guardian technology, and you have Fae magic. You're more different than you can imagine."

She pressed the heel of her palm to her forehead. "You're giving me a headache."

"A Fae is never supposed to be left alone, River, not without a Guardian for protection."

Her insides ached as they hadn't in years, longing for the parents she'd called Mom and Dad, and yearning for the ones who'd called out to her and touched her heart and soul. Hawk drew her into him and pressed his mouth to her forehead.

"If what you say is true," River said, "then I do have protection. If I'm both Fae and Guardian, I can take care of myself."

Hawk laughed and kissed her forehead. "Now you have double protection. Because you also have me."

She tried out the sound of that.

Hawk.

Her Guardian.

It wasn't quite right, but it wasn't wrong either.

"When we made love," she said, "it gave me energy in the same way I draw it from myself. Do you think that has something to do with magic?"

"Maybe." He frowned. "I don't know. I wouldn't expect it. The laws of both worlds forbid Guardians and Fae to interact on a sexual level." He coughed as if suddenly uncomfortable with the conversation.

"Forbid?" She sat up straighter, trying to comprehend the meaning of his words, outraged now and wanting fiercely to defend the parents she'd never known. "Are you telling me my parents did

something *wrong*?" She swept a hand around the bed. "That *this* was wrong?"

"If *this*," he said, catching her hand, "happened in the real world, it could lead to the loss of a host for a Fae soul. A Fae woman can only have one child, and if the father is Guardian, that child will be born without a Fae soul."

"So if the child doesn't have a Fae soul, what is it then, some kind of soulless monster?"

He blinked in surprise at her conclusion. "No, more likely a Guardian, I guess."

"You guess?"

He looked troubled. "We've always been taught that the child wouldn't possess a Fae soul, and Fae souls can't be replaced if they're lost. They're magical, not mortal. I can't say for sure whether the child is actually a Guardian because I've never heard of one. Not until now. But Fae souls are drawn to the Fae. And if there isn't an equal number of Fae hosts, the souls are left with nothing to host them."

What he said made sense, so why did her instincts warn her there was more to it than that?

"If I'm an offspring," she said, "why can't I be a Guardian?"

"Because the magic is tied to the Fae soul. You have magic, therefore you must be Fae." He shook his head and said under his breath, "It must be some kind of miracle that you were born possessing a Fae soul. I've never heard of it before."

"I know I'm different, but—"

He cut off her protest. "The Fae have a great responsibility, River. The Guardians as well. It doesn't really matter how it happened, only that it did, and we can never let the Dark Lord touch your soul. The Fae are the bringers of life. Dark Lords are the destroyers. Somehow you have to be taught to use your magic as it was meant to be used. Uncontrolled magic of any kind is dangerous, whether the user intends it to be or not."

She threaded her fingers together, drawing her knees to her chin and wrapping her arms around them. It felt disloyal to a father she'd never known to simply accept she might be more Fae than Guardian. "And Guardians are the servants?"

He gave her a look that suggested he didn't for a moment think she was funny. "We consider ourselves protectors." He crooked a brow. "And I think of myself as a soldier. In my world, I'm military."

"I want to go home," River said. Her mind was tired. She wanted to end the discussion. "*My* home. I want to find my birth parents. I want to find out what's happened to my team. That means we have to defeat the Dark Lord, and if we want to free the souls that he's trapped, we have to figure out a way to defeat him for good."

"Yes. We do." Hawk was as willing as she was to let the issue of her parentage drop. He lifted his hand and was about to squash a spider as it crawled over the bedsheets. River grabbed his hand to stop him.

"Don't," she said, brushing it off the bed onto the floor. "They're harmless if you leave them alone."

"I don't want you anywhere near a Dark—"

She cut him off. "If we defeat the Soul Man and I go back to my body, what will happen to you? Will you go back to your body, too?"

He nodded. "I'll come for you, and we'll find your parents. I promise. Then I'll bring you home."

She wondered if it could be that simple. He didn't owe her anything simply because they'd made love. Technically, it hadn't even been real sex. She would find her parents herself, with or without him. "You don't need to do that."

"I'll come for you," he repeated. "You should be with your own people. You need to learn to use your magic."

If she were half Fae and half Guardian, she wouldn't have any people of her own. She would have nothing and no one. The thought was depressing.

"I have no other home than the one I grew up in," she said. "I'll be fine where I am. I have been until now, magic or no magic."

He started to say something, possibly to argue, then apparently changed his mind.

"Do you trust Nick?" he asked her instead.

The mention of Nick made her feel guilty. They didn't have a permanent relationship, but still, the polite thing to do would have been to end it before moving on. She would have, but it wasn't as if circumstances had exactly aligned themselves in her favor. He'd understand that. Besides, even though he did tend to be jealous of her, she was fairly certain he'd been sleeping with Marsha behind her back. She simply hadn't cared enough to try to find out.

She felt the need to defend him anyway. "He helped us back in the forest, didn't he?"

"Perhaps," Hawk conceded grudgingly. "But if he wanted to help, why hasn't he pulled you out of here?"

River didn't like what Hawk was suggesting, that somehow, Nick couldn't be trusted. Nick might not be the most upstanding person in the world, but he wasn't bad either.

"He's the medic on the team. Maybe he's worried it will cause brain damage. Maybe the team can't fix whatever's wrong with the game."

"Or maybe he's leaving you in here on purpose. To see how you'll react. I think there might be a lot more going on in your world than you realize. I think this could be a test of some kind and I think there's a good chance that more people than the Dark Lord have managed to take control over parts of your game."

She thought about the old lab they'd found, and the graveyard and what was buried in it. She wondered why the Wizard had sent her to find it. Someone had killed her parents, so someone must know about her. Did someone in her world think she was Fae, too?

Did Nick?

"Why do you suppose my parents are trapped in that graveyard with monsters? Contained behind that fence with magic?" she asked.

Hawk rubbed the back of his neck. "What I'm wondering is who is containing them."

She frowned. "Do you suppose that's why Fae souls are disappearing? Because they're being trapped somehow?"

"I'm not sure," Hawk said grimly. "I was sent to find out what's been happening to the Fae. But I got snagged by the Dark Lord before I had a chance to find those answers. Somehow I think you and your parents must be part of it all."

River gripped Hawk's arm and squeezed. "We really need to find that graveyard. To release my parents' souls."

"I know. And we will. I promised, and I'll help

you." Hawk shot a glance at the door and then at the com-link still strapped to his wrist. "But first we need to finish what we've started here. We need to finish the game once and for all, and get back to our own realities. And to do that, I need to get us some credits so we can move forward. Your good friend Nick told me to haul my ass back inside the level. But how am I supposed to do that? If I go backward, don't I meet with a wall of green?"

River shook her head, returning to gamer mode. "No. In the higher levels if the player enters the safe house for rest or ammunition, but doesn't have enough credits to move on to the next world or summon the Wizard, they can exit the safe house and pick up where they left off. They'll end up in their last location. Back in this level, the player will meet with the demons and weres." She shivered slightly and crinkled her nose in dismay. "Of course when we go back out there, I'm afraid I have no idea what other monsters we'll meet. If there's another wrinkle—"

Hawk threw back the sheets and swung his legs out of bed, not bothering to hide his nakedness. As he stood and dressed River watched him, unable to keep her thoughts from careening off track to how his body had felt next to hers, and how his touch had revived her, breathing new life into her body, mind, and soul.

She could only imagine what it might have been like in reality.

Hawk picked up her gun and tossed it to her, and without hesitation she snatched it from the air. He was testing her, she knew, to see if she was ready to handle whatever the Soul Man was about to throw at them next. She placed the gun in her lap, held her hands out to examine them, and considered the amount of energy now running through her body. She could accept who her parents were because she'd felt them. They'd touched her soul. But could she really possess magic? She angled her head and placed her palm over a shamefully neglected potted plant beside her and watched its wilted leaves bloom.

Yes, she knew she was different. But her green thumb was thanks to her gardener mother. The idea of possessing a Fae soul, a creature who embraced earth magic, was quite a stretch for a girl raised on a farm by two very down-to-earth, nonmagical parents. As River stared at the deep violet blossoms beginning to emerge, she wondered whether the ability to breathe new life into the plant was part of her code, or if it was a part of her.

If she was what Hawk thought she was—half Guardian, half Fae—did that make her a half-breed? If so, it didn't sound to her as if either the Guardians or the Fae would be particularly welcoming to her.

Which likely explained his hesitation when he'd said he'd come back for her.

She also couldn't help but notice the unease on Hawk's face, or the unsureness in his voice when he talked about getting her back to her body on Earth. Why would he be hesitating? Didn't he want her to go home? Did he know something she didn't?

Did she really know him well enough to trust him as much as she did? Or was she trusting him because she had no other choice?

The alarm on her com-link pulled her thoughts back. There was little time for speculation now, not when they were hundreds of credits short of reaching the next level, and any minute they could be timed out. A fine shiver moved through her as she thought about the terrible graveyard that was not part of her game. She did not want a repeat of the modern world. She didn't think she could bear that again. Hawk was right. They needed to make a few kills and they needed to make them now, but they couldn't do it until they refueled.

She watched Hawk move about the room. She grabbed her gun off her lap and dangled it from her fingertips. "We're out of ammunition," she said. "We can't exit the safe house and get those credits until we refuel our weapons."

Hawk closed the distance between them, shackled her wrist, and held it tight. "Not *we*, River. Me."

She yanked her hand back, not liking the sudden caveman attitude. Most Fae might need Guardians for protection, but if she *were* Fae, she wasn't the kind he seemed to know. The mother who'd raised her had brought her up to depend on no one but herself.

"We're in this together, remember?" she said.

He tried to change tactics on her. "I think we can both agree that our common goal is to keep you safe and get you to the Dark Lord's lair in one piece so together we can figure out a way to defeat him. If he captures your soul he can use it to jump out of his virtual prison and back to your earth, so if you care about your world, you can't afford to take any unnecessary risks."

She opened her mouth to protest but he cut her off. "Why don't you go and search the bar instead? Maybe you'll find something useful. I can go take down a few wolves while you do that. Why should we both waste our time and energy on the streets when we can be doing something useful?" He gave her a moment to chew on that, then the teasing light was back in his eyes. "You keep saying you're the brains to my brawn. Prove it to me."

She rolled her eyes, honest enough to admit that maybe he was right. Besides, in her game it always bought more time when she handed the reins over to Sever, and time was something they desperately needed so they didn't have to repeat the level. Maybe they really would be better served if she looked around the safe house. It couldn't hurt to strike up a conversation with Andy either. Not that bartender Andy could tell her anything or give her advice regarding the game, because it wasn't part of the design, but still, being around Andy in any form always made her feel better. That was why River had put her in the safe house and made her the Wizard in the first place.

Thinking of the Wizard brought a frown to her face. Why didn't Hawk trust her? The Wizard was the one computer-generated character in the game that could help them.

Why wouldn't Hawk want her help?

CHAPTER FIFTEEN

♦

Someone had made changes to the game.

Deep in his sanctuary, surrounded by the souls he'd managed to call to him despite the prison boundaries established by the long-dead Guardians, the Dark Lord quivered with rage.

Whoever they were, when he was free, they would pay for the interference. The effort it took to get him back in command had cost him dearly.

Great chunks of stone wall were now missing from the sanctuary. One massive fireplace had collapsed completely. Light from the planet outside—the physical world that housed his prison—gleamed like flame through a deep fissure in the vaulted ceiling. Sparkles of red dust drifted on currents of air.

His face twisted.

The Guardian and the Fae were well within reach. They couldn't stay inside a safe house forever, and when they emerged, it would be to a level the little Fae could not possibly manipulate.

♦ ♦

River pulled on her clothes, grabbed up their guns, and stepped into the main bar.

Hawk stayed close beside her and she knew he was scanning the establishment for anything out of the ordinary. Even though this was the safe house, they'd already found out the hard way that a wrinkle in the program could skew everything. No matter what, they needed to be fully prepared and alert at all times.

Hawk coughed, and River glanced at him sharply. His eyes had a feverish glow to them. Hawk looked like he might be coming down with something. She hadn't felt well herself when they'd entered the safe house, but now she felt fine. They were close to the next level. A cold virus might slow him down but it wouldn't kill him.

River passed by Andy, who stood motionless except for her eyes, which followed their actions closely. Since River had written that into the program she didn't think anything of it. By the way Hawk was fidgeting, however, he didn't care for it.

"Why is she staring at us?" he asked, suspicion darkening his voice.

"She's programmed to anticipate our needs," River replied. "If we'd had more credits, she'd be offering us anything we need for free. Since we have only a few credits, we have to figure out what we need for ourselves. The fewer credits we have, the higher the cost of asking her questions."

"You don't understand the whole concept of 'steal from the rich and give to the poor,' do you?" Hawk said, and River laughed.

"It's more like paying for convenience," she explained. "Andy could do it for us, or we can do it for ourselves. Plus, I know how to cheat."

Widening her nostrils, she drew in the aromatic lemony scent emanating off the towering peanut tree hovering in the corner, its broad leaves dangling over one end of the oaken bar countertop. She pushed aside a branch full of dark green, egg-shaped blades to reveal a cluster of red, leathery, boat-shaped pods approximately three inches long.

Hawk watched in mute fascination as River touched the muzzle of her gun to one pod and it split open to reveal black seeds the size of a peanut. The sound of the seeds snapping open broke the quiet surrounding them. As her gun absorbed the energy from the nut, the seeds clattered to the floor and began to disintegrate.

Once the Glock was nourished, she turned it over in her hands, opened the chamber, and checked for silver bullets. Satisfied that the refueling had been successful even without credits, she handed Hawk's gun over to him.

He popped the chamber to check it himself and examined the contents. His brow furrowed as he counted the bullets. "That's not going to take me far."

She pointed toward the decomposing pile of broken shells on the floor. "No worries. You now have enough stored energy to automatically reload your gun five times."

Hawk holstered his weapon and glanced at the door. A worried expression crossed his face, and a muscle along his jaw rippled. "Hang tight. I'll be right back." He hesitated a moment, and he met her eyes. "Sorry, River, but I don't trust your Andy. Watch yourself. If anything happens, and I mean *anything,* contact me on the com-link and I'll be back as fast as I can."

She nodded. "You be careful, too. Go easy on the innocents. And try not to cough on them," she added. "I think you might be coming down with something contagious."

He sneezed, and the look he shot her made her laugh again.

As she watched him disappear through the door without her, she couldn't help but worry about his well-being. He wanted to protect her soul at all costs, but what of his own?

She chewed her bottom lip as she plunked herself down on the bar stool in front of Andy.

She planted her elbows and rested her chin on her palm. "I need a drink." Hawk would get enough credits to cover the cost.

Andy's eyes focused on her. "The usual?" she asked.

River nodded. If a snake could taste like a big juicy burger in this reality, then surely a fake drink would hit the spot. And right about now she could use a Red Bull and rye.

Andy reached for the bottle behind her and the scent of sage hit River hard. Sage. The smell of magic, according to Hawk. But River had written that into her code. It had nothing to do with magic and was all part of the program.

Wasn't it?

Something else gnawed at River as she watched

Andy prepare the drink. Something wasn't right, but she couldn't quite put her finger on it. Perhaps it was the ringing of gunfire outside, or the sound of wolves howling and demons splattering on the pavement—not to mention the way her conscience was screaming at her to get out there and help Hawk—that prevented her mind from figuring out what was bothering her.

Andy slid the glass across the counter, and with a smile and a drop in their credits that Hawk and his killing spree quickly replaced, River accepted the drink and took a big sip. Perfect. Just the way she liked it. She settled her drink on the counter and focused on her friend's familiar face. The peppery smell triggered her memories and River's heart twisted with longing, aching to be home. But the truth was, if she hadn't known better she'd already think she was home. If she closed her eyes she could hear her team chatting about the latest conspiracy theories, and Johnny's monsters hiding under his bed. River smiled and twisted around, half expecting to see the gang behind her, but the smile quickly fell from her face when her search came up empty.

She pressed a button on her com-link, wanting at least to hear Nick's voice again, then remembered Hawk's warnings. Was Hawk right? Was Nick leaving her in here on purpose?

"Where are you, Nick?" She slapped the countertop. "Where is everyone?" Frustration and helplessness worried her insides.

"I see some things aren't quite as they should be."

Incredulous, her eyes darted to Andy. "What?"

Andy's nervous gaze shot to the door before returning to River. She lowered her voice and leaned close. "I see some things aren't quite as they should be."

River's lungs froze. Andy wasn't supposed to talk without being asked a direct question, and she was being cautious, choosing her words carefully. But why? Who was she worried about overhearing them? The Soul Man? Hawk?

And weren't those the exact same words the Wizard had used when she and Hawk had summoned her in the primitive world?

River had designed both the Wizard and the bartender after Andy from the real world, but in the program when Andy was the bartender, the two had no common code. They shouldn't be reciting the same sentence. In fact, Andy shouldn't be initiating conversation at all when River didn't have enough credits. This felt far too real, and far too personal.

With ribbons of fear creeping through her veins, River grabbed her gun and wrapped her palm around the warm metal. Either she was losing her mind or this was another wrinkle. But if it was a wrinkle, who or what was causing it?

Should she be calling Hawk to come back?

As the warm, peppery aroma of Andy's pub enfolded her, she recalled the arrow that had saved her from the Uultur. Another thought struck. Were Andy and the Wizard overlapping? Was that the wrinkle in the program? By using her for the Wizard had she dragged the real Andy into the game by accident?

She glanced at her com-link. If she gathered information from Andy and it cost her in credits then it had to be part of the game. If not . . .

Then maybe Hawk was right, and there was a lot more going on in her world than she realized.

"What makes you say that?" River probed.

"You seem different."

The amount of energy on her com-link stayed the same. River wasn't sure if that was a good thing or not.

"In what way?"

A large, hairy spider dropped from the peanut tree at the end of the bar and scurried across the countertop as River studied her friend, impatient for answers. The spiders must have come in on their clothing. River removed her elbows from the scuffed countertop to give it a clear path, but the horrified look on Andy's face as it scuttled past didn't escape her. Why would Andy be so afraid of a simple spider?

Once the spider disappeared from sight, Andy relaxed. She picked up a glass from the counter and began to polish it. "Oh my soul, look at how dirty this glass has gotten. That's what I get for trusting it with someone else."

Andy was being cryptic with her. She wasn't supposed to be cryptic. She wasn't supposed to be anything.

Andy offered her a smile that didn't spread to her normally vibrant green eyes. Instead, her gaze contained caution, offering a warning to River as River tried to decipher the meaning of those words.

Then Andy shut down, standing motionless now except for her eyes. River guessed she'd said all she was going to, or perhaps was able to.

River mentally repeated the words, trying to pick out something that held some sort of meaning. *"Oh my soul, look at how dirty this glass has gotten. That's what I get for trusting it with someone else."*

River calmed her mind and concentrated, repeating the words over and over and pulling the sentence apart until she could make sense of it. After a moment, comprehension dawned brightly. It wasn't the glass Andy was trusting with someone else, it was her soul.

Andy was warning River about trusting someone

with her soul. Was she talking about Hawk? A
Guardian of Fae souls?

The sound of gunfire outside ceased and the pub
door creaked open. She turned to face Hawk. His
eyes narrowed in suspicion and his blood-smeared
face tightened as he inhaled deeply, and she knew
what he smelled. He did a quick scan before his
eyes settled on her. "Learn anything?"

"Nothing that made any sense," she said truth-
fully.

"What a surprise." He watched her with quiet
suspicion and she tried not to squirm. When her
com-link chimed and two doors materialized on
the other side of the pub, River jumped from her
stool.

"We should move."

Tight on her heels as she raced across the room,
Hawk reached past her when she identified the door
they needed to use.

"Allow me," he said, and pressed the barrel of his
gun into the panel beside it. The panel creaked
open, leading them into the final and hardest level
of the game before they entered the Soul Man's lair.

Despite the days without sleep, and the unexpected rise in the personal stakes for both of them,
anticipation sang to River's soul. This was the level
she loved the most, but it was also the one that terrified her. If they wanted to make it through this

alive they would have to call on every ounce of strength, willpower, and wit they possessed.

River held back, allowing Hawk to pass her, deciding to be gracious rather than argue over who went first because she didn't like to lose.

As she followed him across the threshold and into the postapocalyptic world, it finally occurred to her what had been bothering her when she first sat down with Andy. Her computer-generated bartender would never know what her "usual" was.

Only the real Andy would.

♦ ♦

She was back and she was alive.

Unfortunately, that asshole Sever was still with her. Nick crumpled the paper with River's handwritten code on it in his fist as he watched them cross into the postapocalyptic world. If Nick and River made it out of this whole mess alive, the one silver lining would be that Sever would be stuck in the game. Nick would gladly pull the plug on him, too. He'd never liked the character, but now he didn't trust him either. Not trusting a virtual character made him feel about as crazy as Kaye—although maybe not quite as homicidal.

But Sever had gone back into that last level with guns blazing, and the asshole had managed to kill everything and then some. Only River had reflexes that good. Nick considered that for a moment. No, River's were probably better.

He rubbed his eyes with the heels of his hands, trying to rid them of the gritty feel. He couldn't see River when she was in the safe houses so he'd snatched a few hours of sleep, curled up next to her comatose body with the defibrillator nearby in case of another emergency, but he'd been afraid to sleep for too long. He didn't know when Kaye would make his next appearance, only that he'd be back.

Nick could hardly wait.

He'd also better be prepared. The fact that he'd interfered already in the game made him break out in a cold sweat. Fortunately—depending on one's point of view—River looked as if she'd never moved. And, too, Kaye had told him to keep her alive. He'd also said Nick was to let him know of any changes, but Nick couldn't be expected to remember everything, could he?

It occurred to him that he might be able to put off a visit from Kaye if he called him first. He hated the thought—it made him sweat even more— but it would be worth it to keep the creepy fuck away.

Kaye answered on the first ring. Nick looked at the clock and realized that it was the middle of the night. That didn't bother him as much as the fact that Kaye apparently never slept. He didn't sound as if he'd been hauled out of bed. He sounded far too alert for that.

"Has she come out of the game?" was Kaye's first demand. Caller ID was a wonderful thing.

"Hello to you, too," Nick said. He was scared shitless of the maniac, but he wasn't about to let him know it.

Kaye laughed softly, and Nick's hands started to tremble. He picked up the wadded ball of paper and bounced it off the monitor screen a few times, trying to distract himself from revisiting those photos of Tanner that Detective Dipwad had shown him. Kaye was waiting for a response.

"No, she hasn't," Nick said. "But she's made it to the last level before she enters the Soul Man's lair. She kicks ass at this part of the game. She sucks when she gets to the end. She's never managed to beat it yet."

"How is she physically?"

"Great. Never better." Too late, he realized what he'd just said. The knot in his stomach turned into a blazing, red-hot coal. River had been in the game for several days. Physically, she should be showing signs of stress. If he weren't so stressed out himself he would have thought of that. "For a woman in a coma."

There was a heartbeat of silence that echoed so loud his ears rang.

"Which is it, Nick?" Kaye asked, his words quiet and cold. "Is she great, never better, or a woman in a coma?"

"You told me to keep her alive," Nick reminded him. He caught the ball of paper and set it on the desk in front of him. He began to uncurl it, his fingers smoothing over the wrinkles. "I'd say thanks to me, she's pretty freaking great for a woman in a coma."

"Vitals?"

Nick rattled them off, fudging the figures, glad he was such a talented liar. To think that his mother used to get mad at him for lying. She'd be proud of him now.

Again, there was that little beat of silence that said so much. Unfortunately, Nick didn't understand the words.

"You wouldn't be lying to me by any chance, would you, Nick?" Kaye asked finally.

Nick raced through the figures he'd quoted in his head, frantic to think if he'd made some mistake. Kaye was a doctor. Nick needed to remember that bullshitting him any more than absolutely necessary was not a good idea.

"Those were off the top of my head. I could double-check them for you if you'd like."

"Not necessary." Nick could hear a shuffling sound in the background, as if Kaye were leafing through papers. "I'm on my way. If she's that close to the end of the game I want to be there to see what happens."

Nick gave his ass a mental boot. He'd taken a bad situation and made it worse by calling Kaye. Then again, how could it possibly be any worse? Sooner or later, Kaye would have shown up anyway. He was going to have to make a decision. Did he try to save River, too, or did he save himself?

"I can tell you what happens," Nick said. "She gets in the level, the Soul Man turns on her, and whatever she throws at him gets thrown right back. She fucked up royally when she programmed that character. She just won't admit it."

"I'll be there in the morning," Kaye said. There was a soft click as Kaye disconnected. Nick set the phone down and cradled his aching head in his arms on the top of the desk.

How was he supposed to get River out of the compound without anyone seeing them? Even the idiot security guard was going to notice him walking out with an unconscious woman draped over his shoulder.

Nick tried to remember when the security guards changed shifts. He'd only ever had much to do with one of them. In fact, it occurred to him that the same security guard always seemed to be on duty whenever the team was working on its game.

He sat in silence for a few moments and digested that information. Then he looked at River, noted she was still the same, and went to the door. At the ell in the hall he peered around the corner to the far end of the hallway, through the glass doors and into the foyer. The same familiar security guard sat at the front desk, slumped back in his chair, his eyes closed.

Nick moved quietly down the hall to the foyer, making as little noise as possible. As he pushed open the glass doors, the tinkling of a small bell sounded and the guard started upright.

When had that door been fitted with a bell?

"Hey," he greeted the guard. "Working late?"

The guard rubbed at his nose and blinked his eyes a few times. "Picking up a few extra shifts," he replied. "I can use the money."

"Couldn't we all?" Nick said agreeably. Looking for easy money was how he'd gotten mixed up in this shit in the first place. Kaye seemed to have found someone else looking for the same thing. "I'm cleaning up after the team. Now that they're gone, I'm finishing what I can and waiting to hear if the investors still want to move forward. We were pretty close to finished."

"Sorry to hear about your friends."

He'd be even sorrier if he'd seen the pictures. Nick couldn't get those out of his head. They were like a big psychedelic slide show on instant replay.

Nick shrugged. "Me, too. Life goes on. Want to order a pizza?"

The guard stretched. "It's too late. Everything's closed." He looked at his watch without enthusiasm. "I should probably be making my rounds."

Nick turned to go back to the gaming room.

"Hey," the guard called after him. Nick stopped, half turning, his hand on the glass door. "Whatever happened to the cute one? The girl with the big eyes and black hair?"

There was something too bland about the way the guard asked the question, and he avoided Nick's eyes. Nick started to sweat again. He and River were in deep shit. No doubt about it.

"No idea. She'll probably turn up eventually," Nick said vaguely.

He went back to the gaming room and straight to the monitor.

CHAPTER **SIXTEEN**

♦

"River?"

Their com-links crackled to life as they stood at the edge of a war-torn world.

Hawk tightened, immediately recognizing the voice.

"Nick!" The pleasure and the relief in River's

words were unmistakable. "I've been so worried about you!"

"The feeling's mutual, babe," came the cheerful response. "What have I told you about playing the game by yourself?"

The cock-sucking bastard. Hawk clenched his fists. He was going to pretend that he hadn't abandoned River in the game.

"I'm fine," River assured him. Hawk glared at her, trying to telegraph to her that she shouldn't tell Nick anything, but she made a face and ignored him. "What's going on? Where is everyone?"

"Food poisoning, or so they claim. I bet it's hangovers. You've seen those losers drink."

Hawk had caught the split second of hesitation before the response, and the over-the-top cheeriness. He could see that River had noticed as well. Worry lines deepened between her brows.

"Nick, I don't bel—" she began, but Nick cut her off.

"Listen up, babe. You and I have a bit of a problem. The investors are on their way to the compound and I don't think I can hold them off any longer."

Hawk had to admire his ability to tell a lie. He might be able to fool most people, and he'd sure as hell been fooling River, but he didn't fool Hawk.

Nick was afraid of these so-called "investors," and Hawk could practically smell the fear.

"And I'm passed out on the gaming platform," River said. She tried to smile, but Hawk could see how worried she was. "I bet I don't look all that great either."

The com-links crackled again. "You look fabulous. I've stripped you naked and propped you up against a wall. I'm taking pictures of you as we speak."

"You'd better not have!" River cried, outraged, and Hawk wondered how she'd ever gotten involved with a man—and he used that term loosely—she clearly suspected had the potential to pull such a juvenile stunt.

If he had, Hawk was going to beat him black and blue. This was one person in River's life he fully intended to meet. He couldn't believe this was the person left responsible for the fate of a Fae.

"He's charming," Hawk said to River. "A real gentleman. I can see why you were attracted to him." Hawk hoped Nick caught his words, and the past tense he'd deliberately used.

River shushed him, flapping her hand and making more faces.

"About these investors," Nick was saying. Hawk went still, straining to catch the words, afraid he'd miss something important. "I need to know, River.

Is there anything . . . odd about you? Can you do things most people can't? Other than the acrobatics in bed, I mean."

Forget about beating him black and blue. Hawk was going to kill him instead.

Color flared in River's cheeks and she avoided Hawk's eyes. Hawk tried to grab for her com-link to keep her from responding, but she was too fast for him.

"Quit being an ass," she said to Nick. "And no, there's nothing odd about me. What kind of question is that?"

"Speaking of asses," Nick replied, "tell Sever to keep his eyes off yours and his mind on the game."

"Tell Nick," Hawk said loudly, "that the next time he wants asses hauled, maybe he should concentrate on hauling yours out of this game." He didn't believe for a second that Nick would actually do so and he wanted River to know it.

"I'm working on it, River," Nick said softly. "Believe me, I am. But things have gotten complicated. There are some . . . safety issues. Something's coming. I can't hold it off any longer. Watch yourself, okay?"

"Nick?" River cried, tapping the com-link, but Nick had signed off and wasn't responding.

"Still think he's being helpful?" Hawk asked.

River looked at him, her clear blue eyes wide and filled with concern. "Something's happened to everyone. Nick's afraid."

So River had picked up on that as well. Maybe she knew Nick better than Hawk gave her credit for. Did she know he was a selfish, self-serving bastard as well?

And she was worrying about her friends when she should be deeply afraid for herself. He could only imagine what they were up against next. Not only was he uneasy about the obstacles River had written into her program, but he was also fearful of the ones the Dark Lord had planted. And now, with Nick warning them that something was coming, and he could no longer hold it off, a growing sense of urgency dwelled in Hawk's gut.

River was in danger, in her world as well as in this one. They had to make it through this level, get to the Dark Lord's lair, and defeat him once and for all. And they had to do it fast.

"We're going to get through this," he said. "When we do, whatever's wrong, we'll do our best to set things right again."

"How are we supposed to do that when you're in your world and I'm in mine?"

"Guardians travel," Hawk reminded her. "You're going to have to trust me. Now let's get moving."

She nodded, but he wasn't certain she believed

him. He'd have to make his promises to her come true.

He examined his clothes and took in the military-issue garb, the sword attached to one leg, dagger on the other, and the big-ass Uzi in his right hand. It could cut a building in half. The corner of his lip turned up. *Nice.*

Then his grin dissolved when he thought about the creatures that could only be killed by an over-sized Uzi.

Even though they'd left daylight behind in the modern world, they met with night in this one. He glanced into the darkened streets, noting the broken buildings, the blood-stained sidewalks, the eerily quiet alleyways, and the not-so-distant howls that carried on the wind. He guessed that this was what River's world would look like after complete devastation.

The Dark Lord would love it. Hawk could only imagine the number of people who'd be willing to sacrifice their souls in order to escape this.

A firefly flew by his head and as he dodged it, River reached out and with her exceptional speed, snatched it from the air, and secured it in her ruck-sack.

His eyebrows shot up and she said, "We need all the energy we can get."

Which meant things were going to come at them

fast and furious. Keeping a firm grip on reality was going to become all the more challenging. Hawk clenched his jaw and fought off a yawn. If he wanted to keep River safe he needed to be wide awake in this round.

He drew a sharp breath and narrowed his eyes as he peered into the darkness. "What are we up against?"

There was a moment of silence as River thought it over. "Only time will tell," she finally admitted.

He shifted on the balls of his feet like a runner waiting for the signal to enter the starting blocks. "You mean you don't know?"

"No. Not really."

Hawk pressed the butt of his hand to his forehead as he cursed under his breath.

"The early levels are fairly consistent because they're for beginners, but as we go deeper, things get more intense and more complicated," she said. "That's when the game really begins to take on a life of its own."

"Due to the software-defined radio system, I take it," he sighed. Technology was great when it worked, but programming randomness into it didn't make it safe.

"This is the best part of the game," River said, her eyes alive. "What sets it apart. Users don't want a repeat of the experience, and this is what enables them to have a new adventure every time." She got quiet for a moment, sadness on her face. "It was going to benefit so many people."

He understood her sadness better than she did herself. As a Fae, it was her way of bringing back a quality of life to those who'd lost the will to live. Her way of giving them the ability to move, and play, even if only through their minds. It might have started off as a gift to her Earth mother, but giving life was as much a part of her nature as breathing. She needed to accept that she was Fae—that being Fae was the most important part of her—but it wouldn't hurt for her to receive some technical guidance from the Guardians as well. With her untutored magic and her raw technical skills, she could as easily prove a danger as a hope to mortal worlds without ever intending it. She could also be a serious danger to herself.

Hawk moved close until their bodies touched. "I'm sorry, River."

She blinked up at him. As her vivid blue eyes locked on his he pulled her tight and brushed her hair from her face.

"I'll never be able to help anyone now," she said.

He dropped a soft kiss on her forehead and put his mouth close to her ear. "Once you accept what you are, and understand your abilities, you'll be able to help people in so many ways. You're going to save worlds. But first we need to save you."

He inched back so he could see her and caught the slight grin of disbelief tugging at the corners of her mouth. She didn't believe him, but she thought it was nice of him to try to cheer her up.

Time and the proper training would prove him right.

She blinked her eyes and instantly returned to gamer mode. "We need to save both of us," she corrected him, and he didn't bother to argue the point.

A dark figure stepped from the shadows and Hawk raised his Uzi and took aim. A full-length, black leather duster billowed around the figure's feet. Something poked from the hem of the duster and swished against the ground. "Looks like the monsters are coming to us."

"Wait." River put her hand over the barrel of the Uzi and lowered it. "It's an innocent. This level is constantly changing, so Nick always meets us at the door and gives us a basic rundown to get us started."

"Nick? As in your Nick?" Hawk brought the barrel of the Uzi up again. Cutting him in half with submachine gun fire would send quite the message to the real Nick.

"He's not *my* Nick."

"So you wrote him into your program just for his pretty-boy looks?" Okay, yes, he was feeling jealous.

He was actually feeling jealous, here. And yes, he knew it was juvenile.

"I didn't write him in. Tanner did. He wanted to piss Nick off." She cast Hawk a quick glance as if trying to gauge his mood. "Tanner might be a little jealous of Nick. I think they're both sleeping with Marsha. Of course, to be fair, I think half the town is sleeping with her, too."

Tanner and Marsha being two of the missing team members, he presumed. And Nick was also sleeping with River. His finger inched toward the trigger guard again.

"Is that why he gave Nick a tail?"

"Tanner's got a sick sense of humor like that."

Or maybe Tanner was a good judge of character.

Virtual Nick stepped up to them and got right to the point. "The Hellhounds are closing in from the east and they're hungry. The demons are restless, and they've set traps all over. The imps are lurking in the buildings, and are causing a great deal of chaos."

Imps were an interesting, if unwelcome, complication. Back in the Dark Lord's lair those two-foot little demon worshippers caused Hawk nothing but trouble, making him walk into walls and fall down holes. They liked seeing him hurt himself even more than they liked inflicting the damage on their own.

River frowned.

"What now?" Hawk asked, tightening his grip on his weapon.

"I don't have imps in my program."

Hawk let loose a frustrated breath. "Since creatures you didn't create only seem to show up in a wrinkle, I'd say we're in for one hell of a ride."

"I honestly don't see any wrinkle," River objected, her forehead furrowed in a thoughtful frown. "Everything looks exactly how I meant it. When we had that big wrinkle and the wichtlein appeared in the primitive world's safe house, everything changed. When we found that swamp, and then the cemetery, I never programmed those either. I don't see anything here out of—"

The ground shook beneath their feet, knocking River off balance and into Hawk's arms. He carried her with him as he fell backward, striking his head and shoulder against one of the crumbling buildings. River went down on one knee and threw an arm over her head as loosened brickwork rained down around them. Hawk caught the crablike movement of an imp as it scurried up the side of the building.

The little monster was tossing bricks at them.

A crack split the sidewalk. Bright streams of white light shot skyward, blinding Hawk for a few seconds, and he squeezed his eyes tightly shut against it.

When the light disappeared and he could see again, River stood on one side of a wide, deep chasm and Hawk stood on the other. Virtual Nick was gone.

Hawk surveyed the damage around them in silence.

"This is different," River admitted. "So are those."

She pointed to a stream of imps swarming up the sidewalk behind him. He half turned, his stomach lurching. One was no real problem. Thirty of the bloodthirsty little ghouls were a bit more of an issue. Their intent was to force him into the chasm.

Hawk raised the Uzi and opened up a spray of bullets. Chunks of monkeylike imp flesh and blood-soaked clumps of matted fur spewed everywhere, the bullets exploding the imps on impact.

Hawk could hear River gagging as the last of the imps splattered against the side of the building after the gunfire ceased.

"Gross," she said, her face crinkling in disgust, then added, "I wish I'd thought to add those."

"I wish you'd thought of a way to cross that canyon," Hawk replied. He eyed the stretch of empty space between them. Tall buildings blocked the way on one side. The chasm stretched as far as the eye could see on the other. It was too wide to jump. He checked their credits.

Then again, maybe not.

"Wait!" River cried as he prepared to put it to the test, crouching slightly and drawing his arms back for leverage. "You can't move backward in the game!"

River was on the side closest to the start of the level. Hawk hadn't thought of that. Hitting a wall of green halfway across would have come as a big surprise. Maybe too big.

"You'll have to come this way," he said reluctantly, not liking to put her in danger. But how was she supposed to get across?

She was scuffing her hand in the dirt and rubble at the foundation of the building as if looking for something.

"Weeds," she said when he asked her. She paused, then cupped something in both her hands. "Here we go."

A long-stemmed dandelion sprouted from between her fingers, and seconds later its giant fluffy head dropped at Hawk's feet. He grabbed the head and pulled, wrapping it around a nearby streetlight to secure it. The stem was thick and tough, and nearly impossible to break when he tested it.

A few minutes later, River was back at his side.

"Let's get moving," Hawk said grimly. "Which way?"

River looked around, frowning. "I have no idea.

We should ask for directions, but I don't see any innocents."

Once again a figure stepped from the shadows, and this time Hawk didn't care what River said, he was fully prepared to shoot Nick.

Except this time it wasn't Nick. Judging by the smell, it could only be the Wizard.

"What is the Wizard doing outside of the safe house?" River whispered. The worried expression on her face was good enough for Hawk. He lifted the Uzi, preparing to fire.

The Wizard smiled at him and the weapon in his hands began to melt like overheated plastic.

"Crisos," Hawk swore, dropping the remains of the Uzi and shaking his stinging palms.

"Patience is a virtue," the Wizard said to him, her thick-lashed green eyes filling with a secret humor. Hawk didn't see the joke. Neither did he like being the brunt of it.

"At least let her speak," River chimed in, sounding annoyed. "She's no threat."

River would have moved closer to the Wizard if Hawk hadn't held her back. He couldn't understand why she accepted the Wizard as an ally so readily, not when the game kept changing.

"Make your way to the old abandoned automobile factory at the corner of Fifth and Ninth," the Wizard advised River. "Go straight there, and hurry."

"What's there?" Hawk challenged, but the Wizard ignored him, all her attention on River.

"Why the automobile factory?" River asked. Her whole body had tensed in a way Hawk didn't like. "Why not the movie theater?"

"Just do it," the Wizard warned.

Hawk made a grab for the Wizard, thinking it was time to shake some real answers from her, but she began to dissolve beneath his fingertips. His glance darted between the disappearing Wizard and River. "What's going on?"

River was frowning. "The Wizard is meant to be cryptic, and she was pretty specific with her help. The automobile factory is an alternate safe house near the first of the level, and we're not supposed to go there unless we run into trouble. The experience is in playing the game, not charging straight to safety." She lifted her eyes to Hawk's. "Unless we're in a lot of immediate danger."

Tension reared inside him and he stepped protectively toward her. "Part of the wrinkle?"

"Maybe." She shifted restlessly on the balls of her feet, lost in thought. "It could be the game rewriting itself."

Hawk caught her unspoken thoughts. Yes, it could be the game.

But no matter what it was, they had to get moving.

CHAPTER **SEVENTEEN**

♦

River examined the shadows skittering about on the rooftops as she moved down the sidewalk, her boots echoing in the blackness of the night. She stole a quick glance at Hawk, then a closer look at the exhaustion lines framing his eyes, noting how deeply those lines ran. How much more of this could he take?

She didn't know how much more she could take either. The real Nick had warned them something was coming. Virtual Nick had warned them the program had been altered, and the Wizard had urged her to head straight for the old automobile factory. Half of her brain was telling her to run, to get to the safe house double time before all hell broke loose. The other half of her brain cautioned her to go slowly, and take extra care because they were playing with life and death.

She ran over her conversation with Nick. The fear she'd heard in his voice had definitely made her stand up and take notice. That, and the fact that he'd lied about the rest of her team. Something had happened to them, of that she was sure, and he wasn't telling her what or why. And just exactly why were the investors coming? They had never shown up at the compound before. What were they after?

Then she thought about Andy's warning and tried to fit it into the puzzle, but couldn't. There had been nothing remotely cryptic about her words. That in itself was cause for alarm.

She needed her full concentration for this level. She gathered her focus and listened to the howls carrying on the wind as she and Hawk came to an intersection. Steam rose around rusted manhole covers, blanketing the surface of the uneven pavement, hiding from sight whatever lurked on the dirty asphalt beneath. River fought off a shiver of fear, slid her hand down her thigh, and tightened her palm over the hilt of her sword. She wished she'd had an Uzi, too, but it would have been awkward for her to carry along with the rucksack, so when they'd designed the level it had been given to Sever.

And now her Wizard had melted it. River's heart picked up speed. That had cost them quite a few credits. If she didn't know better she'd think the Wizard didn't want them to reach the final level, except the Wizard had been programmed to help them.

Hawk looked to his left and then to his right. "Which way?"

She nodded to their left. "That's the fastest route, but in my game it's also the most dangerous."

Hawk shot another glance to the right. "Since you're not the only one running this game, I doubt if this way is any safer."

"Let's go the fastest then," River said, her palms sweating despite the chill in the air, and her legs itching to flee from the fog-shrouded street before whatever was prowling in the filthy sewers could crawl out and catch them.

She shifted her rucksack from one shoulder to the other, ready to run, but Hawk gripped her elbow and pulled her close. "No taking any chances, okay?" he commanded.

"Okay."

His eyes narrowed. "Not even for me."

A burst of coldness seeped into her bones. He didn't know what he was asking of her. She could no more stand by and let harm come to him than he could allow it to her. She nodded anyway.

He released her elbow and positioned himself in front of her. "Let's move."

After only a few steps down the blanketed street, Hawk stopped and twisted around to face her. She could read him easily now, and the blank expression he wore warned her he was hiding something.

"Hold still," he said. "I'm going to carry you for a few blocks."

The ground heaved beneath her feet as if the street were alive. Something slithered over her foot and her stomach dropped. She knew what that had to be. "Oh shit."

Hawk ran an arm around her waist to steady her. "Hang on. They aren't real."

Hysterical now, she pushed him away and began shaking her leg, certain she could feel one of those rats crawling inside her jeans, making its way up her thigh. She felt a set of sharp teeth cut through her flesh. Warm ribbons of blood dripped down her leg, the fresh scent driving the sea of rats around them into a feeding frenzy.

"Oh, God, one just bit me," she cried out, frantically brushing at her leg, but the rat was gone. She grabbed for her sword and began hacking into the swirling mist around her ankles, scared to death another rat would take its place.

Hawk wrested the sword from her fingers, lifted her clear off her feet, and positioned her face close to his. "River, listen to me," he commanded. "You need to keep your focus. The closer we get to the Dark Lord's lair, the more control he seems to have over the game. I'm not positive how he knows about your fear of rats, only that he does, and you need to remember that they can't hurt you unless you let them. Got it?"

She sucked in air. "Okay, I got it. They can't hurt me unless I let them," she repeated.

Without releasing her, Hawk made his way down

the street and she knew she needed to pull herself together. Hawk was tired and in no shape to be hauling her sorry ass around. Not only that, but she'd just wasted a great deal of their remaining credits by swinging her sword. Killing rats wouldn't earn them back.

That realization doused her panic better than cold water. "You can let me down now."

He stopped, uncertain. "You sure?"

"Absolutely."

"The rats are still down there, River," he warned.

She lifted her chin, determined not to be the one who held them back. "I can handle it," she assured him. "They're not real." Already, the throbbing in her leg had eased.

Hawk slowly set her on her feet and under her breath she sang the words, "They're not real," until she had herself semicomposed.

"How far away is this building?" Hawk asked tensely, trying to get her to focus on something else, and she knew he was waiting for her next mental meltdown. He handed her back her sword.

"It's still a fair distance but I know a shortcut," she responded, checking her com-link. "Although now we can't get inside until we gather more energy." She felt her face redden. "Sorry."

Hawk squeezed her arm in sympathy. "Let's get moving. Tell me if it reaches a point where you can't handle it and I'll carry you."

"I'll be fine."

River distracted herself from thinking about what they were walking on by collecting fireflies as they continued down the street toward the shortcut.

Soon the road disappeared behind them and ahead, the sound of rushing water drew her attention. She followed the noise, letting it guide her to a small clearing backed by an old-growth forest.

The hairs on her nape began to prickle.

"Demons," River said tensely. Normally she would have made a run for it rather than face them head on, but thanks to her, they now needed the kills for energy. "The good news is, if we kill enough of them, we'll have no trouble entering the safe house and moving on to the Soul Man's lair." She bit her lip. "The bad news is that they're a bit more of a challenge than they were in the subway."

"Bring them on." Hawk patted his sword, and River rolled her eyes. He was in for a surprise.

So was she.

River's pulse hammered and the com-link let out a bleep. These creatures no longer even remotely resembled the wichtlein she'd created. These were massive, ugly monsters with blood-red skin as hard as steel, and arms and legs like tree trunks, and they swarmed from the shadows of the forest like an angry rogue wave. Hungry, crazed eyes gleamed as the demons closed in on River and Hawk.

She'd never faced demons quite like these before,

but from Hawk's stone-faced, determined expression, it would appear that he had.

"Crisos," he murmured, and she read a caution in his tone that was out of character for him.

She touched his arm and when he turned to her she also saw confusion, and that scared her more than the demons. They both worried about losing their grip on reality, but he'd been the strong one all along and now was not the time for him to lose it.

"Are you with me, Hawk?"

"I'm with you," he said. "But when we're done, we just might wish we were dead."

She remembered the deep purple scars once marring his flesh, and suddenly, she knew. These were the tools the Soul Man had used to try to beat Hawk into submission.

Rage unfurled inside her, exploding like shrapnel. She opened her rucksack, letting loose a brilliant white cloud of the fireflies she'd collected. They flew into the faces of the demons, flitting back and forth, blinding them.

River then drew her sword from its sheath and lifted it high over her head. Energy poured off her body and clouded the air like blackened soot. Wind picked up around them, blowing dirt, twigs, and rocks until the gusts reached hurricane force.

The battle was back in Hawk's eyes, and she smiled at him, knowing just what to do to goad him to action. He would never let her head straight into danger without him.

"Come on," she cried over the howling wind, and pressed forward, dancing away from Hawk's reach so he had little choice but to follow.

In return, the platoon of demons let loose blood-curdling cries and struggled to step forward, but River controlled the wind and it held them immobile. She moved so quickly behind the wind that her hands seemed to blur in front of her face. She struck out, dropping demon after demon, the sound of her com-link dinging as it quickly accumulated credits dimly registering with her. Out of the corner of her eye she saw Hawk, his sword buried deep in the belly of a demon, a happy *fuck you* written all over his face.

As her mind cleared and the wind died down River sucked in air, her heavy breaths cutting through the sudden silence, her heart still beating madly. Even she was amazed at the number of dead and dying demons spreading pools of slippery red blood across the trampled grass.

A touch on her shoulder had her adrenaline pumping again. She spun around, ready for combat.

"Easy, River. I like my insides where they are."

She lowered her sword, noting the spray of stinking blood on both their clothing but glad to hear the humor back in Hawk's voice. She offered an apologetic smile for almost filleting him. "Sorry about that."

His answering smile was slow as he looked past her shoulder at the dead demons. "Remind me never to piss you off."

She was so glad to see that smile, she could have wept. "You mean more than you already do?"

He chuckled and squeezed her shoulder. "Seriously, River. Nice work. I'm not even going to yell at you for doing exactly what I told you not to do."

"I appreciate the self-restraint. I know how hard that is for you." She scrunched up her nose. "To be honest, I have no idea what I did."

"You did what the Fae do," Hawk said. "You reacted. It's instinctive. Fae can calm the winds, quiet the earthquakes, control the fires, and so much more. The Fae are responsible for all aspects of nature and can restore its balance." He looked again at the dead demons, sounding troubled now and trying to make light of it. "You certainly restored balance. I'll give you that. Although you did it in reverse." He rubbed the back of his neck as if realizing his words might have been poorly chosen. "Not that I'm complaining, mind you," he added hastily. "It seemed to work for you."

Some of her pleasure at winning a battle with demons dimmed. If she was Fae, apparently she wasn't a very good one. She wouldn't make a very good

Guardian either. She couldn't control her own game and make it work.

She glanced around, checking for any more signs of danger. The air reeked of blood and rotting demon flesh—in other words, Hellhound bait. Using her pant leg, River wiped the blood off her sword and drove it back into its sheath.

"River." Hawk caught her hand. "You aren't any different from any other Fae. You simply need to learn to control your magic."

"You keep calling it magic," she replied, annoyed. "To me it's energy."

"You can call it whatever you like," Hawk said with a shrug, releasing her hand. "It's still the same thing."

He had a point. If she had energy, then who was she to say that others couldn't have something similar as well?

That gave her something to think about.

Leaving the decaying corpses behind, they walked a leaf-covered footpath that wound along the river. Save for a few birds overhead, and the soft, rain-soaked earth squishing beneath their boots, all was quiet and for that she was grateful. After the demon encounter she needed a moment to regroup and get her mind back in the game. Something other than magic and energy niggled at her thoughts.

"How did you do it, Hawk?" He looked down at

her walking beside him, and she searched his face, thinking about all those months he'd spent as the Soul Man's prisoner. "How did you keep your sanity for so long?"

He rolled one shoulder. "I kept thinking of the bigger picture and how important it was to get home to warn everyone."

"I don't know if I could have done it." She frowned and shot him a cautious glace, the sight of those thick, ugly scars permanently etched in her memories. "Those demons must have done a real number on you."

"They just got what was coming to them." He gave her a sly grin. "And then some."

His obvious enjoyment made River feel better about the way she'd used her energy, even if it had been backward. Besides, her energy was just that—hers. How, or when, she used it would always be up to her.

They came to another small clearing in the path, close to the wide river near a sandbar. The current was strong but without whirls and eddies. A strong swimmer could cross with little difficulty.

She began to strip down.

Hawk ran a hand down his face. "What are you doing?"

She paused, her arms crossed in front of her with her hands on her shirttail. "Getting rid of these smelly clothes. We don't want to be in that water with the scent of blood all over us. Who knows what we'll attract? When we get to the safe house we can cash in a few credits for new clothes if being naked with me bothers you so much." She lifted her eyebrows in teasing challenge. "Being naked with you doesn't bother me."

Hawk didn't take the bait. He glanced out over the horizon to the far side of the river instead. "We have to swim?"

"We have two choices here," she explained. She pointed up, and he followed the direction, taking in the old utility cable that dangled between wood-rotted poles. "We can take the wire, or we swim. Since I know you're not a fan of heights, I assumed you'd choose water over wire."

He gave her another one of his looks, half amused, half resigned, that always made her want to laugh. "I can't believe you included two choices."

"I wrote the river into the program because my mom and I used to love to swim in the river near our house. That's where they found me," she reminded him. "By the river." She peeled off her shirt and tossed it aside. "But not everyone knows how to swim, so I included a second choice."

"You made the second choice pretty unappealing," Hawk replied, eying the rotting poles. "Who did you think those were going to support?"

"If you think that's unappealing, wait until you see what's in the river," she said. Her boots followed the shirt. "You've got to be fast. Ever hear of snapping turtles?"

"Crisos," he said, resigned.

She liked the way he was looking at her, with warmth and a touch of humor in his eyes. It was far different from how he'd looked at her just a few short days ago. A lot of the grimness was gone.

But he still looked tired, and River was afraid for him.

He ran the tips of his fingers down her cheek, then traced the soft swell of her bottom lip. "When a Fae uses magic involving love the magic is strongest by a lake, or a river," he mused. "I wonder if your parents knew that when they named you?"

Her parents had been plain, practical people, firmly rooted in reality. Magic hadn't been a part of their lives, or hers either.

Not until Hawk.

"I think it was a coincidence," she said.

Hawk didn't agree with her, she knew, but he let it drop. He drew his hand back, and River instantly missed the light touch.

As night turned to day, and warm rosy rays of sunlight crept over the horizon and spread across the water's smooth surface, they finished peeling off their clothes.

River strapped her weapons to her naked body, tossed her rucksack over her shoulder, touched her toes to the cold water, and shot Hawk a glance over her shoulder.

"Warm as bathwater," she lied. "Ready?"

"Not yet."

She glanced at the river and then back at him, a hand on one hip. "My hero. Don't tell me you're afraid of water, too?"

"No. But I don't like the unknown, and with the way the program is changing, we don't know what we're up against. I want you to try something for me." He gestured toward the flowing river. "I want you to manipulate the water and create a path for us."

She gave a quick shake of her head. "I can't do that."

"Yes, you can. You're ready for it. You whipped up a hurricane and blasted demons," he pointed out.

"It's not part of the program."

"No. It's part of *you*. Take control of your game."

River glanced at the water, then back at Hawk. He wasn't afraid, she knew that, but they were getting closer and closer to the place he'd been held prisoner and tortured. Swimming the river would take up mental energy he'd need for that final level.

"Okay," she said. For his sake, she'd try. But she didn't have to be happy about it. "What do I do?"

"I want you to dig deep, just like you did when you summoned the wind and fought off those demons."

Standing on the edge of the sandbar, her bare toes buried in mud, River closed her eyes and concentrated, channeling her energy. She clenched her fingers and tightened her whole body as she pictured waves and wind and chaos. Seconds led into minutes as she struggled with the task. After a short while she let loose a frustrated breath, opened one eye, and peered at Hawk.

"It's not working."

"You have to believe in it." He moved close and touched her shoulder. "Believe in yourself and your magic."

She blew out a breath. "I can't. It's impossible."

"Then we'll swim." Hawk squeezed her shoulder, then turned and waded out into the water.

"What are you doing?" she called after him.

"We need to get to the other side, so we'll swim."

He was nothing if not practical. She hadn't been able to do what he asked of her so he was going to do the next best thing.

"Hawk, wait," she said, hating that she'd disappointed him, but it was too late. He was already swimming away.

River stepped forward and dipped her muddy toes into the water, frustration swirling around her. She was just about to dive in and catch up with

Hawk when off in the distance she spotted movement. The hairs on her nape stiffened, a sure sign that Hawk wasn't about to meet with the easily avoided snapping turtles she'd coded.

She narrowed her eyes to get a better look at the danger, needing to know which weapon would be best to take it out. If she couldn't see it, she had no idea how to kill it.

Blood pulsing, she waded farther into the water until it splashed around her waist.

"Hawk, look out!" she shouted, but the rushing current swallowed her warning cries as a long, lizard-like tail shot from the water, curled around Hawk's body, and dragged him under the rapids.

River dove in, desperate to see where he'd gone, but visibility underwater was only a few feet and she was too far away.

She surfaced, water washing over her head, taking in a mouthful and choking on it.

Warmth brewed in her chest as energy raced up her spine and down her arms, stirring the water around her. Waves erupted, spreading until the swells engulfed the entire river.

She widened her arms and lifted the flow of the river into an enormous aqueduct, clearing the river's rocky bed. She found her footing and took off at a run beneath a cascading rainbow of water, colorful droplets showering around her.

Hawk lay motionless on the rocks, his sword in his hand, the long tail that had snagged him streaming blood as the creature slithered back into the river's waters farther upstream.

She dropped to her knees and put her fingers to Hawk's neck to check for a pulse. "Hawk!"

When he didn't answer, she bent forward and began to resuscitate him. She worked his chest, her palm pumping, one, two, three, four, then pressed her mouth to his to give him air.

"You'd better not die on me," she warned, and went back to pumping his heart. "So help me if you do, I'll—"

"You'll what?"

Relief burst through her and she made a noise, a half laugh, half sob, as she dropped her head onto his chest.

Hawk lifted her chin until their eyes met, then glanced around and took in the ceiling of water above them. "Now do you believe me?"

What she believed was that he'd scared the shit out of her. River climbed to her feet and wrung out her hair. "I should have taken your advice."

Hawk stood, too, his head tipped back, eyes that were filled with respect still on the water flowing above them.

"What advice was that?" he asked.

He wasn't paying any attention to her, or the scare

he'd given her. He was far more interested in some stupid trick she could do.

That pissed her off. "To take no chances. I should have let you drown."

Her tone must have warned him. His eyes went to her face, softening in understanding.

"I saw that lizard coming, River." He tapped his sword. "I was prepared. And you were a fair distance away, out of the danger zone." He lowered his voice. "I'd never do anything to put you in danger."

She was still angry with him. "I wish you'd do the same for yourself."

She made a move to leave but he cupped her elbow, spun her around to face him, and pulled her close, anchoring her body to his. His heat and warmth wrapped around her, pushing back the chill of fright that had invaded her body. Dark eyes met hers. He wet his lips and put them close to her mouth.

"Next time you should probably take that advice, because from here on in, I think things are going to get a lot more interesting."

She opened her mouth but her words were lost when he pressed his lips to hers. He kissed her long and deep, indulging in her mouth until her knees wobbled beneath her.

He pulled back and let his glance rake over her nakedness. His eyes widened and she took a step back.

"What is it?"

"Your leg."

River looked down to where the rat's sharp teeth had pierced her skin. She cringed when she saw the red, spiderlike veins spreading to her thigh. "It's a virus. Insects are the only part of the program able to introduce a change into a character. The Soul Man must have planted something similar in the rats."

"How do we heal it?"

"If it's anything like my spider virus," and she fervently hoped it was, "it will go away when we move into the next level. If we don't make it through in time, I lose my life in this level. If the virus was caused by one of my insects, I'd have to start the level over again."

But this virus wasn't caused by an insect, and she had no idea what the effects might be—either on her character, or worse, and the one that truly worried her, on her mind.

She could see in Hawk's eyes that he'd come to a similar conclusion. His mouth settled into a hard line as fat, sparkling droplets of water showered steadily around them.

"Let's go see what your friend Nick has in store for us," he said.

CHAPTER **EIGHTEEN**

♦

The boot to the ribs came as a shock.

"For Christ's sake," Nick complained, shooting upright and rubbing his side. "Can't a guy take a break?"

Kaye was already halfway across the room from the gaming platform, his eyes on the screen.

"If they're better timed," he tossed absently. "You're missing all the action."

Nick tried to shake the sleep from his head. He glanced at his watch, then at River lying warm beside him. He hadn't had nearly enough rest. At least by curling up close to River he'd been able to monitor her somewhat.

"How did you get in?" he asked Kaye, although he already knew. But he didn't want Kaye to know that he knew. He threw off the blanket and rearranged it around River. "This is a secure building."

Kaye didn't bother answering. Instead he asked, "Is she supposed to be able to control water this way?"

"Jesus," Nick breathed, coming up behind Kaye and looking over his shoulder. A huge geyser of water spewed off the riverbed, arced into a shining bridge, and plunged earthward again in a massive waterfall several hundred feet downstream from where it began.

"I take it that means no." Kaye's dry response brought Nick crashing back to reality.

"How do you know River's controlling it?" he said. "The game is programmed to change on its own."

"If she lifts her arms and the water lifts, too, then I'm going to assume she's in control."

Nick decided it was better not to insult the man's intelligence. He had that crazy-ass glow in his eyes that scared the shit out of him.

"Where is she?" he asked, wondering where she'd gotten to. He couldn't see her around the river anywhere, and the monitor was supposed to follow her progression.

"She's underneath it."

It took Nick a second to realize that Kaye meant she was underneath the actual waterfall.

Kaye's eyes narrowed. "Can we see what's happening in there?"

Nick punched a few keys, curious himself as to what was happening, and there she was.

In Sever's arms, buck naked, kissing the bastard. Nick's knuckles turned white. He was going to have a little talk with her about her overactive imagination when this was over.

Assuming he got the chance.

Kaye poked a finger at the monitor. "See this?"

River's bare ass? Yes, he saw it. Anyone who wanted could see it. Then he peered closer and saw what Kaye was really looking at.

Fine red lines, like tiny veins, crept up one of River's thighs toward her hip. Nick zoomed in, and there they were—tiny puncture marks on one calf. She'd been bitten by something.

Something a lot bigger than a mosquito.

"All part of the game," Nick said, hoping like hell he was telling the truth for once. "She programmed a virus to slow down the players. It's spread by bug bites."

Kaye leaned forward, his nose nearly touching the screen. "That's not a bug bite." He turned his head to look at her behind them, lying on the gaming platform. "I wonder if she has those in reality?"

"Of course she doesn't," Nick said. His shoulders started to sweat. "It's all part of the game."

"Still."

Kaye rose from the chair and went to her, looking down at her for a long moment. Short of Nick tackling him to the ground—and it occurred to him to do just that—there was nothing he could do to stop what Kaye did next. Kaye drew back the blanket and slapped River sharply on the face.

"Hey!" Nick said, starting forward in protest, but the cold look Kaye shot him froze him in his tracks.

He wondered wildly what he could use for a weapon. Kaye might be an old man, but Nick would have to kill him. If he left him alive, he'd be running for the rest of his life.

As quick as the thought of killing Kaye occurred to him, what stopped him was the memory of what Kaye had created in that lab that River had tapped into.

Killing Kaye was a death sentence. Better men than Nick had tried. He didn't need something even worse than a werewolf coming after him.

Kaye had so utterly dismissed him as a threat he'd immediately turned back to River and was in the process of lowering her denims so he could get a better look at her leg.

Don't get mad, get even, Nick thought. Someday Kaye was going to get his. And Nick was going to sing and dance while it all went down. Maybe one of his monsters would turn on him.

Sweet.

Visions of Kaye being torn into little pieces distracted him so that at first he didn't see what River's clothes had concealed. Tiny red veins marred the creamy smoothness of her otherwise perfect skin.

◆ ◆

When they reached the rocky embankment on the other side Hawk shook off a wave of exhaustion, climbed the rocks, and held his arm out to River. She took the hand he offered and let him pull her from the slippery riverbed.

He was anxious to get through the level before that virus eating up River's leg spread even farther. What had she been thinking to write a virus into the program in the first place?

Hawk surveyed the somewhat familiar setting on this side of the river.

They were back in her world, but it was drastically different from the one they'd left behind. Gone was the sun, eclipsed by an ash-clogged sky. War-torn streets bustled with innocents resembling the homeless—their clothes, what little they wore, were ragged and torn. No one noticed his and River's nudity. Or if they did, she hadn't programmed them to care.

Something small and furtive flashed out of the corner of his eye. He turned in time to see an imp scurry past, snickering like the evil little hellion it was. Irritated enough to want some revenge and figuring to earn a few credits, Hawk reached for his gun, but River touched his arm to stop him.

He put his mouth close to her ear. "What's going on?"

"The rooftops," she murmured. "The demons are organized and they're trying to draw us out of the crowd."

"With imps?"

"I didn't add imps to my game. That means they've been planted on purpose. They have to be from the Soul Man's program, and they're something you hate. Just don't react, and follow me. It's our reactions that will draw attention to us. The building is just up ahead."

Hawk followed her glance and spotted the dilapidated old brick building at the end of the street. Two large windows leered at them from above a sealed garage door. Hawk gauged the distance, noting that the factory was some fifty feet away. Close, but still far enough out of reach that a demon attack was inevitable.

"Oh," River said as an afterthought. "Don't let any of these innocents get too close to you, and whatever you do, don't try to kill them."

A loud purr sounded at Hawk's feet and he glanced down to see one of River's freaking Tabinese. The Dark Lord must have given up on the rats and wanted to try something different to get a reaction from her.

Too bad. River's reaction to rats tended to be something spectacular.

When he felt her start beside him, he touched her shoulder in warning.

"It's another trap," she whispered, not bothering to do more than glance down although he saw her throat work a couple of times. "It doesn't belong in this level."

She hadn't fallen for it, and thank the gods neither had he, but it worried Hawk that the Dark Lord seemed to understand a lot more about them than they realized. Sooner or later, however, the attempts to draw them out were going to become a lot less subtle.

No sooner had that thought crossed his mind than a bolt of lightning struck from above, hitting a lamp-post beside them. Static electricity coursed through his body, lifting the hairs on his limbs. Startled, Hawk and River stopped in their tracks.

As if provoked into action by the sudden burst of energy, the crowd of innocents began bumping against them, and instinctively Hawk pushed them back, wanting to protect River. A flurry of hands reached out to them, snatching at their weapons and her rucksack. Hawk raised his gun, but River stopped him.

"Don't. We can't waste credits."

"I don't consider this a waste, River. They're drawing attention to us."

River grabbed her rucksack off her back and began swinging it. From Hawk's peripheral vision he spotted the demons, triumphant grins of discovery turning up the corners of their ugly faces as they zeroed in on them. One by one the demons jumped from the rooftops, losing themselves in the crowd.

Hawk grabbed River's hand and pulled his sword

from its sheath. "Run!" he yelled, and used the cold steel edge to slice his way through the crowd. He stole a glance over his shoulder.

The innocents he'd killed had begun to morph into wichtlein.

"Crisos," he swore. Could things be any more fucked up?

"I told you not to kill them," River said.

Hawk dodged a wichtlein that dove for his head and countered, "You could have told me why."

Their feet pounded on the pavement as they ran, and Hawk, feeling the hot stench of demon closing in on them, feared they weren't going to make it to the building in time.

"Which weapon to get in?" he bit out as they approached the garage door.

"I'm on it." River drew her sword, but it wasn't to enter the safe house, it was to cut the head off the demon that materialized in front of them. It fell with two distinct thuds, its head and its body, and River jumped over the twitching remains. A second later she drove her sword into the slot above the numbered keypad and the garage door creaked open. They bolted inside.

Hawk gave a quick scan of the factory floor and checked his ammunition.

"We need to get dressed and recharge our weapons before moving on."

She tipped her head to the side. "Upstairs."

Hawk stalked across the cold cement floor and pulled open the heavy metal door leading upstairs. Guiding the way, he bolted upward. River followed, taking the steps two at time. When they reached the upper level Hawk stepped across the threshold first, registering what appeared to be an employee lunchroom.

Although the world outside was ravaged by war, River had made this safe house somewhat more pleasant. A rectangular table sat in the center of the room, the chairs pushed in and neatly lined up. Floral sofas skirted one wall, facing a polished blue countertop complete with a coffeemaker, sink, and microwave. At the end of the counter sat a refrigerator, its door slightly ajar, most likely knocked loose from the blasts outside.

As River walked to a console, disguised as a paper towel dispenser, on the wall beside the sink and jammed in her sword, Hawk moved to the window to glance out. The street below was silent. Beyond was a thick wall of green. Because they were armed with enough credits, there was no going back now. They could only go forward. And forward meant one place and one place only.

To the Dark Lord's lair.

◆ ◆

"I want inside that safe house," Kaye said.

He was leaning intently into the screen, blocking Nick's view.

"If I could get inside a safe house don't you think I'd have done so by now?" Nick said.

Kaye looked up at him, then lifted the back of his jacket to show the gun holstered at his hip. "You have ten minutes to get me inside. After that, I start blowing off the little gamer's toes, one by one."

Nick wondered how throwing up in front of Kaye would be received. Crapping himself probably wouldn't go over any better. "I can't get you inside," he said, thinking fast. "I'm not that good. River is the software engineer. But I can get you audio through the com-link."

It wasn't going to be good enough. Nick could see it in those freaky, maniac eyes.

I'm sorry, babe. Not even for River would Nick risk the chance of those lab experiments being unleashed on him. Losing a few toes to gunfire wouldn't be half so bad.

Kaye dropped his jacket back into place. "Get me the audio." Before Nick could feel even a flicker of relief, he added, "Then get them out of that building. And here's how I want you to do it."

♦ ♦

The feather-light touch on his shoulder had Hawk turning around. River stood before him, fully dressed now. Looking slightly worn and weary, she folded her sleeves to her elbows then held a pair of fatigues out to him. When he reached for them, he noticed the spiderlike veins running toward her fingertips. The virus was spreading. Quickly.

A worried look danced in her eyes when they met his, but all she said was, "You'd better get ready."

"Thanks." He unhooked all his weaponry, then shook out the pants and hastily climbed into them. The shirt and jacket followed. He dropped all his weapons, the metal now somewhat flimsy and bendable in his hands, onto the table to begin the refueling session.

He looked around to pinpoint their energy source and spotted weed-choked pots and yellow star thistles, hearty beneath the ash-coated window. River had a Fae's take on life. Weeds could be beautiful as well as useful, and were often underrated. The Fae valued them equally. These would most likely be the plants hardiest enough to withstand the destruction of a postapocalyptic world.

Hawk had seen other worlds devastated by war. The ashes and dust of ruin drifted upward into the planet's atmosphere, filtering its sun's rays for decades, even centuries, making life all but impossible for plants that thrived in the light. More people starved to death after those wars than were killed in the wars themselves.

Silence settled in, both of them lost in their own

thoughts as they walked the room and touched their weapons to the plants.

Once complete, he turned to River. His heart pounded erratically against his chest as he pulled her close. This might be the last chance he got to hold her. Her virtual world was about to end. Even if they survived the Dark Lord's prison, even if he found her again—and those were pretty big "ifs"—in the real world their relationship would have to change.

River was Fae. He was a Guardian.

Whatever she'd been about to say fell off when she caught the look in his eyes.

His throat worked. Rattled, his voice came out gruffer than he'd intended. "I need for you to know something. It's been a long time since I've truly felt alive. Not since I lost my wife and daughter. No matter what comes next, I want you to know how much I value the life you've brought back to me."

River's hands went to his face, and unbidden, before he could stop it, a memory of his daughter popped into his thoughts. She'd been smiling that final morning before she'd gone off with her mother, excited at the prospect of her first transportation, all skinny legs, rosy cheeks, and curly dark hair. She looked so much like him, and yet was as beautiful as her mother.

Or she would have been if she'd gotten the chance to grow up.

"Thank you," River whispered, pulling him back to the moment, and he realized she was thanking him for the memory he'd just shared with her.

Sharing it hadn't hurt nearly as much as examining it alone.

His hungry gaze slid over her and then settled on her face. His throat dried as the air around them charged. He touched her hair, lazily running the strands between his fingers. He put his mouth close to hers, his voice soft and full of every conflicting emotion he had when he confessed, "I can't seem to resist you."

River moaned, and ran her fingers through his hair, holding his mouth to hers. He inhaled her scent, slipping his tongue into her mouth and kissing her so deeply he could actually feel it inside him. Beginning in the center of his chest warmth blew through him and moved onward and outward as their souls intertwined. He absorbed a part of her, her body trembling against his, the soft sounds from her lips driving him mad. Hunger consumed him, a need unlike anything he'd ever felt before burning his blood. The peppery scent of Fae magic perfumed the air.

When she gasped Hawk inched back, but the look on her face told him she'd felt the effects of her magic every bit as much as he had.

He rested his forehead on hers, trying hard to steady his breathing. He and River had been through a lot together in a short time. She was going to be impossible for him to give up. It would be the same, if not worse, than losing his wife and daughter all over again.

But the worst thing of all would be in his losing her soul to a Dark Lord. Now that he'd touched it, he knew precisely why it was so precious. Losing it—losing *River*—would destroy him.

He brushed his thumb over her cheek. "We need a plan."

She nodded. "I've been giving it some thought. If I'm Fae like you say, and my soul is reborn, then doesn't that in a sense make me an immortal? If only an immortal can kill an immortal, shouldn't I be able to kill him?"

She hadn't been able to do so in the past, and he didn't like the idea of her trying it again. If anything, he wanted to keep her as far away from the Dark Lord as possible. He frowned. "How did you program killing him in the game?"

"I gather energy throughout the level, then use the credits to call on lightning from a chimney in one of the fireplaces. When my sword is fully charged, I drive it into his heart. Or I'm supposed to. So far I haven't had much luck." She crinkled her nose. "But if he can't be killed, then the game doesn't work. And if the game doesn't work, he has no claim on my soul. Right?"

"Wait a second," Hawk said, cold terror seeping through his insides and turning his lungs to ice. He was gripping her arms too tightly and she tried to shrug him off, but he didn't let go. "What exactly does it take for your game to work?"

She was looking at him as if he were mad. "Either the gamer or the Soul Man has to be defeated in the final level. If the gamer dies, they surrender their soul."

"Crisos." Hawk thought he might be ill. "And you are the gamer, because Sever is simply a character in the program." River was so anxious for her game to work that she hadn't thought this through. She'd accepted the Dark Lord's help. She'd traded her soul. The Dark Lord couldn't collect her soul if he were dead. Therefore, the only way River could have traded her soul for the game to work was for her to lose at her own game.

"I'm going to win," River was saying.

"Don't you see?" Hawk loosened his grip, trying to steady his shaking hands. They'd almost made a terrible, terrible mistake. "You can't win. It's not possible. You already offered him your soul. If you fight him, you lose."

Understanding, then shock, crossed her face. "He's been toying with us. He's been driving us to the safe houses to get us to the final level faster."

Hawk didn't like the defeat he read in her eyes.

They weren't finished yet, and the Dark Lord hadn't won. "Your game has to fail," he said. "And since his program and your game overlap in that final level, if it does, his program will fail as well." He took a moment to think things through. "The electrical charge from a sword might not be enough to kill him, but maybe it can destroy his program. No program, no Dark Lord." He pressed his lips to her forehead. "Or at least, no program for him to control. He'll still be contained on the planet by Fae magic, but without some sort of reality, virtual or otherwise, to give him substance, he'll be nothing more than a consciousness."

She inched back, doubtful. "Just like that?"

"Just like that. You have software running software," he reminded her. "He must, as well. That's got to be how you've both crossed programs." He lifted his wrist to show her the com-link. "When I take your micromachine out of this com-link, I disappear. If we find his console, and destroy its signal, the same thing should happen to him."

"I've been in that lair dozens of times," River objected. "I've searched every corner."

Hawk's mind raced. "You've searched the level you programmed, but remember, he has a program as well. That's what he's using to manipulate your game. By destroying his program, we ruin the game." He didn't want to take River into the final level, but he didn't see that he had any choice. "I'll keep the Dark Lord busy while you look for anything you didn't build into your game, or that looks out of place. He'd keep his console close to him. Once you find it, drive your charged sword into it and see what happens."

He tried to think of anything the Dark Lord kept nearby, some clue to help her search, but his mind came up blank. He had to be missing something and he couldn't figure out what it might be.

"It's worth a try. Maybe we'll get lucky and it'll work," River said. The gamer look was back on her face, the one that always scared the shit out of him because it meant she was going to dive in headfirst without testing the waters.

"Maybe, or maybe nothing can kill him," Hawk warned her, wanting her to be careful. "Which is why he was put in a virtual prison in the first place and contained with Fae magic."

River shrugged, gripped the back of his shirt, and leaned into him to plant a kiss on the corner of his mouth. "Or maybe no one knew how to kill him and so they put him in prison while they were trying to figure it out. But they got distracted by other things." She gave him a small, wistful smile. "I really want for my game to work. But I want it to work because I made it happen, not because someone else did."

Hawk rubbed the top of her head. "You know you're crazy, right?"

She laughed, which was what he'd intended, then her face grew thoughtful. "Everything has a beginning. Have you ever wondered where he came from in the first place?"

"I've done nothing but wonder since I realized what he is," Hawk said. "I won't know those answers until I get back to my world and talk to my bosses. They might not know anything either. He's become a children's fairy tale to us, nothing more."

They clung to each other, both unwilling to break the intimate contact. Hawk dipped his head lower and spotted the red veins on her neck now. The virus was climbing higher, surfacing along the line of her jaw. Fear erupted inside him again and he worked hard to hide it. Not wanting to alarm her, he swallowed the knot in his throat and whispered, "We'd better get a move on."

"Okay, let's—" River stopped, groping for her rucksack as if suddenly remembering something. "The fireflies," she said, answering his unasked question. "How many are left? We need all the energy we can get."

She lifted the flap, then dropped the bag and jumped back as if stung. Hundreds of spiders crawled from the fallen bag and spread out over the floor.

Hawk started to stomp on them but there were

too many, and they were too fast, peppering the walls and skittering around the room like hungry locusts.

"Stop it," River cried. "You're making it worse." She stood still, letting them crawl over her feet, and they immediately lost interest in her. Hawk did the same, and the wave of spiders parted and swarmed around them.

River looked at Hawk, worry in her eyes. "Fireflies don't morph into spiders."

"Maybe Nick's rewriting the code," Hawk suggested.

"Nick wouldn't do that. Spiders might hurt us."

Before Hawk could voice his opinion on that, the floor at his feet began to vibrate and crack.

"Not again," he bellowed, bracing himself.

River's com-link chimed and her eyes widened.

"River? Babe, tell me. What's going on?"

"Nick," she cried out and leaned against the brick wall behind her. "What's happening? What are the spiders for?"

"What spiders?"

River waved her hand around wildly. "*These* spiders. Can't you see them?"

"No. I can't."

He was telling the truth for once. Hawk could hear the underlying edge in the little shit's voice. He was scared, no doubt about it.

"You're not rewriting the code?"

Instead of answering her he said, "I need you to listen carefully, River. I need you to do something."

"Why should we trust you?" Hawk cut in, anger coiling through him as the floor split down the center, widening, once again separating him from River. Nick had to be rewriting code, and River knew it. It was the only way he could get into a safe house. Software running software or not, there were still areas in the game she'd protected from it.

"Look around, Sever," Nick shot back. "Right now I'm the only hope you got."

That made him feel good.

"What do you want me to do?" River asked, waving a hand at Hawk to shut him up.

"Look for a brick marked with an 'X' in the outer wall near the window."

River spun around, scanning the wall, her fingertips flying over the rough surface. "Found it. Now what?"

"Work it free from the wall, then pull it out."

She cast a glance over her shoulder, hesitating. "Hawk?"

"What are you asking him for?" Nick said, disgust in his voice. "He's the beefcake, babe. You're the brains."

She ignored Nick, keeping her focus trained on Hawk, and Hawk didn't know what to tell her. Something was wrong. He and River had been separated

again, so there was a good chance that whatever Nick
was planning, he wasn't planning to harm them both.
If Nick meant to harm only one of them, chances were
especially good he was gunning for Hawk.

Hawk gave a curt nod, telling River to go ahead,
and in a calm voice that contradicted the storm in
his stomach at taking a gamble with her life, he said,
"But protect yourself, no matter what."

River proceeded to scratch away at the mortar
with her fingernail until she could free a brick. As
particles of lime and sand trickled to the floor, she
worried the brick until she had it free.

She raised it in triumph, opening her mouth to
call something to Hawk, but the words went unspoken. The entire wall collapsed, dust and debris clouding the air, tilting the world on its axis.

The floor heaved beneath him and Hawk lost his
footing. He fell into the hole, scrabbling with his
fingers to find something solid to grasp onto, unable
to see what had happened to River and panicked
by that. Chunks of broken brick and mortar rained
around him, smashing off his body with enough
force to crack bones.

Adrenaline pumped through his veins as he fell.
If he hit the ground, would the shock kill him instantly? Or was that only in dreams?

Before he could find out, two warm, familiar arms
wrapped around him. In the next instant he was lying
on the pavement outside the wreckage of the building,

River beneath him. Something in his wrist snapped as he shifted to adjust his body weight to keep from crushing her. Billows of debris settled around them.

Concern hit him first as he checked her for injuries. Save for the virus now creeping up her neck, she looked to be all in one piece.

"Are you okay?" he asked her.

"Yes."

It took him a few seconds to figure out what she'd done to rescue him. When he did, anger nipped at the heels of his concern. She had jumped—transported herself—without any instruction or idea of what she was doing. She might have been killed.

He wanted to shake her, but as angry as he was, the anger was mostly with himself. No matter how hard he tried he couldn't seem to keep her safe.

And he was going to take her into the Dark Lord's lair.

"I told you to protect yourself," he said, fighting for calm through the red haze of his kindling anger. "Do you have any idea what you just did? Do you have any idea how dangerous that was?"

"No. I don't have any idea what I just did," she shot back. "All I know is that I didn't want you to get hurt. I wasn't thinking about anything else." She got quiet. He could see the wheels turning in her head. "Wait. If I did exactly what Nick told me, why would that building collapse?"

As much as Hawk disliked Nick, he hated hurting River even more. From what little she'd told him about herself, he knew she valued her friendships very much because they were few and far between. The truth of what Nick had done was going to hurt her, but if Hawk could make her see the truth, at least it might keep her alive.

"He told you to pull it because he's testing you," Hawk said. "Fae react in the face of danger, and that's exactly what you did. He's not your friend, River. Something's wrong in your world, and Nick's up to his ass in it."

She looked at the dark, cheerless sky, her brow furrowed, and in a low tone she said, "Nick must have been who Andy was warning me about back at the safe house."

Hawk didn't like what he was hearing. "What are you talking about? What did she say?"

Guilt crept into River's eyes. "Nothing, really. Just that I needed to be careful who I trusted with my soul."

"You call that nothing?" Hawk bit the inside of his mouth, briefly pinching his eyes shut. "Why didn't you tell me?"

"I just . . ." She made a face and shrugged.

She didn't trust him. Son of a bitch. After everything they'd been through, Nick, the bastard, rated higher with her.

Damn right, the truth hurt.

He slapped his palms to the concrete on either side of her, then pushed himself to his feet. Clouds of settling dust from the collapsed building rolled low across the sky like a carpet of fog, blanketing the city for as far as the eye could see.

The demons would be back.

"We have to move," Hawk said, taking River's hand and pulling her to her feet. She squeezed his fingers, sending him a silent apology. He wasn't going to think about that right now. They had more immediate problems to worry about.

But another thing he wanted to think about later, when he had the time to consider its ramifications, was what it meant that River had not only successfully transported herself from that collapsing building, she'd transported Hawk as well.

CHAPTER **NINETEEN**

"She jumped," Kaye breathed in satisfaction.

To the best of Nick's knowledge, it was the closest Dr. Frankenstein had ever come to expressing excitement. Yes, River had jumped. Out of the frying pan, into the fire. Wasn't that the expression?

"What's the big deal?" Nick asked, truly bewildered by Kaye's reaction. "It's a game. She can do all sorts of freaky, death-defying things in it."

"The 'big deal,' as you call it, is that River Weston is what I've been looking for all these years." Kaye whirled in the chair to look at River where she lay, unconscious and unaware of the very bad turn her life was about to take. "She can control things you couldn't even begin to imagine."

If it meant imagining more than the things he'd already seen in Kaye's creepy lab, Nick was okay with the deficiency. But Jesus, he hated to think about the things Kaye would likely be doing to River when he got her there.

And that she was about to end up as some lab experiment, Nick did not doubt.

Kaye pushed away from the monitor and gathered his cell phone and the jacket he'd discarded. "Keep her in the game for a little while longer," he said. "I need to prepare a few things for her return." He chuckled, and the sound made Nick shiver in spite of his best intentions not to show fear. "Little Miss Fae won't get the chance to jump from this reality. I've found a new drug that should see to that."

He walked to the door, and if there was any jumping going on, Nick could have jumped for joy. Kaye paused with his hand on the doorknob.

"She'd better be here when I return," he said softly.

"She hasn't moved in three or four days," Nick replied. He kept his hands steady on the arms of his chair. "I doubt very much if she'd be able to stand, let alone jump around."

Kaye opened the door. "Don't fuck with me, Nick. I'm warning you. I want her, and if she's gone, I'll find you both. When I do, I can make you beg for mercy for days on end." He smiled. "And then I can make you wish you were dead."

Nick stared at the closed door for a long time.

He was tempted to walk away. River was as good as dead and there was nothing he could do about it. She was the real prize Kaye was after. Nick was nothing. A nobody.

But Nick couldn't get past something Kaye had said. Kaye thought River could transport herself in real life, just as she'd done in the game. And in the game, she'd taken Sever with her.

If he could get River out of the game and convince her of the danger, could she also be convinced to transport the both of them to somewhere Kaye wouldn't be able to find them?

He turned back to the monitor. River and Sever were standing in front of the ruins of the former safe house, flanked by a thick wall of green. They had nowhere to go now but into the Soul Man's lair.

Nick rested his chin on his hands and pondered

his options. Kaye had said he wanted River here when he returned. He'd said nothing about wanting Nick.

So, did Nick get River out of the game and hope she could—or would—do everything Kaye thought she could do?

Or did he run and leave River to fend for herself?

♦ ♦

The ruins of the safe house were gone now, replaced by a wall of green.

Hawk brushed dust and debris from his clothes, then lifted his eyes upward and sniffed at the air. A storm was brewing. The wind picked up speed and whipped around them, ruffling their clothes and blowing River's hair across her face. "Where's the door to the final level?"

"Look," River said, pointing.

Hawk glanced over his shoulder. The building might be gone but two doors remained standing, a few spiders clinging to the frames. One door would lead to the Dark Lord.

Outside the second door stood River's Wizard. She waved them over, her long gown billowing in the breeze.

"River, hurry," she called, her voice carrying on the wind.

The Wizard was again standing on the wrong side of her door, in the level of the game, and they

had no choice but to approach her. There was nowhere else for them to go. Hawk prayed the woman
with the mystical green eyes wasn't about to spew
more cryptic shit, but he doubted very much if his
prayer would be answered.

"This way, River." The Wizard gestured toward
the door leading to the Dark Lord. "Watch yourself,
and choose your weapons carefully. From the spiritual world, practice the principle."

River got quiet for a moment, and Hawk could
almost hear her brain spinning. A second later, her
eyes widened. "She's talking about the spiritual principle." When Hawk raised a questioning brow, she
explained it in terms he'd understand. "GIGO, in
computer lingo."

Hawk knew what that meant. *Garbage in, garbage out.*

"What you put out comes back threefold," the
Wizard stated.

River checked her weapons. "Which weapon
should I use carefully?" she asked, almost frantic.

"The one inside you." The Wizard placed her hand
over her heart and in a soft tone intoned, "The one no
one can see."

"Enough of this," Hawk said. "She's talking garbage, all right." He kept his sword carefully out of
her reach. He didn't want her to melt it on him. He
was going to need it.

The Wizard's green eyes lit on him and for the first time, Hawk felt the full touch of her magic. It flowed over and through him, reaching deep into his soul in a way the Dark Lord had never managed. Only River had been able to do so.

It was creepy as hell, but on the other hand Hawk didn't feel threatened by it. If nothing else, it calmed him and helped force his tired mind to focus.

"Patience, Guardian. Stay strong. Remember what is important."

Hawk had so many important things to remember, he couldn't keep them straight. Of them all, River was the only one that truly mattered to him anymore.

River reached for his hand.

"Ready?" she asked, and he nodded.

They stepped through the door that led to the final level, and back into the Dark Lord's sanctuary. Hawk was as ready as he'd ever be for that. As the door creaked closed behind them, Hawk finally thought to wonder.

How did River's Wizard know to call him Guardian?

◆ ◆

The door to the Soul Man's lair slammed shut and River tried desperately to quiet her thumping heart.

Hawk's presence beside her gave her a measure of comfort and she pressed closer to him, thankful that he wasn't about to stand by passively waiting for instructions the way she'd programmed Sever to do.

Yes, she was scared. Never before had she had so much to lose.

Cold air stroked her face and a fine shiver ran down her spine. Her denim-clad legs brushed against each other, and the slight sound of the fabric echoed off the walls.

She looked at Hawk. They exchanged a silent message, both knowing what they had to do. Hawk had the harder of the two jobs—to distract the Soul Man while she searched for the console. Exhaustion etched lines in his face that hadn't been there two days ago. The Wizard had known he was weakening and River hadn't wanted to see. The Wizard had forced her to do so.

The room they were entering was familiar to River, and yet somehow not. Their footsteps rang on the polished granite slab that carried them down the center of the long medieval-styled hall, with its low ceiling and tunnel of carefully pillared archways. The deep, smoke-blackened fireplaces lining the outer walls were unchanged.

A sense of déjà vu hit River hard. She'd been here and done this before. Except this time would be the last, and the outcome would be final.

The Soul Man stepped into the mouth of the hall, his black robe billowing around his long legs, and instantly, the peppery scent of sage overwhelmed her. The spice was similar to hers, but yet different. Hawk's face turned to stone, and it was then that she truly understood the level of his mistrust for her Wizard, because her Wizard and Hawk's Dark Lord gave off the same scent.

But River's Wizard was crafted from everything she knew to be true of Andy, and Andy was someone River trusted more than anyone except Hawk.

And Hawk didn't trust the Wizard.

Bony fingers stretched out to her, and the Soul Man crooked his fingers to draw her closer. "Welcome, girl."

The Soul Man's awful mouth twisted into a grotesque smile that was far from welcoming, and Hawk stepped protectively between them.

Think, River.

She'd never properly explored the fireplaces. River ducked into the one where she called on the lightning to charge her sword. As she did so, a rumble of displeasure rolled from the far end of the hall. Satisfaction washed through her. The Soul Man hadn't expected that. He'd expected her to try to finish the game quickly, as she'd done every other time she'd faced him, because always before she'd had too little time.

Not that she had a whole lot of it now. She only had what Hawk was attempting to buy for her.

She tossed her rucksack behind the blackened andirons and examined the inner walls of the fireplace.

She'd paid little attention to it in the past. It was a funnel for lightning to charge her sword.

The walls concealed nothing she could see. She looked up, then looked again. The fireplace had a flue.

River started to climb the jagged, interior crocks. As bright light flared in the hallway, and a cluster of fireballs lit the hearth beneath her feet, she shimmied upward as fast as she could. When she reached the top she climbed out.

Above her burned a brilliant red sun. In the far-off distance, in a dark, angry sky, masses of storm clouds were brewing. Thunder rumbled from deep within them, and River sat on the top of a lightning rod.

What lay around her, however, made her forget any approaching danger. An expansive domed grid encompassed the Soul Man's program. More than likely it encompassed the entire world. Never, not in her wildest imaginings, could she have created something so massive and complex.

If she hadn't believed Hawk about the prison program already, this would have confirmed it for her.

She looked through the grid straight into the Soul Man's lair, and she caught her breath in amazement. Every object in the room, including Hawk and the Soul Man, was nothing more than streams of code. Some flashed green while others, those on the brink of a failure, flashed red.

She inspected the strings of code for a flaw she could use, a glitch of some sort, and noticed the black holes—spots where the program had completely failed.

Returning her attention to the room below she watched the two coded figures fight with their swords, metal ringing against metal, sounding for all the world as if the battle were real. To them it was, and she had to help Hawk.

The clouds swarmed closer, red and roiling, the rumble of thunder moving in tandem with them. Sitting on the peak of the chimney was no longer safe, not even for a virtual character.

She peered into the room through the grid, searching for any sign of the Soul Man's main console. Strings of numbers and letters paraded along the outer walls, all leading to one main column near the Soul Man's throne. It was somewhere nearby. She crawled onto the roof of the grid dome on her hands and knees until she spotted another black hole just off to her right.

That was her entrance back into the game.

◆ ◆

Hawk held his sword steady, widening his legs as he met the Dark Lord's cold, dead eyes.

He'd been waiting long months for this moment. If not for River, he'd gladly do this for himself. He might not be able to defeat the Dark Lord, but he could inflict a little pain of his own.

"It seems you have a soft spot for my latest pet," the Dark Lord said.

"I know what you're after," Hawk replied. He listened carefully for any movement behind him, and watched for it from the corners of his eyes.

The Dark Lord's eyes narrowed. "I'm after you, Guardian. It's always been about you."

"What you want is to escape from a prison you more than deserve."

"Isn't that what you want as well? To escape from here and return to your body? Or better yet, maybe you'd prefer to be reunited with your family. I can make that happen."

The Dark Lord waved an arm, gesturing to the crucible filled with seeing stones, but Hawk didn't dare take his eyes off the bastard for a second.

"Daddy, come with us."

Hawk's throat dried, nausea welling inside him. *Crisos, no.* Tell him the Dark Lord hadn't somehow captured his daughter's soul.

He turned, unable to help himself, and everything around him went fuzzy. Standing before the crucible was his daughter, dark eyes glistening with laughter, one hand reaching out to him. Exactly the way he remembered her on the last day of her life.

"Come, Daddy." Her other small hand was secured in the palm of her mother's. *His wife*. When their gazes collided, his ears began drumming and his head ached, the pain radiating to his shoulders and down his arms. With the way his heart was beating against his chest he was certain it was about to erupt. Every emotion he'd bottled up came rushing to the surface, and Hawk searched his mind for some explanation.

How? How had the Dark Lord known? Hawk had never let those thoughts surface, not the whole time he'd been trapped in the Dark Lord's virtual prison, for fear the Dark Lord would use them against him.

But he'd shared those memories with River when they were in the last safe house.

He turned back to the Dark Lord. "You couldn't have known."

The Dark Lord's grin widened. "It seems you and my pet have been sharing your secrets."

Hawk gritted his teeth. He was dead tired on his feet, and so damned burnt out that he couldn't take any more. Not this.

Warm, peppery sage filled his senses, the fragrance sweet and aromatic. It wasn't the Dark Lord's magic he smelled, it was River's. She was getting closer to them and as she did, she was drawing on her powers, summoning lightning to charge her sword.

As rumbles of thunder sounded in the distance and electricity crackled in the air, the Dark Lord widened his hands, closed his eyes, and drew in a deep breath.

Hawk couldn't take his eyes off him. *Son of a bitch.* The bastard was drawing strength from River's magic and using it against her. No wonder she could never defeat him. He recalled the Wizard's warning to River to use the weapon inside her carefully.

The Wizard spouted that cryptic shit to keep the Dark Lord from figuring her words out, not River. That was why she'd been so direct about the automobile factory. It hadn't mattered to the Dark Lord if they got to a safe house.

But if the danger hadn't been from the Dark Lord, why had the Wizard sounded so urgent?

"Daddy," his daughter said again, drawing him back to the moment. Her voice filled with disappointment. "Why won't you come with us?"

As equal measures of exhaustion and rage pulled at him it became harder and harder to separate what was real and what wasn't, but real or not, he didn't want his daughter connected with this place.

He turned on the Dark Lord, the rage erupting inside him, and readied his sword just as River dropped from the ceiling and materialized behind the Dark Lord. With her own sword raised high, now partially charged, Hawk saw she was about to draw on more lightning.

He needed to stop her. It wasn't lightning she was drawing on, it was magic.

"No!" Hawk shouted. With his sword in hand he stalked toward River, predatory now. The Dark Lord stepped from between them, a look of triumph on his face.

"Hawk?" River asked, her eyes wide. "What are you doing?"

"What I should have done the second I set eyes on you."

Her glance went from Hawk to the Dark Lord, to the wife and child Hawk had loved and lost, then back to Hawk again. He could see fear in her eyes, but he also could see that she wasn't afraid of him, she was afraid for him.

"How did he know about them?" she asked.

"Because I made a mistake," Hawk said, inching toward her, needing to get closer. Despite the rage in his eyes, and the sword he was wielding, she did not back down from him. His heart warmed at her show of trust.

Hawk got close and lowered his voice for her ears only. "For not recognizing immediately what you were, and teaching you to block your thoughts." Everything the Dark Lord knew, he'd gotten from River. And Hawk blamed himself for that. He'd worked so hard to block his own thoughts, but River's were an open book to the Dark Lord.

"Your weapons," Hawk commanded. He met her glance straight on. "Hand them over. Even the ones I can't see. Let's finish this once and for all." River was smart. He prayed she'd understand the underlying meaning.

Confusion slowly morphed into understanding, and he almost wept that she'd gotten it. She passed him her charged sword, now humming with electricity, and in a silent message, cast her eyes toward the Dark Lord's throne.

The crucible.

Of course. That was the power source for the Dark Lord's program. It tied the magic of the seeing stones with the technology of the Guardians.

Once again his daughter's voice sounded. Hawk swallowed. He loved and missed his family dearly, but it was time to let them go. Somewhere out there his wife and daughter's souls were at rest. He knew it in his heart, just as he knew that if they were to remain at rest, he had to move on. He would hate for his pain to cause them distress.

"Time to finish this, Guardian," the Dark Lord urged.

"Indeed," Hawk said. He would finish this all right, but not in the way the Dark Lord wanted. He'd waited too long for this. He raised his sword high above his head, tossed the Dark Lord a grim, satisfied smile and drove his well-aimed blade into the crucible of seeing stones. The crucible cracked, and the stones scattered across the floor before vanishing from sight.

As the program flickered, the Dark Lord roared and lunged for Hawk. Hawk dodged the attack and turned to protect River.

But River was gone.

♦ ♦

River moaned and opened her eyes, head pounding, only to discover the pounding wasn't just in her head, it was coming from the compound door. Her mouth felt like she'd swallowed a thick wad of cotton.

"River, can you move?" a frantic Nick was asking, glancing back over his shoulder at the bolted door.

Why was the door to the gaming room bolted?

River pressed her palm to her forehead and tried to swallow, but her throat was too scratchy. "What happened?"

"I pulled you out of the game." Nick held a glass of sugared water laced with Red Bull to her lips and she drank from it greedily until he drew it away.

As her brain came back into focus, panic set in. She gripped his shoulder, angry voices growing louder on the other side of the door. "Put me back in the game, Nick. I need to go back."

He frowned. "The game is the least of your worries. You need help." He tugged her none too gently to her feet.

Pins and needles set in, making standing almost

impossible. She fell against him. "Why haven't you helped me before now?" she demanded, and she nearly cried at the guilt she read on his face.

"I'm sorry, babe. I never meant for things to get this out of hand."

River rubbed at her legs, working to get the blood flowing as she carefully picked her way to the monitor. She'd hoped to see Hawk inside, still alive, but met only with the words *game over*.

Her heart skipped a beat. Oh no, this was not game over. It was far from it. She had to save Hawk.

"River, you need to listen to me." Nick pointed to the door. "There is a lot more going on than you know. Those men are after you, and I don't know how to stop them."

She tapped her monitor, uncaring about who was on the other side of the door, worried only about Hawk. "I need to get back in the game!"

Nick shook his head, his mouth setting in a stubborn line. "You can't. The program is fried. It must have happened when I pulled you out."

"No. It happened when Hawk took out the program's console. But he's still trapped." She pressed her fist to her stomach. "I can *feel* him. If I can feel him, surely I can jump to him."

"What are you talking about? Who the hell is Hawk?" A loud boom sounded on the door, and the hinges groaned. Nick grabbed her arms. "We're the ones who are trapped, River. You've got to get us out of here."

The compound door crashed open. Six men rushed into the room, guns aimed. Five of the men swarmed around River. The sixth walked up to Nick.

Nick held his palms out. "You said she had to be here when you returned, Kaye. You never said I couldn't lock the door."

The man had the craziest eyes River had ever seen. "True enough," he said to Nick. "I also never said I'd let you live. And you're making me angry."

A gunshot rang out. Nick crumpled, half smiling, and River shrieked as she broke free and dove for him. She caught him before his head could hit the floor. On her knees, she looked up at the man who'd shot Nick and at the pleasure dancing in those scary eyes.

"You are fast," he murmured, admiration in his tone. He turned to the men. "Hold her down. She's quite strong for her size."

One of the men had a syringe in his hand.

River didn't waste any more time trying to figure out what was happening. Heat moved through her body, her energy levels building to dangerous proportions. As several sets of hands reached out for her, and the needle of the syringe touched the skin on her arm, she gripped Nick tight.

She jumped. Back into the Dark Lord's lair.

CHAPTER **TWENTY**

♦

Something was wrong.

She was in two places at once.

Hot wind whipped her hair and she shielded her face with the crook of her arm to protect her skin and eyes from the blistering sting of a sandstorm. The air was so thick with grit she could barely breathe.

She crouched over Nick, covering him with her body as best she could, gasping for breath. Something round and hard dug into her knee as she knelt. She shifted her leg and saw it was one of the seeing stones from the crucible. Several more lay nearby, slowly being buried by blowing red sand. This could only be the real world that housed the Soul Man's prison.

And yet they were also in the Soul Man's lair. She could see it as clearly as if standing in the room. The demons were there, waiting for the Soul Man's command. Two Hellhounds flanked the Soul Man while Hawk knelt before him in nothing more than a loincloth, blood streaming from the fresh lacerations on his shoulders and back.

The Dark Lord raised the whip in his hand, prepared to deliver another lashing. So intent was he on what he was doing, he hadn't yet noticed River's return.

She staggered to her feet against the force of the wind, her body stiff and uncooperative from days of inactivity. Reality had twisted, overlapping her worlds, and she was scared—for herself, for Nick, and for Hawk as well. Nick was far too still.

And Hawk . . .

"Stop," she cried out to the Soul Man, but the sound she released came as little more than a croak. It felt as if she'd swallowed ground glass when she tried to speak, but the pain could be no worse than what Hawk had to be suffering. Both he and Nick were going to die while she stood and watched, and she could think of no way to save them.

Hawk's shoulders tightened, muscles bunching as he lifted his head to look into her eyes. She tried not to react to the swelling on his face.

"Get out of here," he growled at her from between clenched teeth.

The Dark Lord gestured to one of the waiting demons. It hauled Hawk to his feet.

Hawk twisted his head and spoke to the Dark Lord through bleeding lips. "I'd sell my soul for you to release your claim on River's."

"Hawk, no," River whispered, terrified.

Deep laughter erupted in response. "A weakness,

Guardian?" The Dark Lord raised his hand, and the demon delivered a blow that cracked ribs. Hawk toppled and dropped to his knees, but the demon jerked him to his feet again. "Why not sell your soul for the two of you to be together for all eternity? Then you'd never have to lose her as you did your family." The Dark Lord paused as if in thought. He looked at River, then back to Hawk. "The little Fae is in a bit of trouble in her real world, so I believe I'll pass on your tempting offer. No, it's going to be winner take all. And I plan to win."

The wind eased abruptly, allowing River more air to breathe, although it remained unbearably hot in her lungs and on her skin. She drove her nails into the soft flesh of her palms, glancing down in surprise at the sudden, sharp pain, but it was the spiderlike veins racing up and down her arms that caught her attention.

Her mind raced. She was here in her physical form, not as a gamer. Why would she still have the virus?

Spiderlike veins. She remembered the fear in Andy's eyes when a spider crossed her bar in the safe house. River's fireflies morphed to spiders, and the spiders spread viruses. It was a virus that had taken out half the earth, mutated, then killed her mother. Viruses mutated. She'd written her game to mutate as well.

Perhaps a virus was the key to finishing off the Dark Lord. Perhaps on some unconscious level she'd written the spiders into her game on purpose. Characters in the game could only be affected by insect bites. Software running software couldn't touch them any other way.

But the virus she'd acquired in the game was in her physical form as well. There could be only one way for that to be possible.

Through magic.

Hawk, too, had seen what she'd noticed and drawn the same conclusion. Understanding lit his eyes and filled them with hope.

"Forget anything I've ever told you. This is your game now. You need to believe in who you were born to be, River," he urged her. "Dig deep to what's inside you."

Another powerhouse blow to Hawk's midsection drove him backward, and River cried out. She felt that blow as if she'd received it herself. She separated from it, buried it, and concentrated on pulling her energy from within her.

She smiled then, a strange new calmness coming over her as she took a step toward the Dark Lord. He could feel her calling her magic. She could see in his eyes how much he loved the touch of it. Through her magic he'd managed to defeat her every time she'd called it when she'd faced him before.

But before, she had faced him as a gamer, not as a Fae. The magic felt different to her now that she wasn't filtering it through the game. She could smell it, too, and it smelled more marvelous than anything she'd ever imagined.

It made her feel alive. Powerful. In control.

"That's my girl." The Soul Man crooked a finger and urged her close.

She directed the magic to her fingertips. She held her hand out and tapped one of the Hellhounds on its head. Its body cracked in response, morphing into a troop of spiders that immediately spread out, skittering across the cold stone floor.

The Dark Lord stepped back, a sudden caution in his eyes. The spiders touched his feet and he stepped on them. The more he killed, the faster the remaining swarmed around him. They crawled up his robes, covering his skin, his face, his arms. He shouted in anger as they started to bite. "What have you done to me?"

But River, secure in the knowledge now that Hawk would be free, had already turned away from the Dark Lord.

She had to save Nick.

◆ ◆

The walls of the prison flickered, cascaded, and began to collapse. Hawk began to lose definition as well.

A brief flash of euphoria sang through him. Any moment now, he'd be free. And, just like that, the euphoria passed to be replaced by cold fear.

River was in danger with no one to protect her.

She was bent over Nick's motionless form, crying now, and it hurt Hawk's heart to see how desperately she tried to use her magic to heal a bastard who'd brought her so much harm. Nick didn't deserve such loyalty from her.

Hawk reached for her hands, trying to stop her, to take her in his arms, but that was no longer possible. She'd gone back to her body while his remained elsewhere. He could return to it now. She'd given him that. But he'd be returning to it without her, and the thought of doing so was more than he could bear. He'd go crazy trying to get back to her.

He dropped his hands to his sides. "It's too late for Nick, River," he said as gently as possible, crouching beside her. "His soul is gone."

"Then I'll call it back," she said stubbornly.

"Right now there are so many souls newly freed around you, you'd have no idea which one you'd be calling." The souls were already departing. Hawk could feel them as they flickered out of the program, one by one.

Nick's, however, was nowhere to be found. It gave Hawk an idea.

"River," he said urgently. He wouldn't leave her, not if he didn't have to, but they were almost out of time. "Listen to me." She glanced up then, and by the expression of dawning awareness he saw on her face, she'd only now realized what was happening to him. "You aren't safe in your world. You have to let me help you." He pointed to Nick. "Can you heal his body?"

She didn't understand at first. He stepped closer to Nick. As her eyes widened, unsure, bits of the wasteland superimposed over the flickering program. She reached out to Hawk, trying to keep him from disappearing, but her hands passed right through him.

"Is there no other way?" she asked, rocking back on her heels, looking from him to Nick. "Can't you go back to your home, then come to me from there?"

"Nick is gone," he said, desperation forcing him to be cruel with her. "Can you defend yourself against the people who killed him? Do you want to find out what happened to your parents? Do you want to save their souls?" He was being more than cruel. But he had no more time to persuade her. And the idea of assuming Nick's body was no more appealing to him than it was to her. "It's the only way," he said to her, wishing it weren't the truth.

With that, he stepped into Nick's body. She would either heal him or not. The decision was now hers.

Crisos, it hurt. With a gasp Hawk opened his eyes. He'd forgotten how it felt to be alive. And so nearly dead. It hurt to breathe, it hurt to move, but

River's hands were on him now, already healing the worst of the pain.

"Fae. Get us out of here," he commanded her when he finally could speak. There would be time for kindness with her later.

She helped him to his feet. He slipped his arms around her and held tight, but before she jumped with him—destination unknown—she cast a glance over her shoulder. They both watched as a bundle of blood-blackened veins paraded upward, consuming the last of the Dark Lord's virtual body.

When the Guardians came back to secure the Dark Lord's prison once more, there would be no more compassion. Hawk hoped the little bastard enjoyed what would have to be the closest thing to a living hell a Dark Lord could experience.

The program flickered from existence, leaving nothing in its place but sand and heat and wind.

River's eyes met Hawk's, hot with angry triumph.

"Now it's *game over,"* she said, and pressing her face to his chest, she jumped.

◆ ◆

She'd brought them to a bright meadow near a wide, slow-flowing river. Sunlight glittered on the water's surface. Hawk didn't need to hear her confirm it to know that she'd brought them to the place where she'd been born, to the place she felt safest.

He wondered how long she'd really be safe here.

She looked at him with a mixture of wariness and sorrow, the triumph gone, and it nearly broke his heart.

He shivered in the wind, cold in a way that went straight through him and made him wish on one hand that he had a jacket, but on the other convinced him he was flesh and blood once more.

The wind lifted a swath of her black hair and blew it across her cheek. She crooked it back with a finger. Her wide, almond-shaped blue eyes, even more beautiful than they'd seemed in the game— whoever had created her virtual self had not done her justice—met his.

"Hawk?" she asked tentatively, and her eyes filled with tears when he took a step forward and reached for her.

He stopped and dropped his hands to his sides. He didn't like this any better than she did. He didn't like it that River, his kick-ass Fae, was crying over a former lover who'd betrayed her. The sooner he found a way to return to his own body the happier they'd both be, because he certainly didn't like the idea of touching her while in the asshole's body either.

First things first.

"If you're angry with me," Hawk said cautiously, "I just want you to know that these boys aren't made of titanium. They feel pretty real. So take that into consideration."

River laughed.

And Hawk knew for certain then that whatever they were about to face, they'd face it as a team.

TOR
ROMANCE

Believe that love is magic

Please join us at the Web site below for more information about this author and other great romance selections, and to sign up for our monthly newsletter!

www.tor-forge.com

PB
R
(mm)